THE HAUNTING
OF OAK SPRINGS

What Reviewers Say About Crin Claxton's Work

The Supernatural Detective—*Foreward Review Winner*

"This was an extremely tense, but amazing thriller with an amazing touch of comedy that helped lift it from being too dark and twisted. That formula made the story so enjoyable and a lot of fun to read. The paranormal and thriller genre can be quite scary, but I loved how this provided some relief and made it a story that anyone could enjoy. The humour didn't detract from the depth and excitement of getting caught up in the intense drama this story provided, but it was brilliantly executed to only attract the reader more and offer personal connection to the characters. A great story that I highly recommend."—*LESBIreviewed*

"*The Supernatural Detective* is a sexy, supernatural thriller. A perfect read for the beach."—*Diva Magazine*

Scarlet Thirst

"*Scarlet Thirst* is a book for those who like their erotica to be a little more subtle but still sexy—a la Anne Rice or Mary Renault. Surely a fangtastic read for fans of Buffy, Willow, and Tara!" —*Gay Voice*

"Claxton's descriptions of Granada are sensuous and entirely in keeping with her characters. Claxton manages to pull the disparate threads together with prose and plotting that is never overwritten or superfluous. Claxton has created an entirely believable other world. *Scarlet Thirst* is a great big fun, sexy, smart novel. Look out for it."—*Rainbow Network*

Death's Doorway—*Rainbow Awards Honorable Mention*

"I loved this one. I like the flow and writing style of the author. The story is packed full of twists and turns and keeps the reader engaged. The characters mesh well together! Really enjoyed it—the setting in London England, the main characters were entertaining, the suspense and the humor were spot-on."—*Elisa Reviews*

"There was enough action to keep me excited and enough twists and turns to keep me wondering, though the final thrill. All in all, this was a fun read, with interesting characters and an intriguing story. I recommend it to lovers of diversity, paranormal mysteries that involve ghosts and private investigators, and romantic stories with realistic issues."—*Butterfly-o-Meter*

By the Author

Death's Doorway

The Supernatural Detective

Scarlet Thirst

The Haunting of Oak Springs

THE HAUNTING OF OAK SPRINGS

by

Crin Claxton

2023

ISBN 13: 978-1-63679-432-7

This Trade Paperback Original Is Published By
Bold Strokes Books, Inc.
P.O. Box 249
Valley Falls, NY 12185

First Edition: September 2023

Credits
Editor: Cindy Cresap
Production Design: Susan Ramundo
Cover Design By Tammy Seidick

Acknowledgments

Without the following people, this third Supernatural Detective novel would be the poorer.

Thank you to my trusty band of beta readers. You read it first and potentially weep. Your comments and suggestions improve my ideas and my writing, and you keep me on track. Hiraani Himona, Kate May, Susan Purdue, Sarah Purdue, and Semsem Kuherhi, your contributions are invaluable. Thanks to Martina Laird for consultancy on all things Trinidadian. And to Kate May for helping me with details on farming in rural Derbyshire. To Deni Francis and Luca Claxton-Francis for allowing me to disappear into worlds of my own making. To all the people who keep me writing with your support: Campbell, Rita Hirani, my sisters, Victoria Villasenor, readers, and reviewers. I must also thank Sandy Lowe, who is the most delightful person to email and couldn't be more helpful. To Rad and all at Bold Strokes Books for keeping on believing in queer literature. And my editor, Cindy Cresap, your skill and support have polished this novel and lifted my words. The last shout goes to all the butches, wherever you are. Keep on being you.

Dedication

For Luca,
And the joy you bring

Chapter One

A rickety gate, strung with rusting barbed wire, swung in the wind. It crashed against the gate post and blew open again, revealing a rutted, muddy track.

The wind was bitter, and Tony Carson wasn't dressed for it. Four short hours ago, London had been alive with the heat of late summer. Up here in Derbyshire, the land was firmly in autumn.

The track ahead threaded through a wild copse. It was impossible to see what lay beyond untamed branches of oak and elm.

Tony turned to the ghost at her side. "Are you sure this is the place?"

Bryony nodded toward a flat piece of wood nailed to a tree.

Tony squinted at it. "No trespassers?" she asked.

"Not there. There." Bryony stabbed a finger at a crumbling sign stuck on a rotting post to the left of the tree. It was hanging from one nail. Faded lettering spelled out the words *Oak Springs Farm*.

Bryony didn't seem happy to be home and looked as nervous as when she'd appeared to Tony asking for help. She passed clean through the gate, barbed wire and all, and started walking along the sodden track.

Tony gingerly pushed the gate open.

The path was dark ahead. Shrouded by thick, black cloud, the light was fading fast.

Tony passed another sign nailed to a tree, *No hawkers. No cold callers.*

Bryony waited ahead at a bend in the track staring into the woods. Tony followed her gaze to yet another sign. *Danger. Keep Out.*

"What's the danger?" Tony asked.

"Later," Bryony said in the lilting Irish accent that had made everything seem simple and possible four short hours ago.

Tony opened her mouth to press Bryony further.

A click at her back froze the words in her throat.

She spun around.

To stare down the barrel of a shotgun.

The butch holding the weapon stood nearly six feet tall and stocky with it. Their eyes were masked by the peak of a gray tweed cap. They had a weathered, rugged face with a dark brown complexion, and when they spoke, their words were gravelly and succinct.

"What do you want, boy?"

Tony swallowed. The older butch was damned cool and twice as scary. "I'm not a boy. I'm a lesbian," she said.

The older butch straightened and appeared to consider Tony's words. "Well, lesbian, you're trespassing."

They crooked an arm, still pointing the shotgun, and leaned on a sign hammered into the ground. The sign read, *If you're close enough to read this get off my land.*

Bryony crossed the few feet between them, smiling affectionately at the person holding the shotgun. She patted their arm lightly, and the butch's shoulders twitched.

"This is Red," Bryony said.

Tony cleared her throat. "I've come to see Chris," she said.

Red pushed their cap back, meeting the driving rain with flint-cold eyes. They considered Tony for a moment and then waved the shotgun toward the track.

"Let's go then. You first."

❖

As they started up a long track pitted with potholes, the wind picked up, and rain came down in sheets. Bryony disappeared.

Tony turned around.

A prod from the shotgun forced Tony onwards.

There were barren fields on either side. In their depths, Tony made out the occasional tree and dark shapes huddled together.

Over the squelch of boots in mud, Tony caught an occasional murmur. And a howl that had to be the wind. She had seen a nature program that talked about bringing back wolves. They wouldn't really do it, though, would they?

Tony began to shiver, and not just from the biting cold. She had taken on Bryony's case on a whim. Leaving without telling anyone where she was going had seemed adventurous a few short hours ago.

Now it felt bloody stupid. She was alone on a deserted path with a shotgun at her back. And there was something out there in the fields.

People disappeared in situations like this. Cut-into-pieces-and-fed-to-the-pigs-disappeared.

They passed a large barn. Things snuffled and moved inside. Tony hoped it was animals and not previous trespassers.

A two-story farmhouse loomed ahead. Squat to the ground, its gray stonework and dark slate roof blended into the stormy sky. Smoke puffed upwards from the chimney. A light flickered behind a window on the ground floor.

Tony stopped at a low front door.

"What are you waiting for, Christmas?" Red grunted.

Tony pushed the door open, stumbled over the doorstep, and fell into a pile of boots.

"Wipe your feet," Red said, looking unimpressed.

They passed through a run-down kitchen into an equally tired sitting room.

A woman sat in a threadbare armchair pushed close to the fire. "I've just made a brew if you want one, Red," she said without lifting her eyes from the flames. She was around the same age as the butch and the ghost. Tony guessed this was Bryony's spouse, Chris. She was white with shaggy gray hair and carried some weight on a muscular frame. Her skin looked like it had been knocked up and down the hill, rained on, sun-dried, and wind-battered.

"Found someone poking around down by the copse," Red said. "Said they've come to see you, Chris."

Chris turned without getting up. She scrutinized Tony in a silence broken only by the loud ticktock of a heavy mantel clock.

"What do you want?" Chris asked in a tone colder than the wind that had blown Tony along the track.

Tony bulked before the glare of her. This was crazy. She'd been foolish to turn up at nightfall in a strange place. She wasn't even getting paid.

"I've made a mistake," Tony stammered.

"Spit it out," Chris said, and Tony saw the grief then in her red-rimmed eyes.

There was a photo of Bryony in a frame on the mantelpiece with a dying red rose beside it. Candles flickered on either side of the frame.

"I'm intruding," Tony said. It was a long walk, but maybe there'd be somewhere to stay in the sleepy village they'd passed through. She turned toward the door.

Red stepped in her way. "Intruding?"

Bryony materialized. "Tell them the cover story." Her voice was warm and insistent.

Red snapped the shotgun together. "Start talking."

"Selena Moonspirit's my aunt," Tony said in a rush.

Chris blinked. "You know Lena?"

"Hang on," Red muttered. "What do you mean, Lena's your aunt?"

Bryony tutted. "Lena doesn't have any siblings."

"Well, not my actual aunt," Tony embellished. "She was a friend of the family, of my parents, and I called her Aunty Lena."

"How is Selena?" Chris asked.

"Oh, fine. You know, busy," Tony said.

"Go on," Red prompted her.

"Aunty Lena told me about this place, how she lived here with you, with all of you." Tony looked around, trying to conjure the houseful of lesbians from years past that Bryony had described. "That's why I came."

Red laughed, cocked the shotgun, leaned against a second, equally faded armchair, and laughed some more. "Welcome to wimmin's land, child. You're only thirty years late."

"Flatter Chris like I told you," Bryony said. She floated over to her partner and kissed the top of her head.

"I thought you would be bigger," Tony said to Chris. "Aunty Lena said you were as strong as an ox. Brave too."

Chris didn't smile.

Red laid the gun on a rack. "You're soaked through. What on earth are you wearing, a jeans jacket?"

"It's my summer coat," Tony protested. "This is summer, isn't it?" Her words were punctuated by a steady drip from the sodden coat hem. It joined the pool spreading from her muddy feet.

"Not from Derbyshire, then," Chris muttered. "You can have a cup of tea before you leave." She poured walnut brown tea into a chipped earthenware mug and sloshed milk on top.

Tony took the mug gratefully, burying her face in the steam. Chris nodded toward a chair. Tony held her hand out to the fire's heat, suddenly feeling lonely and stupid.

"I shouldn't have come," she said quietly to no one in particular.

"It's bad out there," Red said. "Rain coming down hard."

Chris sighed. Then tipped her head up in exasperation.

Red turned to Tony. "One night," they said.

❖

The rickety old staircase was covered in a blue carpet that had seen better days. Tony followed Red cautiously, straining to find her footing in the feeble light of a flickering bulb.

Red opened a door on the first-floor landing, nodded toward the bed, pointed down the hall at another room where Tony made out the outline of a bath, and left.

If the stair carpet had seen better days, the bedroom couldn't possibly be expected to remember them. A dubious patchwork quilt lay on a single bed with brass knobs dulled by lack of polishing. A small wardrobe and a huge dressing table took up one wall. A latticed window filled most of another. A beautiful rocking chair sat in the corner. Tony sensed its loneliness. The room had known life and laughter, but not for a long time.

She opened the ancient window, and a blast of wind knocked her backward. Quickly, she pulled the window closed, only for it to jam an inch from the frame. A gale shrieked through the gap. It was as disturbing as it was freezing.

Bryony appeared in the rocking chair. "This used to be my favorite room," she said.

Tony eyed the peeling wallpaper, the moth holes in the curtains, and the worrying stain on the carpet and suppressed a shudder.

"That bed's seen some action," Bryony said with a wink. "So has this chair. And not just Chris and me. There were quite the goings-on when the house was full of women. But I'll save that story for another time."

Under the current circumstances, Tony sincerely hoped that other time was never.

"I chose the paint, morning blush. The sunrise comes through that east-facing window, you know."

Tony made out flakes of pale pink on the blistered, cracked woodwork. Sleet blew in, leaving a glistening trail.

"The frame's out of true. Give it a thump if you want to close the window. We'll dig the jewelry up tomorrow, give it to Chris, and you can leave knowing you did some good." Bryony tossed Tony a smile as she faded away.

Tony stood in the freezing room and sighed. Since starting the Supernatural Detective Agency with her girlfriend, Maya, and best friend, Jade, Tony had been on more than one wild ghost chase. This was turning into another. Bryony had materialized at the breakfast table with her crinkly green eyes and soft brogue, talking of train rides and retrieving lost jewelry. In the bright London sunlight, the case had had the promise of adventure.

In this cold, forgotten room, not so much.

She should call Maya.

Tony's stomach twisted with the remembering. Oh.

Well, she should call Jade. Tony patted her jacket pocket. Then all of her pockets and then she emptied her backpack. She'd had the phone in her hand when she'd fallen asleep on the train.

And no memory of it when she'd woken in a panic with the train about to pull away.

She sank onto the bed. She was well and truly alone now. All that had gone before pressed down onto her chest, and she only just kept the tears from falling.

❖

The kitchen was warm and comfortable with a red tiled floor, pine units, and a well-used range cooker throwing out proper heat. Tony found Red sitting at an ancient rectangular wooden table eating breakfast.

"Late riser, then," Red said without looking up.

Tony looked at her watch. It was half past seven. "I think you have a sick bird." She shuddered, recalling the horrible sounds that had plagued her sleep.

"We do?"

"Or dead maybe by now. It was groaning all night."

"When you went to bed?" Red scooped up a spoonful of something thick, gray, and lumpy and swallowed it.

"Actually, no. The terrible shrieks started in the middle of the night."

"Harvey. Crows at first light as cockerels generally do on farms." Red nodded at a saucepan. "Help yourself."

A serving spoon was standing bolt upright in the pan. The porridge could repair the wallpaper in Tony's room, but she was hungry. She ladled a portion into a chipped, blue and white enamel bowl. Red slid a sugar bowl across the table.

Tony put a spoonful of the lukewarm mixture into her mouth and chewed.

"What are you running from?"

Startled, Tony tried to answer, but her jaw was glued firmly shut. She demonstrated her confusion with a shrug.

"It's not rocket science. You show up late at night with a haunted look."

If only you knew. Tony shrugged again, noting the twang of Birmingham in Red's voice and warmer notes from one of the islands. Jade would have known which.

"Chris doesn't want you here. I don't know if I do. Tell me what you're running from, or you can pack your stuff and go."

Tony straightened, rubbing her back. The bed hadn't wanted her to stay either. "I'm running from nobody."

Red's eyes drilled into her. They were deep, dark, and almond-shaped. "You're lying."

"I'm not," Tony said. "I meant it literally. I'm not running from any person. I'm running from life."

Red frowned, and Tony sighed. This was precisely what she didn't want to talk about. Probably exactly why she'd taken off so quickly the day before. The stubborn tilt to Red's jaw told Tony the butch wouldn't be brushed off.

"I lost my job," Tony said. "My daughter came to live with me. I had to cancel shifts. They let me go."

Red studied Tony without blinking. Much as she didn't want to, Tony felt compelled to elaborate.

"I didn't care about the job. Not at the time. Having Louise was everything. Even though my girlfriend wasn't happy. Not that that matters now. Louise's mother showed up and took her away." Tony bit down on her lip. That pain was easier to bear. "I only see my child when my ex needs a break. She left Louise with me for a year this time. We were settled, happy. Even though Maya and I weren't getting on. But she's gone."

"Your girlfriend?" Red asked.

"No. Well, yes. But I didn't mean Maya. I meant Louise." Tony looked down at the porridge. She shoveled a spoonful into her mouth and then another. No more talking. Slamming down the lid was the only way to get through the day. If Red wanted her to leave, so be it.

"I see," Red said quietly. "We used to take any woman in when they needed a safe space. I'll talk to Chris."

"Talk to me about what?" The back door swung open, revealing Chris in dirty overalls swinging an empty bucket. "Pigs are hungry this morning."

"Pigs are hungry every morning," Red said.

"Saw Nick out in the fields." Chris scratched her head. "The Rawlings family farm has been sold. Can't say I'm upset to hear their lad won't be coming back to run it."

"He's a mechanic, isn't he? A lot of water's run under the bridge, mind. But maybe you're right. Probably better all round." Red finished their porridge.

"You're still here, I see," Chris said to Tony.

"About that," Red said quickly. "I thought we could do with the help, maybe. The kid can work for her keep."

Chris looked skeptical. "Know anything about crop growing?"

"I water my friend's houseplants when she's away," Tony said.

"Pigs? Sheep? Poultry? Any experience with animals?"

Tony didn't think having a cat and two goldfish counted. She shook her head, deciding now wasn't the moment to say both goldfish had died.

"Carpentry? Plumbing?"

"I can do electrics," Tony said quickly. "I can lift stuff, and I'm quite good at repairing things. Not plumbing, though. At my last job, they tried to get me to fix a urinal. It didn't go well."

Chris shuddered. "You can help me lift the potatoes. And then we'll see. No promises, mind."

❖

Hills rose beyond the line of trees in fading leaf. The green slopes were marked into rectangles and strips by the gray curving ridges of dry stone walls. The trees hid the valley but not the foreground rolling away from the house in great, green swathes.

There was no rain falling from the huge, empty sky. That's because all the rain in all the world was already in the saturated soil. Chris's potato "patch" was a field. Tony had toyed with vegetable growing, mostly in containers. She'd thrown a few seed potatoes in a black sack, tipped compost on top, and left them alone for a few months. It had been a delightful harvest. Jade had made a small Cajun potato salad. Tony smiled at the memory.

"We haven't got all day." Chris startled Tony into the present.

She turned to the alarming number of withered green rows. "Are these all potatoes?" Tony asked.

Chris laughed. "All potatoes." She shook her head. "Of course not. Half the field's beetroot and carrots. We'll get to them, don't you worry."

Tony was worried. Worried about her back. Chris put a foot on her garden fork and sliced through the wet earth, scooping potatoes from their muddy bed.

Copying Chris's style, Tony plonked her borrowed Wellington boot on her fork and pushed. Nothing happened. She put her weight behind it. The fork disappeared into mire that could have featured in a B movie entitled *The hideous life-sucking swamp from another planet*. Tony tried to wrench the fork back to the surface. The swamp was reluctant to relinquish its prize and even more reluctant to relinquish any potatoes. There were two. Speared onto the tines of the fork.

Chris walked back from four perfectly lifted potato plants ahead. The grim look on her face spoke volumes. She removed the damaged potatoes with disgust, slid Tony's fork back into the mud, and, a hot second later, unearthed a bounty of ten.

The hideous swamp liked her. Maybe they were from the same planet. Perhaps Chris was, in fact, a swamp in human form. She handed the fork back to Tony with a scowl. "Go on to the next row."

The adjacent row was on higher, dryer ground. The fork slid down more easily, and a good armful of large potatoes tumbled out. Tony picked two up, waving them at Chris. "Hey, I did it this time," she said proudly.

"Handle them gently. We need them to see us through the winter," Chris grunted.

Tony started walking to the next plant but was stopped by a loud ker-hum. She turned back.

"Stay there. Get them all up, even the tiny ones. You don't want them passing on diseases come next year, do you?"

Tony didn't care if they infected the whole of the potato universe, but she didn't share the thought.

Chris watched Tony for a while. The sun rose overhead, warming the air. The inside of the borrowed boots felt damp. Tony didn't like to think how many women had worn them before and what manner of foot infections they may have had.

"Why didn't you go after your child?"

Tony stood stock upright, staring at Chris, and breathing hard. She couldn't bring herself to speak.

"Red told me your ex took your daughter away," Chris said. "Why didn't you go after her?"

"Amy won't answer me. She's blocked my number. Her mother said Amy and Louise aren't staying with them and she wouldn't tell me where they've gone. I've got no legal rights. Amy is the biological mother, and I didn't adopt her." Tony spat out the words, furious with her stupidity and with Chris for asking.

Chris leaned on her fork. "There was a small army of women here once. Children too. Some stayed a few days. Others lived here for years. That was a long time ago. I've got used to it being me and Red." Her eyes dipped. "And Bryony…" Chris coughed and started turning potatoes over as if there were a shortage, with the world relying on Chris alone to resolve their potato needs.

Tony worked her rows. It was hard on her back and harder on her thighs. By the time Chris called, "Lunch," Tony had blisters on her hands, mud in her hair, and the potatoes she'd dug were as sorry-looking as Tony felt.

Chris peered disapprovingly at her small pile. "Tip those into the wheelbarrow and try not to mash them completely in the process. I'll meet you back at the farmhouse. Make sure you wash up and don't be tramping mud all over my kitchen floor."

Tony stared after Chris's retreating back. There was no need to be rude, and she was doing her inadequate best. There were machines for this sort of work, surely? It was just her luck to rock up at the farm that time forgot.

❖

Red pulled up in front of a buff brick building just outside the village of Wooly Mill and parked in the middle of a sloping forecourt.

At lunch, Chris had asked Tony to go with Red to the local garage. She'd offered to drive. Chris and Red had laughed.

Red hadn't said a word on the journey. Just winced when the truck sputtered and groaned when it occasionally backfired. Now Red was frowning at a discolored patch above the workshop entrance.

"Where's the sign gone?" they muttered.

A middle-aged white man in overalls that were more sludge gray than royal blue wandered out as Red swung open the truck door. He wiped his hands on a rag and pushed a strand of hair behind his ear. The rest of his hair was tied loosely into a ponytail. He had a sweet smile, and Tony warmed to him.

"Was that you coughing or the truck?" he asked.

Red shook the man's hand firmly. "I need your help, Ed, old friend."

"Summit wrong with Emily P? Pop the hood then. Get yourself a coffee while I take a look. We're not supposed to offer it to customers now, mind." Ed's voice dropped.

"Sorry? What do you mean?" Red asked.

"I'll fill you in later. Let me look at her first," Ed called from under the bonnet.

There was no one in the workshop, although there was a mud-encrusted Range Rover on the ramp. At a stained machine, Red passed Tony a paper cup filled with coffee so thick and strong it smelled burnt. It tasted good, though. Just the stuff you'd need when you were knuckle-deep in engine grease.

"Emily P?" Tony asked.

Red smiled. "Named after Emily Pankhurst. Naming vehicles is an Oak Springs tradition. The tractor's called Audre, after the late and great Audre Lorde."

When they walked back, a highly polished, new pickup was parked behind Emily P. A white man in his early fifties fished a long, rectangular parcel from the cargo bed. He had a ruddy complexion, chapped lips, and was tall with a stocky build, probably standing around five foot eleven. He could have been handsome under the several days' worth of stubble if it wasn't for the mean frown and narrowed, hooded eyes.

"Why is that old banger blocking my workshop?" he growled, speaking to the raised bonnet.

Ed whipped his head out. "Oh, hi, Arnie. Need to get your truck in?"

But Arnie was staring at Red. "Thought I recognized that pile of crap. Can't believe you haven't replaced it. But happen, maybe you can't. Money tight up at Oak Springs, is it? Oak Springs Eternal, we used to say. That was before *she* took it over. Before you lot run it into the ground. Oak doesn't spring anymore, does it, love?"

"What's it to you?" Red said with an emphasis on to. They spoke slow and even, though Red's hands were clenched.

"You remember Arnie Rawlings?" Ed said quickly.

"I do." Red nodded crisply.

"He's moved back into the village and bought the garage." Ed's voice was upbeat and bright. Some might say over bright.

"And I don't want your business." Arnie's eyes darted to Tony. "None of you, Oak Springs women."

He ripped the brown paper from the package revealing a sign that read *Arnie's Autos.*

Red's eyebrows lifted a quarter inch.

"Now, Arnie, Wooly Mill's a small place. Old Mr. Jessop said we should never turn people away," Ed said quietly.

Arnie grunted. "And that's why he ran the business down and jumped at the chance of selling it to me. That truck is past fixing and not worth our time. Ed, put this sign up. And, you." He turned to Red. "Move that heap off of my property."

Red chewed the inside of their cheek, staring at Arnie's back until he disappeared through the workshop into the reception area. "Back in five," they said to Ed.

Tony trotted behind Red along the street to a small corner shop. The bell tinkled as the door swung open, bringing a young man to the counter. Red went to the fridge and picked up two pints of milk.

"Hi," the young man said pleasantly.

Red took out a twenty. The young man scanned the milk and opened the till.

The bell tinkled again.

"You can put that back." Arnie stood in the doorway, blocking the light. "We don't want your type in here either."

The teen's eyes dropped to the floor.

Tony stepped forward, barely containing her rage. "You can't refuse to serve Black people and lesbians."

Arnie stared at her for a long minute.

The teen behind the counter coughed. "She's right, Dad."

"Who said it was that?" Arnie shot back.

"Why won't you serve us then?" Tony demanded.

Arnie looked at the twenty-pound note in his son's hand. "That looks fake. We've got the right to bar people passing counterfeit money." He took the twenty and held it to the light. "I have to keep this." He pocketed it. "It's the law."

"An' he call me a teef," Red muttered, shaking her head.

"That is not fake money," Tony said, her throat so tight the words came out as a growl.

Red dumped the milk on the counter and walked to the door passing the aging mechanic with barely a look.

"Shame on you, Arnie Rawlings," they said.

CHAPTER TWO

Bryony was annoyingly insistent. But then she was the reason Tony had haul-arsed two hundred plus miles.

"You can go now. They're both busy." Bryony stood in a large muddy puddle winding a strand of hair around her fingers.

Tony had dutifully returned to the veg field as soon as they'd returned to the farm. She ran her eyes along the line of heaped earth and browning leaves. "Chris wants me to finish this row by teatime."

Bryony raised one eyebrow. "In this weather? That's foolishness, and Chris knows it. You don't want to be lifting more potatoes. You want to be drying those out in the barn." Bryony nodded at the muddy spuds heaped in the wheelbarrow. "Pick that up and come with me. Bring the spade."

"But—" Tony started to say and stopped herself. Why did she care about a pile of dirt-encased vegetables? She felt gloriously rebellious until she remembered Chris was grumpy and more than a little bit scary.

"You need to get the necklace. And then you can go home," Bryony reminded her.

The ghost was right. Oak Springs wasn't where she should be. Tony should be in London. Even if the thought of being there made her feel weak and nauseous. *Don't think. Distract.*

Bryony led Tony onto a small path that wound around a dilapidated barn. Chickens ran in and out of it, pecking in the dirt.

They didn't look the friendly type. Were poultry friendly? Tony decided not to find out.

"Dump the barrow in there for now."

Tony did as she was told and followed the recently deceased sixty-something farming lesbian along the track to the grove of trees by the entrance gate.

Something about the grove made Tony uneasy. A cold wind snaked under her jacket collar, stealing her body's warmth away. The oak and beech trees looked innocent enough. Leaves the color of copper, and ochre, and hot red chilies fell from the branch to the damp ground beneath. The air smelled of leaf litter and fungi tinged with wood smoke. It was autumn in a breath. None of that unnerved Tony. But something unpleasant hummed just out of reach of her senses.

Bryony stood at the gate. She walked to a tree taking long strides and counting. She stopped, pointing to a clump of earth near a large rock. "Dig here," she said.

Tony went to the spot. She tested the ground with her foot sensing a peculiar vibration.

"What are you waiting for?" Bryony said.

Tony lifted the spade.

A twig snapped in the still air. A decidedly human voice cleared their throat behind her.

"What the hell are you doing?" they said.

Chris glowered at Tony and then down at the spade in her hand. "I said, what are you doing?"

Tony opened her mouth to speak but couldn't form words. Chris looked furious. Her ruddy complexion had turned a shade to rival the reddest of the leaves.

"I, well, I filled the wheelbarrow, so I took the potatoes to the barn." Tony swallowed, her mind racing to think of a reason, any reason, why she'd be in the woods. "And then I thought, well, I've always wanted to dig for truffles. So I decided to give it a go."

Chris stared at Tony for a minute. Then she tipped her head back and laughed and laughed. She laughed until she was in danger of falling over.

"Truffles," she said between guffaws. "Truffles," she repeated, wiping a tear from her eye. "Unbelievable."

Tony frowned. She didn't see why the idea was so funny. "You find them under trees, don't you?"

"You need a forest, not a few trees, and you must know where to look. Southerners, honestly. But it was a good idea to lay the potatoes out in the barn. I hope you spaced them out properly."

Tony took a breath. "Actually, I was going to do that next."

"Best get on with it then," Chris said crisply. "Feed the chickens while you're there."

Bryony complained as Tony picked up the spade and set off toward the farm. But there was no way out of it. And no sneaking back. When Tony turned to check, Chris was standing in the copse, watching as Tony walked away.

The flock of chickens and two ducks were pecking in the dirt outside the barn. The ducks paid her no attention, and their waddling walk was comforting in a Beatrix Potter kind of way. The chickens were surprisingly intimidating. They stared up at her with contempt in their beady, chicken eyes. Thankfully, they scattered when she stomped toward them. Tony didn't mean to stomp. The boots were too small, and they hurt her feet. There was no way she was wearing her trainers. Not with all the dirt and, quite frankly, crap underfoot. Animal farming seemed to involve lots of poo.

As she turned into the barn, Harvey, the rooster, planted himself firmly in her path. Tony narrowed her eyes, and he narrowed his.

"Shoo," Tony said, forcing confidence into her voice.

Harvey seemed to snort. Were chickens even capable of snorting? They were certainly capable of aggression if Harvey was anything to go by. It wasn't fair to Harvey Milk to name this bird after him. He should be called Attila the Hen. He put the toxic in toxic masculinity. Harvey strutted forward, and Tony instinctively stepped back. Big mistake. Harvey flew at her sinking his beak into her thigh.

After she'd hopped for a bit, rubbing her leg, Tony took a breath. "Out of the way, chicken," she snarled, flapping her arms at the bird.

Harvey stalked off across the yard with a look that suggested this wasn't the end of the matter.

Tony turned to the big pile of potatoes and started laying them out on the drying rack. After a few minutes, she settled into a rhythm. Take wet spud, separate it from the clump of other wet spuds, plonk on cleanish bit of wood, wipe muddy mess from hand onto tatty, two-sizes-too-big-jeans cinched unflatteringly at the waist by an old belt, both borrowed from Red.

Soon there was a long row of potatoes bathed in glorious shafts of sunlight. The clouds had sailed away, leaving a sky full of nothing but blue and birds circling on the wing.

Tony felt a strange sensation. Something she hadn't felt for weeks. Peace.

But then weird scratching noises broke the moment. They came from a corner of the barn somewhere behind her. Tony didn't bother turning around. Harvey hadn't backed off. He had just regrouped. Tony could picture his claws scraping the floor as he performed some kind of aggressive chicken dance. Well, she refused to be bullied by a bird. Toxic Harvey could make whatever frightening noises he liked. Tony fixed her attention on the potatoes.

Until Harvey strutted past in the yard, his bottom turned pointedly toward her.

Tony swallowed. If it wasn't Harvey, who or what was making the creepy, rustling noises?

She inched around, telling herself, *It's only a chicken. It's only a chicken.*

It wasn't a chicken.

It was a woman in her seventies stabbing at a bale of hay. Her shoulder-length gray hair was tied loosely back. Strands of it flopped onto a burnt-orange shirt embroidered with flowers worn over jeans tucked into Wellington boots. She prodded the very real hay ineffectually with a ghostly, long-tined fork.

"This is harder than it should be," she said.

Tony's heart sank. Was this someone newly passed over, ignorant of her corporeal state? Tony took a breath. "You won't have much luck with that. What is it?"

"A pitchfork," the ghost said.

"Right," Tony said. "The hay's real, and the pitchfork won't be any use on account of it being…" Tony trailed off, searching for a sensitive way to explain life, death, and the universe to a recently departed person.

"Ghostly?" the ghost filled in. "I see. I just wanted to help out. Even if this isn't my farm. I know where I am with animals, you see. Mostly they're no trouble. Predictable once you've gone a season or two. A farmer's life is much the same day to day. It's the years that go and change everything." The ghost leaned on the phantom fork. "I'm Vera," she said.

"Tony." Tony turned away from the potatoes to give the older woman her full attention.

"This is all very strange. I don't mind it." Vera dropped her eyes. "But I can't leave him. He's not ready."

Sadness breezed over Tony, salty as the sea and lemon sharp.

"Your husband?" Tony asked.

"Son," Vera replied.

Ah. Sometimes the ghosts were ready, but the living weren't.

"It was just the two of us on the farm. Hard work even before I got ill. He's desperate to speak to me. Unfortunately, he can't hear me. Even when I'm right next to him talking as plainly as I am to you now." Vera tucked a loose strand of hair behind her ear. "Will you take him a message from me?"

It was a reasonable request. Not one Tony could easily explain to Red and Chris. "I have to lay these potatoes out," she mumbled.

Vera nodded. "Space them further apart. Making yourself useful, that's good. How are the girls?"

"The girls?" Tony asked, wondering if Vera meant the chickens. Or the sheep, or perhaps the two cute ducks?

"Red and Chris. How are they?" Vera asked.

Tony suppressed a smile at hearing Red and Chris referred to as the girls. "Not brilliant. They're grieving."

"Of course, with Bryony gone," Vera said. "They were close."

"Oh, and there's some trouble in the village. The shop won't serve them."

"What?" Vera said indignantly. "Why ever not?"

"Well," Tony relayed to Vera the info Red had passed on during the return journey. "This bloke, Arnie Rawlings, he inherited a farm."

Vera nodded. "The Rawlings farm is the other side of ours. Arnie is the only child, but he lives in Sheffield, doesn't he?"

"Not anymore. He sold the farm and bought the village shop and the garage."

Vera raised her eyebrows. "Oh. I can see how that wouldn't bode well for Red and Chris. They've got history, and Arnie can hold a grudge for England. So have the girls got milk?" Vera asked.

"No. And Chris is struggling without it," Tony said.

"Problem solved. In fact, two problems solved," Vera said with a smile. "Go and see my Nick. He'll give you milk."

"Are you sure?" Tony asked. "What if he doesn't have enough?"

Vera chuckled. "There'll be enough, pet. We're a dairy farm."

❖

Vera's farm was in better shape than Oak Springs. Tony walked up the track past a field of black-and-white cows chewing contentedly on rich pasture. They made a tourist-board-perfect picture with a patchwork of fields rolling away into the distance. The farmhouse was a gray stone two-story building with a surprisingly bright red front door.

Tony wondered where Vera was. There had been no sign of her since Tony had left the barn. The activities of ghosts followed no pattern or rule known to Tony. And Tony's spirit guide Deirdre was little help. Now that Tony thought of it, Deirdre had been ominously silent for weeks. Usually, Tony could rely on the New York drag queen to appear at the most inopportune moment wearing something startling. Tony brushed a worry aside. Deirdre had been absent before. She'd turn up eventually.

Tony lifted the cow head knocker and rapped the ring through its nose against the heavy wooden door.

Nobody came. Several minutes later, Tony knocked again.

This time she heard footsteps moving slowly, coming nearer. The door creaked a little and swung open.

A white man in his forties stared at her. Tony saw Vera's vividly blue eyes in a face that also duplicated her nose, chin, and broad cheekbones.

"Are you Nick?" she asked.

He nodded.

Tony opened her mouth to tell him she was staying with Red and Chris and did he have any milk to spare? And then she saw the deep shadows under his eyes. His posture and expression radiated grief.

"Your mother sent me," she said instead.

The effect of Tony's words was immediate. Nick started but held her gaze as if daring her to disappoint him.

"When?" he asked hesitantly. "When did you speak to her?"

"Today," she said.

He ushered her immediately inside, past a cozy lounge into a modernized kitchen. The sun streamed through a latticed window. The back door was a stable door-type, its top half open to let air flow through the room. There was the smell of baking.

Nick took a kettle from the range cooker and topped up a teapot on the breakfast bar. Without asking how she liked it, he poured Tony a mug of tea and passed it to her, gesturing toward a sugar bowl.

Tony took a sip and then a breath. "I'm staying with Red and Chris," she said. "I was working in the barn when your mum, Vera, came to see me. She's worried about you."

Nick tipped his head to one side, regarding her with a steady gaze. The sorrow that lay on him was familiar. Tony's mum had died twenty years previously, and the loss had devastated her.

"You've been trying to contact her, she said. She's tried to answer you to let you know that her love hasn't died with her."

Nick bit his lip at that.

"She said you can't hear her."

Nick shifted in his chair. "I want to. I miss her so much. Every day I wake and remember, and I feel sick. I guess I'm lucky we were that close. She was a good friend."

Tony smiled.

"I was a child when my dad died. Mum put all her energy into looking after me and keeping the farm going. She never asked a thing of me. She wanted me to go off to university, learn something, go somewhere. But I love this place." Nick looked out of the window to the cows chewing grass.

"It is beautiful here."

Nick nodded. "You're over at Oak Springs, then?"

"I am. There's been some bother, though."

"Oh?"

"Do you know a guy called Arnie Rawlings?"

"Yes. I heard he'd moved back with his family. Bought up the garage, hasn't he?" Nick held the teapot over Tony's mug with a questioning look.

When she nodded, he poured more tea. "And the shop," Tony added. "And he won't serve Red, Chris, or me, for that matter. He's taken against anyone from Oak Springs."

Nick sighed a particularly weary-sounding sigh. "That's ridiculous."

"I'm glad you think so," Tony said, warming to the man even more. "Chris is upset about it."

"Of course. It's come at a bad time with Bryony gone."

"Yes. And she really likes milk. She can't bear tea without it, and she drinks a lot of tea."

"Well, I can help you there," Nick said. "We've milk straight from the cow. And butter and cheese too. Take as much as you want."

"Thank you."

Nick glanced at her across his mug of tea. "Tell me, is Mum here now?"

Tony took a breath sensing the air, making sure. She shook her head. "I'm sorry."

"I keep expecting to see her. I find it so hard to accept I'll never, never see her again." He turned to Tony like a child asking her to explain away the pain.

Tony felt his loss. She missed her child. And Maya. They weren't gone forever, but the pain was harsh all the same. She gulped her tea for want of distraction.

"The heart is a long time catching up with the brain in accepting," she said eventually.

Nick took the mugs and dumped them in the sink. "There is something you can do for me, though. You being a medium."

"What is it?" Tony asked.

He brightened up. "Have you ever played the Ouija board?"

❖

A feeling of dread rose in Tony as Nick pulled a sepia-colored games board out of a cupboard, laid it on the table, and unfolded it. The letters and numbers were printed in a curving, old-fashioned font. The sun and moon had faces. The sun looked surly, and the grinning moon smugly malevolent. She shivered. She told herself not to be ridiculous. It was just a parlor game from long ago. Harmless fun.

But her sixth sense wasn't listening, and, as Nick lit candles in a circle around them and switched off the overhead light, her mouth grew dry, and her heart rate quickened.

Nick sat in the chair next to her and put the tips of his fingers on one side of the pointer. Reluctantly, Tony put her fingers on the other side of it.

The pointer moved slowly to the letters portion on the board.

Nick looked surprised. "It's working. It's never done that before."

He must be unconsciously moving the pointer. He wanted to speak to Vera so badly that he probably had no idea he was doing it.

In which case, Tony had no use for the nasty feeling in the pit of her stomach.

The pointer stopped at the letter B. Then it slid to A, then D.

"Bad," Nick said in a whisper.

It took off again, moving quickly now. It barely stopped between letters focusing on the same three.

"Bad, bad, bad," Nick said. "What does it mean?"

"Don't know," Tony muttered.

"Mum? Is that you?" Nick asked.

The pointer sped to the word NO.

"Then who?" Nick's voice was almost a whisper.

The pointer careered across the board, hitting letters, pausing, and moving off again.

T O N Y. K N O W S. W H O.

Tony took her hands from the board.

"Someone's trying to tell us, tell you something," Nick said, his voice shaking. He smiled weakly. "Do you think it is Mum? Having a joke?"

Tony stood up. She wanted to get as far away from the Ouija board as possible.

"When your mum came to me, she was kind. She loves you. Whoever that was, Nick, I'm as sure as I can be it wasn't her."

Nick stared up at her. "Then who the hell is it?"

Tony arrived back in the kitchen laden down with two bags. She lifted out three packs of butter, a big slab of cheese, and two pitchers of milk and set them on the table. Red and Chris stared at them and then at her.

"What did you do, rob a cow?" Chris asked dourly.

Tony laughed. "No. I made a friend of your neighbor, Nick."

Chris glared at her. "You shouldn't have. He's in mourning."

"Now, Chris," Red intervened gently.

Chris snapped her head to them. "It's not how we do around here. We don't go bothering our neighbors. This isn't London. We don't pop in for tea every five minutes."

Tony stared at her. She didn't know the London Chris was referring to. Tony couldn't think of a place where people were less likely to pop in for tea. Pop in sometime next month by mutual agreement if there's a space in my diary, maybe.

"How did you even know to go to Willow Farm?" Chris's frown had deepened while Tony had been distracted.

"I didn't. I went for a walk. Thought I might find a shop. I saw the cows and—"

Chris sat bolt upright. "You went on his land uninvited, begging for handouts?"

"No. I didn't," Tony said. Vera had asked her to go. She couldn't tell Chris that, of course.

"Like that would be such a terrible thing to do," Red said quietly.

"Nick saw me on the trail, and we got talking." Tony edited the truth for the greater good. "He thinks it's terrible what Arnie did."

Chris glared at her for a second, and Tony worried that she'd made it worse. It was possible that Chris would hate Nick knowing her business. She hadn't thought of that. But Chris slumped back onto her chair with a "Hmmph" and let out a breath. "He's a good sort. You, mind, you were supposed to be digging potatoes."

"In this rain? Give the young butch a break." Red fetched a glass and poured milk into it.

They all eyed the rich, cream-colored, slightly frothy liquid until Red held it out to Chris. Chris took a sip. Then she drained the glass and licked her lips.

"Why don't we always get our milk from Willow Farm?" she asked, plonking the glass on the table.

Red shrugged, pulling a knife from the block. "Cheese sure looks good."

Tony lifted the last item from the bag at her feet. "It'll go with this loaf. Nick's taken up baking."

"Listen to you. Nick's best friend, are you now?" Red asked.

Tony just grinned.

"Brew up, Red," Chris said. She smiled at Tony, and the smile changed her face completely. "You're all right, kid. Well done." She cut thick slices of the wholemeal loaf, slathered it with butter, and inserted slabs of cheese while Red made the tea.

When they were all sitting around the table with their sandwiches, Chris looked at Tony and began to chuckle. "Thought I might find a shop." She glanced at Red. "Kid thought she was going to walk to the shop."

Red snorted and then laughed out loud. "Walk to the shop," they repeated. The idea was apparently hilarious.

Tony ignored their teasing. The bread was soft and chewy, the butter was like salty cream, and the cheese melted in her mouth. They could make fun of her all they liked. Tony had saved the day even if she hadn't meant to. And it tasted gorgeous.

Tony's hand strayed to the iPad, lying innocently on the patchwork quilt. She should be exhausted, but she was as far from sleep as she was from London. She couldn't shake Maya from her mind, and that hot mess was a scab that shouldn't be picked. She drew her hand back and focused on the quilt.

It was a fading record of all that was lesbian and feminist in the 1980s. A red power fist inside a women's symbol had been sown next to a black double-bladed axe. Interlinked women's symbols, the symbol meaning lesbian, were dotted across the bedspread in various colors. Some were block printed, some embroidered, and one was made entirely from sequins. There was a lot of work on this quilt. Tony's eye was drawn to a pink, red, and purple oval shape that she realized with a sudden shock was a labia. Well, that was entirely reasonable and very feminist, she told her prudish self. Women should take pride in their bodies. She couldn't quite get her head around displaying herself like the woman in the drawing. But she had to admire the display of self-love.

One patch declared *The Future is Female*. Tony was standing in the future, and it wasn't nearly as female as it should be. And that's without getting into the fledgling impact of being gender-queer in this brave new world. An inverted black triangle gave Tony pause for thought. The Nazis used them in the camps for people they called anti-social, some of whom were lesbians. It had been adopted in the eighties and nineties as a lesbian symbol alongside the pink triangle for gay men.

And lying on top of all that symbolism and call to revolution lay a little slab of twenty-first century technology. A siren urging Tony to pick over the remnants of her relationship.

Sod it. Tony grabbed the tablet and clicked on Facebook, putting Maya's name into the search box.

A second later, there she was. Tony's heart surged and immediately tightened. Maya looked beautiful in her profile pic. Tony's gut and stomach united to encase her heart in a box. At least until Tony had had a chance to read her ex's latest posts.

There were new photos. Tony clicked on them straight away. And it was entirely her fault when she was staring at the handsome, masculine-of-center, annoyingly-muscly new squeeze. Eve Phee was the person's Facebook persona. The butch, or however they identified, smiled softly at the camera, an arm draped casually across Maya's shoulders. Maya was leaning into Eve's neck.

The sparkle in Maya's eyes and the brilliance of her smile were knives cutting a path through Tony's pathetically weak defenses. Her heart burst out of the box, and her head and gut did nothing to quench the pain that overwhelmed her. *What a fool I am.*

Tony closed the tab. She shut her eyes, unable to stop that horrible day from flooding back.

❖

Three months previously

Tony pushed the sofa aside to vacuum it and, a second before sucking it up, spotted Louise's fluffy purple hair tie. She hit the off button with her foot and sank onto the footstool. The hair tie was soft in the palm of her hand. Just eight days ago, Louise had been looking for it. Yelling before school that it was the only one that held her hair properly. Tony had tossed her another hair tie, one Louise didn't want to wear, and stressed they were going to be late again.

If she had that time again, she'd search the house top and bottom for the purple hair tie just to make it all right for Louise. Damn, Amy. Damn that selfish bitch. Tony choked back the tears and made herself stand up. She needed to keep busy. Not that easy to do with no child to look after and no job. But Maya would be here soon. They'd have a lovely evening. Tony would try not to be so down. Try not to go on about missing Louise again. God knows what it was like for Maya. Tony had been so distracted, but, hey, she could make it up to her now.

Tony was about to switch the vacuum cleaner back on when her phone chimed, announcing a text.

It was from a number she didn't recognize. No actual message, just a video. Maybe someone had sent her something funny to cheer her up. Tony watched half-heartedly, hoping there were no kittens involved.

The footage had been shot in a bar. Music was playing low in the background, and people were chatting. The camera was zooming in on a couple kissing passionately several tables away. Tony felt uncomfortably like a voyeur. And then she realized she was staring at Maya in side profile with her tongue down a boyish woman's throat.

The phone dropped out of Tony's hand.

She was still sitting on the half pulled out sofa, numb, with the vacuum cleaner at her feet, when Maya's key turned in the door.

"Hey," Maya said brightly. Then immediately, "What's wrong?"

Tony stared at her. Three years they'd been going out. This was the woman she trusted and shared intimate secrets with. The woman, incidentally, that she'd nearly been killed for.

"Tony? What's happened?" Maya sounded worried now.

Tony pressed play on the film and passed her phone to Maya.

Maya watched. Then gasped. Her mouth opened and shut as if her brain was running at a pace too fast for her lips.

"I…I…" she said. Then she frowned. "Why is the vacuum cleaner in the middle of the floor?"

"Do you think I give a flying fuck about the Hoover right now," Tony said.

"No. Um, can I move it, though, and can we put the sofa back against the wall so we can talk?"

Tony ground her fingernails into her palms. Maya's obsession with neatness bordered on a psychological condition. But it was what Maya needed, so, like many times before, Tony put her needs aside. She stood, shoved the sofa back, and put the vacuum cleaner away. Then she flipped the top from a bottle of beer.

"Tony, shit, Tony, I'm sorry. I wanted to tell you. I was going to tell you last week, and then Amy took Louise away. You were devastated. I just couldn't…" Maya stopped talking. She looked everywhere but into Tony's face.

Part of Tony knew this must be killing Maya. Honesty with a capital H was a huge deal to her. But the moment of compassion was quickly quashed.

"How long?" Tony asked.

Maya drew in a breath. "Since the end of May."

"Two and half months ago. What, you just met her then?"

"No. She came to my practice in March."

"She's one of your herbal clients?" Tony folded her arms. This was another of Maya's hard and fast rules. Absolutely no shenanigans with any of her clients. "It blurred the relationship," Maya always said. She had the grace to look ashamed, at least.

"Yes." Maya's voice was barely above a whisper. "Oh, Tony. I didn't mean it to happen. She asked me out for a drink. Just as a friend. She was new in town."

"You never mentioned it."

Maya bit her lip. "You were stressed. Down. You'd lost your job at the theater."

"Of course. Yes, you start seeing someone else just after I lose my job. Nice."

"Nothing was supposed to happen." Maya reached for Tony's hand.

Tony stood up. "So when did it?"

"What?"

"When. Did. You. Sleep. With. Her?" Tony didn't feel anything except cold.

Maya's eyes widened. She didn't want to tell Tony, so Tony prepared herself. Guessed.

"That night. The same night."

Sometimes there was no joy in being right.

Tony sat down. Took a slug of beer. Let out a breath. "God, Maya. So, do you love her?"

Maya looked surprised by the question. "Tony, it's, um, it's early days."

Suddenly Tony couldn't care less. "Just go, Maya," she said.

Maya flinched as if Tony had struck her. "But, we should talk. We can probably work this out. I mean, I don't know—"

"Go," Tony repeated. She looked into Maya's eyes and knew they were done. She could never trust her again.

And it hurt like hell.

After Maya left, Tony drank a lot of beer, played the film way too many times, and finally, sensibly, called Jade.

In Jade's arms, she cried

CHAPTER THREE

I don't know about this," Tony said. She had a bad feeling that built with each step closer to the dark and gloomy copse of trees at the farm's entrance.

Bryony heaved a sigh. "It's not going to take long, I promise. Look, we're nearly there. We need to start at the gate."

Although it was only September, it was surprisingly chilly in Derbyshire at four a.m. Or maybe it was just cold in this eerie part of the farm. Tony swallowed. There was a strange energy. It thrummed disturbingly beneath her feet.

"Start at the gate and look for the tallest tree," Bryony said.

Thick clouds draped the sky. Tony switched on her head torch. It was her old one, which was why it had been lying about in her backpack when she'd left on the spur of the moment. The strap was broken, and the batteries didn't fit properly, making it unreliable, but a reassuring shaft of light shone out from it. The trees were brooding shapes in the dark. Their branches waved in gusts of chill wind.

"Go into the wood," Bryony said impatiently.

Tony didn't want to. "Does twenty trees a wood make?" she asked to distract herself. Bryony ignored her. Reluctantly, Tony started walking. "We're looking for a cash box, you say?"

"Yes. I put the necklace in a metal cash box and buried it." Bryony floated ahead. "There," she said suddenly, patting a thick, gnarled, ancient-looking tree trunk. "Stand here and walk ten paces east."

Tony remembered the sun rising behind the farmhouse. She took ten steps in that direction.

"Good," Bryony said. "Take three paces south."

Tony turned. A gust of wind blew fallen leaves into Tony's face. It felt like a warning to go no further.

"Now twenty paces west."

Tony stopped to glare at Bryony. "Back to the tree, you mean? Why did you make me walk ten paces east? I could have just walked ten paces west."

Bryony bit her lip, looking sheepish. "There's not much by way of amusement where I am."

Tony glared at the ghost, tempted to go back to bed. The head torch slipped again. Tony righted it. Then she walked back to the tall tree and ten steps beyond it.

"Is there a large rock there?" Bryony asked.

"Ow!" Tony's wet foot made sharp contact with a boulder the same color as the night.

"Excellent. Now walk around the rock."

Tony frowned suspiciously at Bryony. "Walk around it? Really? Fool me once…"

The ghost smiled. "I'm not messing with you, I promise. You need to find a dip in the ground."

Against her better judgment, Tony circled the large rock. She found the dip, fell into the dip, tripped over the shovel, and landed in something wet and slimy. The head torch strap snapped. And then she felt the first drops of rain.

"That's it," Tony yelled. "We do this in the morning."

"No," Bryony insisted. "Chris doesn't want you here. She'll see you digging and throw you off the land for good this time."

Tony wanted to say fine by me, but Bryony looked so plaintive she bit her tongue and knotted the broken strap so that it kept the torch gingerly on her head.

She took a breath and pushed the spade into the ground. The broken strap slipped with the exertion, and the dying head torch lurched drunkenly to the side. Tony shivered. Her summer jacket was sod all use against the bitter winds of Derbyshire. The shovel drove poorly through the soil, its edge too blunt to cut cleanly.

And then, with a dull thud, the spade met something buried there. Excitement surged through her just as the torch slipped entirely from her head, leaving her in total darkness. The rain picked up, and Tony wanted out of the cold, wet night. She dropped to a crouch, feeling for the box.

A chill crept through her as she searched the damp soil. The wind whistled through wet branches, sounding eerily like a voice.

"Get out of my grave."

Tony froze rigid, convinced a man had spoken malevolently into her ear.

"Keep going," Bryony urged her.

But Tony ignored her because she had found something in the earth, and it wasn't the hard metal of a cash box.

The crumbling cylinder between her fingers felt like a bone, long stripped of flesh.

The moon broke through the clouds shining a pale spotlight on the grotesque outline…

Of a skeletal, human hand.

❖

The house was quiet. Deathly quiet. Tony lifted the router to read the password and scribbled it down, her hand shaking so badly the letters were practically illegible. Or they would be to anyone else. How she longed for anybody else to be there at that moment. Especially Jade.

Somehow the thought of her funny, gorgeous, feisty, wonderful, and very best friend got Tony up the creaking steps and into the musty back bedroom. Her throat tightened. She pulled the window open, gulping in the damp air. Outside, the rain dripped steadily. Nothing moved in the vegetable patch. Sheep hunkered down in their field. Her eyes followed the track leading to the copse where a person was buried in the cold, wet ground.

Tony slammed the window shut and fumbled in her backpack for her tablet. It came to life.

Police, that's who she needed.

There was a convenient form. It was amazing what you could do these days without speaking to a soul. Tony could report the whole thing, leave at first light, and that would be that. She clicked on the link.

But would that be that?

She could input the details anonymously, but what would happen when the police turned up? Red and Chris had met her. They could give a description. Had she mentioned she lived in London? And anyway, how quickly would the form be read? What if the police arrived before Tony had left? Could they pin the body on her?

Of course not. There was no flesh on it. The hand and presumably the rest of the body had been there some time.

"What are you doing?"

Tony jumped, quickly turning off the tablet. Bryony stood in front of a chest of drawers painted purple and green with women's symbols painted on the knobs. Bryony had a cold glint in her eye.

"Are they homemade?" Tony asked by way of distraction, nodding at the drawer handles.

"Yes," Bryony said crisply. "Red carved them. Why did you run away just now?"

Tony stared at the ghost in disbelief. "Oh, I don't know, possibly it was something to do with the dead body in the woods," she hissed.

Bryony flinched. "Oh. You found something then."

Tony could tell the ghost knew the body was there. "What the hell's going on?"

"It was an accident," Bryony said.

"What was?" Tony asked in a whisper.

Bryony drifted to the bed, sat next to Tony, and closed her eyes. "It was a long time ago," she began.

❖

9 November 1985, Oak Springs Farm, Derbyshire

The young woman grabbed Bryony's arm, pulling her toward the front door.

"We have to leave now," she said. "My father will be at the station, but he'll come looking if he comes home and I'm not there." Lisa's nose was swollen and crooked. Her right cheek was a vivid shade of purple. Bryony had only known her a day, but she'd seen the bruises on Lisa's arms, legs, and back. The welts. The cigarette burn. Fifteen years old and the butt of her father's rage. They couldn't go to the police. Raymond Walker was the police.

The young woman was scared, but they didn't need to rush. Lisa had come through the network, and Bryony had taken the usual precautions. They'd met in a park in Sheffield, and Bryony agreed Lisa needed to leave tonight. Bryony had fed Lisa at the farm, grabbed the emergency supplies pack, and now they were leaving for a safe house down south. No one had seen her. The Oak Springs women were away, wild camping at Doll Tor for the Full Moon.

Bryony opened the front door. The smell of smoke was still hanging in the air around the gutted outline of the barn. Bryony took a step, and the wind blew her backward. Instinct told her they should wait it out. These sudden storms could be ferocious, but Lisa's hand on her arm was a vice. They got into the truck as the rain started.

The windscreen wipers on the Bedford needed replacing. They hadn't worked right since Jay had tried to clear solid ice. Bryony wouldn't have let her near the pickup truck. But that wasn't the Oak Springs way. With rain coming down in sheets, Bryony drove on sixth sense, gripping the wheel as they bumped over potholes on the rough track.

Out of the pitch-black came a blinding light. Bryony slammed on the brakes.

She stopped inches from a car blocking the path.

Someone was getting out.

"Get in the floor well," Bryony said. She shrugged her coat off and covered Lisa with it. The girl was shaking.

"I'm searching this vehicle," barked a rough, male voice. Sheffield accent. Cocky. He was taller than her and packed with muscle. She glimpsed a thick mustache before a warrant card obliterated her view, and she was pushed aside so hard she fell over into the mud.

Lisa screamed, "Stop it, Dad."

Raymond Walker was dragging her from the truck.

Bryony scrambled to the cargo bed. She fumbled under rope and sacks and crap for the tire wrench, and it wasn't there.

She turned toward the sound of footsteps moving fast, squelching in the mud. Lisa had managed to get away. She was running desperately for the road with Walker steps behind her.

Bryony pulled everything out under the seats in the cab, gasping when her fingers wrapped around metal.

Another scream and her fear vanished. The child was being dragged along the ground by her hair to the bastard's car. He was laughing.

Bryony jumped in front of him and swung the wrench with all her strength. His eyes widened in shock. He staggered backward, bent over.

Bryony reached for Lisa, and Lisa's hand gripped hers.

They got two steps when Bryony's arm was wrenched behind her back. The tire iron smashed into her face, and she thought she was going to throw up. She couldn't see. There was a thumping sound in her ears. A hand gripped her throat, the fingers squeezing her windpipe.

Her feet dangled in midair like a child. She forced her head up. Walker smiled. Her heart screamed for air getting louder until the sound filled her ears. His eyes locked into hers as the light faded, and everything faded to this one moment. His pleasure and her pain.

❖

Bryony's story played like a film. Tony saw the farm and the track as it was thirty years ago. She felt the wind and the rain. Smelled smoke and charcoal. She tasted Bryony's fear. But when Bryony fell silent, Tony was confused.

"So, what happened? You didn't die in 1985."

"I passed out, losing a chunk of time in the process. When I came to, I was lying on the ground with the tire iron in my hand. Walker was dead, and Lisa was in her dad's car cowering in the driver's seat."

"So, how did he die?" Tony asked.

Bryony swallowed. "Delayed reaction. I guess his brain bled out or something. I didn't think about it. I was in shock. I'd been hit on the head myself and half strangled. He was an abuser, but still, I'd killed someone. I wanted to scream, to cry, but I stared into that poor girl's face and kicked into action. I dragged the body into the trees, took the car up to the main road, and left it with the keys in the ignition. I drove Lisa to Brighton, then turned around and came straight back. The car had gone, thank the Goddess. Joyriders, I guess. I didn't care. I was grateful to them. I buried Raymond Walker where I'd dumped him before. No one knew."

"Lisa must have known," Tony said.

"I don't know how much she saw. It was dark and raining. I never told a soul. Not until now. His, his…grave, it's on land that Chris has sold. That's why I needed to get you up here."

"Long lost treasure, you said," Tony muttered. There were lies, and then there was, well, something like this.

"I didn't think you'd come if I asked you to move a body."

Tony nearly fell off the bed. "What?"

"You have to, Tony." Bryony tossed her head back, and her eyes were twinkling emeralds catching the light.

Tony wasn't moved. "Absolutely not. No way. Not a chance in hell." She picked up her backpack. If ever there was a time to leave, this was it.

"Tony, even if you won't move the body, you can't go to the police." Bryony grasped Tony's wrist or tried to. Her fingers slipped through Tony's flesh, sending an icy chill along her arm.

"It's the only thing to do," Tony said through gritted teeth.

Bryony snatched her hand away. "And what will happen to Chris and Red?"

Someone rapped on the bedroom door.

"Breakfast in fifteen," Red grunted. "Don't dither. Those potatoes won't lift themselves."

Out of the window was a sky streaked with pink. Tony looked at her watch.

It was five forty a.m.

❖

The day's porridge was lumpier than the day before. There were dry oats inside the lumps. If a person was marketing the dish, they could call it Stuffed Lump Surprise. Tony didn't think it would be popular.

"How do you like Chris's porridge?" Red asked, chomping heartily down.

Chris glowered at Tony from across the table.

Tony dropped her eyes to the scratched, well-worn surface of the wood. "It's very filling," she said.

Chris seemed satisfied with that. "Hey," she said. "Remember how you wanted to drive Emily P yesterday?"

Red grinned. "Need me to drive the truck?" they said in a passable imitation of Tony's voice.

Tony looked from one to the other and nodded warily.

"You could do us a favor and take the truck to Hatherwell Motors," Chris said. "The potatoes can wait."

They could wait forever if Tony's back had any say in it.

Red put their spoon down. "I'd go, but I did something stupid this morning. I got between a calf and his feed, twisted my foot, and it's brought on my Achilles tendinitis. It's a long-standing problem. You could say it's my Achilles heel," Red said with a grin.

Chris chuckled. "Achilles heel," she repeated, shaking her head.

That was interesting. Tony had thought the repetition-laughing thing was when someone said something stupid. It was for jokes, too, apparently. Not that it mattered. There was no point in Tony trying to work out their odd little ways. Not when she was leaving.

"Even in Hatherwell, there will be someone who knows me. They'll ask me how I'm doing." Chris looked down at her porridge.

Bryony rested a hand on Chris's shoulder. The gesture softened Tony's heart though Bryony was not in her good books.

"Only go if you want to," Chris mumbled. She sounded like it didn't matter a damn to her, but Tony was beginning to know better. Chris was a person deeply in grief. A proud person who didn't want to show their feelings to an almost-stranger. Maybe Tony could take the truck. Actually, it would give her a ride.

"Yeah, I'll take it," she said. She'd drop off the truck and walk to Hatherwell train station.

"Pick up some stuff for us, will you." Red hobbled over with a list, and Tony suppressed a groan. It meant she had to come back to the farm first. That was annoying and would make it a lot later getting a train, but she could still do it. And they needed the damn groceries, thanks to the only homophobe in the village. Tony thought about that. Was Arnie the only homophobe? Possibly not, but it was a nice thought.

Red pressed three twenty-pound notes into Tony's hand. "That should cover it."

Tony had money. It was her phone she didn't have and any common sense, apparently. She stuffed the cash in her pocket, took the list, and nodded at the pair.

"Okay," she said.

"Oh, and there are no truffles on the list but do pick some up if you see any," Chris said, brightening up and punching Tony playfully on the arm.

Tony smiled. Chris was an okay person when you got to know her. Too bad Tony wasn't planning on hanging around.

❖

Emily P started up the first time, making Tony smile. The vehicle had faith in her even if the Oak Springs lesbians didn't.

"Don't get cocky," Chris said. "She likes to mess with new people."

"Like a cat with a mouse," Red drawled from the porch. Red had hobbled outside with Chris to form the opposite of a reception committee. What was that? A departure committee? It was enough to make a dyke nervous driving their beloved truck for the first time.

But Emily P purred like a kitten, the gears responded smoothly, and Tony managed not to stall as she turned the vehicle around and set off along the track. She could feel them shaking their heads after her, but she shrugged it off. She felt a little sad to leave. Taciturn as they were, they weren't all that bad when you got to know them.

But a long-dead body was serious stuff. Tony hadn't decided what she was going to do. She didn't want to get Red and Chris into trouble, especially as Bryony was sure they were entirely innocent. But would the police see it that way?

It was a beautiful day. The sun shone on hills so green you could toss them in a salad. The sky went on forever. The road was clear, and Emily P was a joy to drive. There were no strange noises and no sudden judders. Tony relaxed at the wheel and smiled. *I think she likes me.*

"What do you think I should do, Emily P?" she asked.

"I think you should stay and help us."

Tony started as Bryony materialized in the passenger seat.

"All packed up then," Bryony said. "I take it you're not planning a long hike."

Tony's rucksack was on the seat next to the ghost. She sighed and pulled Emily P over, turning off the ignition to not pollute the atmosphere more than she had to. In the sudden silence, she did wonder if that was a mistake. But Emily P liked her. Tony turned to Bryony.

"I'm going to London. Don't try to talk me out of it."

Bryony wasn't angry. She looked sad. "Sure, that's fair enough. You've been kind to me coming up here at all. Will you do one more thing before you go?"

Tony opened her mouth to say, "No."

And, as if predicting Tony's answer, Bryony shook her head. It was a soft movement reminiscent of a stream flowing over moss. "It's not for me. It's for Chris and Red. There's someone who will help me, but you'll have to find her."

Tony stared at the oak tree ahead. She didn't want to know. She should go back home. But if she did, she'd have to deal with Everything.

"Who?" she asked, turning to the ghost.

Bryony's face softened. "Lisa Walker," she said.

"The daughter of the—" Tony was about to say, "murdered man." Was it impolite to use that term to the person who committed the murder? Even if it was done to save another? "The man you, um, hit on the head."

"Yes. Raymond Walker's daughter. I'm dead, but if the police discover the body, it would be inconvenient for her. She'll move it."

Tony had some experience with people being killed and the police getting involved. Inconvenient didn't cover it.

"The only problem is, I don't quite know where she is."

Tony tapped her fingers on the steering wheel. She should get going. She had to take the truck to the garage, get the shopping back to the farm, and then head back to the station.

"You have to go to Hatherwell anyway," Bryony said.

"You know I do," Tony said, watching a squirrel bound erratically along the branch of the tree. Looking for acorns, no doubt.

"There's someone in the town who may know where she is. Just one visit while you're there."

The squirrel jumped to the next tree, scampered upwards, and disappeared. It wasn't stopping to help ghosts with odd, annoying requests.

"Please, Tony. If they find Raymond Walker, it will finish my Chris. You've seen how she is. And it won't go well for Red either."

Tony sighed. "One visit," she said.

"One visit," Bryony repeated.

Tony turned the ignition, and Emily P purred into life. Then she spluttered and coughed. Tony put her into first gear, and she backfired spectacularly. The squirrel fell out of the tree. It jumped up onto its hind legs, glaring furiously up at her. She half expected it to shake a furry little fist.

A blue van pulled off the road. It came to a halt behind the truck, and a man got out. Tony's spirits lifted when she saw it was Ed, and she wound the window down. "The truck won't start," she said.

"Pop the hood," he said amiably.

Tony found the lever under the dash. In a minute, Ed was humming to himself under the bonnet. Tony got the impression he liked his work. What a shame that nasty Arnie guy had taken over the garage.

"Give it some fuel, but do it gently," he called out.

Tony pressed down on the accelerator, and Emily started up sweetly.

"Let me show you something," Ed said, beckoning Tony over. "Leave the engine running."

"See down there." Ed stabbed a finger at the depths to the left of the engine.

Tony couldn't see much, but she nodded.

"Fuel pump's the problem. If she cuts out on you again, let her cool down before you try to start her up again. Don't push the truck too hard. If she starts to splutter, slow down. Got it?"

Tony nodded again. Ed walked her back to the cab.

"Lucky I was passing, luv." Ed scratched his head. "Or do you prefer, mate?"

Tony thought about it. She wasn't sure. What was the non-binary term? Child? Mate was the closest.

Ed grew tired of waiting for an answer. "It didn't sit right with me not helping Red and Chris. It's not how we do things around here. Now I've seen what the problem is, it's easily fixed. And we've got the part. Been sitting on a shelf for twenty years. Could say we're doing Arnie a favor clearing out junk," Ed said with a wink. "I can fit the part at the farm, but I can't do it now. I've got to get back."

"That's okay. I've got to get some stuff in Hatherwell anyway," Tony said.

"Right then. Remember what I said, and you should get there and back. Tell Chris and Red I'll be over tomorrow with the part." Ed patted Tony on the shoulder and got back in his van.

It really was a shame A1 Autos didn't belong to Ed. Tony pulled out onto the road continuing on her way.

❖

The Forest View Care Home was not, in fact, near a forest. It was in the middle of a residential area close to a main road. Housing Estate View Care Home would have been a more accurate name. The residents had landscaped grounds, at least, with paved paths that meandered through grass and shrubbery. Tony pulled into the car park outside a two-story, stone-fronted, sprawling modern building. She walked past a row of potted plants to the front door and buzzed. A voice said to "come in."

The white woman working at reception was probably in her late forties or early fifties, carrying a little weight with shoulder-length blond hair and a soft smile. A name badge pinned to her right epaulet identified her as "Madeline."

"Can I help you?" Madeline asked. She had a West Country burr, twinkly blue eyes, and an open, kind face.

"Yes, I've come to see Sandra," Tony said the name of Lisa Walker's friend. Lisa visited, apparently. And, although Sandra had early-onset dementia, Bryony thought there was a good chance Sandra would know where Lisa was living.

"Friend, relative?" the receptionist asked, reaching for a book titled Visitors.

"Yes," Tony replied.

The receptionist frowned.

"I'm a friend, and we're both friends of Lisa Walker," Tony embellished on an impulse.

Bryony raised an eyebrow and then made a thumbs up sign. She could have spoken. It was highly unlikely that the receptionist was going to hear her.

In fact, the receptionist visibly relaxed. "I see. Sign in here, please. You'll find Sandra down the hall, third door on the right, number five. She will be pleased to see you, I'm sure."

Tony walked to a corridor that led off from the reception area. The walls were painted a soothing pale green color. Paintings of flowers hung on them. Tony found number five and knocked.

"Hello?" someone called out from within.

Tony was unprepared for how young Sandra was. She looked in her mid-forties at most. The dementia that had brought her to the care home was early onset indeed. She had long, dull, dark hair that contrasted sharply with pale, practically translucent skin. She had a downturned rosebud mouth, a small, somewhat stubby nose, a splattering of freckles, and hazel eyes. She looked curiously up at Tony from a heavily padded, red armchair. She pulled a shabby cardigan around her and repeated, "Hello?" in the same tone as the first time.

"Hello. I'm Tony," Tony said.

"I know you are," Sandra replied.

"Go along with her," Bryony whispered. "She'll get upset if you don't, and we'll get nothing from her."

"The survivors' group, Hackney. I remember you." Sandra nodded at Tony. "Do you remember me?"

"Um, yes," Tony said hesitantly. It didn't feel right lying to the woman, but Bryony wafted in front of her with a desperate expression.

"That group helped me so much. How are you doing now?" Sandra said.

"Er, I'm fine," Tony said.

"That's good because you were in a bad way."

Tony looked at Sandra and wondered what it was like to hold on so vividly to some memories while others were confused or lost entirely.

"Have you seen Lisa lately?" Tony asked.

Sandra stared off into the middle distance. "It was bad for you, very bad," she said. "It was for me too. But you know that. Justice is important, Tony. No one's going to give it to us. I love you for what you're doing. Keep doing it, won't you?"

Tony frowned. Sandra not only had dementia but was a survivor of something horrible, clearly. She started to moan. "You will, won't you, Tony?" Sandra wrung one hand with the other, agitated and fitful.

Bryony stirred beside Tony. "Say yes, for goodness' sake."

"Okay. Yes, I will," Tony said quickly, and Sandra relaxed immediately. Tony took a breath and tried again. "Lisa Walker, Sandra, do you remember her? Have you seen her lately?"

Sandra looked into Tony's eyes. "You're the only one that matters."

Bryony sighed. "She's very confused today. I don't think we'll get anything more out of her. Sorry to waste your time."

Tony smiled at Sandra. "I have to go now. Nice to meet you."

Sandra looked up and reached forward to grasp Tony's hand. "Good to see you again, Tony. Don't leave it so long next time."

Tony tried to make eye contact, but Sandra was staring over Tony's shoulder, fixated on the wall.

Bryony led the way back to the main door. The reception desk was empty. Maybe visiting hours were over. Tony glanced back at Sandra's room, feeling sad. There was a door open on the floor above. The receptionist was inside the room. She wore a plastic apron and gloves and was standing beside the bed of an elderly male patient. His eyes were closed. Even in the dim light of the bedside lamp, Tony could see he wasn't well. His breathing was shallow, and his skin was pale and clammy. An air of finality radiated from the room. The receptionist raised a hypodermic syringe. She pushed it into the man's arm and turned her head. Her eyes caught Tony's, and she smiled as her thumb pushed the plunger home.

❖

Tony pulled up outside the farmhouse with mixed feelings. She got out and walked to the cargo bed to pull out the groceries.

"Ed will sort you out Emily P." She patted the sky blue metal, and the truck gurgled. It was probably water cooling in the radiator, but it sure sounded like a sigh of contentment. Maybe it was. Tony had known far stranger things to happen.

She'd miss Emily P. And, bizarrely, maverick Red and grumpy Chris. Chris was grieving, of course. She had a right to be angry. Red was grieving, too, Tony realized. She'd assumed all their behavior was to do with Tony. How self-obsessed was that? Tony had reasons to be self-centered, and she wasn't looking forward to heading back to them.

She felt sick at the thought, but she had to go. She scoured the sky for signs of rain. It looked clear enough, and quite frankly, she'd have to risk it. She'd checked train times, and she could walk to Wooly Mill in time to get the bus to Hatherwell to pick up the connecting train.

She hadn't decided what to do about Raymond Walker. Even his name made her uneasy. She felt his presence malingering in the ground beneath the copse. Tony didn't need Bryony to tell her he'd been a horrible man. It wasn't good for Chris or Red to have that energy on their land. Tony shouldered the box of groceries and sighed.

At least in London, there would be Jade.

Her best friend would know what to do.

Sidestepping the worst of the mud and chicken droppings, Tony walked toward the kitchen, and then she paused.

Laughter pealed from inside. Tony smiled. Someone was in a good mood. That would make it easier to leave even if she did feel a stab of loneliness.

Tony was struck by how familiar the laughter sounded as she pushed open the heavy, old door. And then she stopped. And stared.

At the sight of Jade perched on a chair, her knees tucked into the table, and her hands wrapped around a mug of coffee.

"I thought you were out of coffee," was all she could think of to say.

Red beamed at her. It was an unsettling sight. "Jade found some at the back of the cupboard. We're celebrating."

"Blue Mountain, no less." Jade sounded as delighted as a child at a birthday party, a party complete with balloons, streamers, cake, and a bouncy castle. She jumped up. "Tony, Tony, Tony." She threw her arms around her and squeezed hard. "Why was your phone in Manchester?"

Tony blinked.

"You didn't sell it to that pot-hound, did you? I didn't believe him and demanded it back." Jade fished a cell phone out of her pocket and handed it to Tony.

It was the one she'd lost on the train. Tony opened and closed her mouth as shocked as a fish on the wrong side of an electric eel. "What? When?" she managed.

Jade took the groceries from Tony, passing them to Red. Then she steered Tony to the table, sat her down, and poured her a cup of coffee. Jade was remarkably at home in the space. That was the least of Tony's questions.

Red hummed as they put the shopping away.

The kitchen door blew open, and Chris strode in. "Emily P's back then…" She caught sight of Jade and tailed off. "Who's this?" she asked, as tense and unwelcoming as the day Tony met her.

"Jade." Red stretched the name and added a lilt. "Tony's friend."

Chris glared at Tony before turning to Red. "This isn't women's land anymore."

Red glanced across the table to Tony and Jade. "Why don't you go to Tony's room? You'll have some catching up to do, I'll bet. And Chris and me, we need to talk."

❖

Jade's, some might say, eye-wateringly bright exuberance dampened when she stepped inside Tony's bedroom. She took in the rickety single bed, the threadbare rug complete with alarming stains, the peeling paint on the draughty window, and the general air of not being lived in, loved, or even dusted for many a long year.

She patted the faded lesbian symbol eiderdown before gingerly sitting on the bed. "Are they hygienically challenged?" she asked in a whisper.

Tony bounced down next to Jade and rested up against the lumpy pillow. "I haven't seen Red's room or Chris's, but from the sitting room, the kitchen, and this room, I'd say yes, ma'am."

Jade frowned. She didn't like dirt. Cleaning wasn't an obsession like it was with… Maya's face popped into Tony's mind, and it hurt. The pain was in that region between the stomach and chest where a person wanted to but couldn't let go.

Jade slipped her hand into Tony's. "You really worried me, y'hear?"

"I'm sorry. I couldn't phone you because, well, you know why." Tony turned her cell phone over, staring at the dark screen.

"How come you don't know my number by heart?" Jade dipped her eyes.

Tony said nothing.

"You disappeared, Tony. Scared the life out of me."

Tony exhaled slowly, feeling guilty. Breathing out was calming. She concentrated on that and not on the reasons why she'd left.

"You couldn't let me know you were going? Not one text?" Jade sounded annoyed, but when Tony looked into her face, all she saw was concern.

Tony shrugged. Jade didn't know how dead Tony felt inside, how hopeless. "I needed a change of scene."

Jade sighed. "Well, I found you. So, it all worked out in the end."

Tony sat up on the bed. "How?"

Jade went to the window, shivering. She tried to pull it completely closed, failed, gave up, and peered out. "Hey, you can see sheep from here."

Tony crossed the room. "How did you find me?"

Jade frowned up at the ceiling. "That's a real bad crack. You think it's safe?"

"Jade," Tony said sharply. "How did you know where I was? And how did you find my phone?"

"Well," Jade said, picking at her nails. "You remember things didn't go so well for me recently?"

"Of course, I remember." Tony would never forget Jade's abduction and the awful women who carried it out.

"Now look, Tony, don't get mad." Jade grabbed Tony's arm. "In fact, why don't we sit down?"

Tony let herself be led back to the bed.

"I put a location finder on your phone and your iPad."

Tony opened her mouth to protest, then she looked at Jade's stricken face. It was bizarrely understandable after what Jade had been through. "How did you get past my passwords?"

Jade shifted awkwardly. "There are ways. You should change your passwords probably. Ghostsareannoying was strangely easy to guess."

Tony sighed, and then she squeezed Jade's hand.

"And I'm not sorry," Jade said in a rush. "This is a dangerous world, and I'm worried about you, Tony. You've been distant since—"

Tony flinched. "Don't want to talk about it," she said firmly.

"Okay." Jade backed off. "So why are you here?"

The draught from the window intensified, making the tattered curtains dance. Jade shivered violently at the same moment Bryony materialized on the small armchair in the corner.

"So cold in this room," Jade muttered.

Bryony stared at Jade. "I'll come back later," she said before disappearing.

"Ah," Jade said immediately. "You're on a case." Jade was clairaudient. She could hear ghosts but not see them. A skill that had both advantages and disadvantages.

"What else do you think I'd be doing?" Tony said.

"I don't know. I thought maybe this was a retreat for lesbians. Lesbians who don't mind the run-down, dirt-encrusted look," she added as an afterthought.

"A lesbian B&B? Hilarious thought, Chris cooking breakfast and Red changing the sheets. I can see the advert now: Like your scenery with a side order of swamp? Come to Oak Springs, the women's land that time forgot."

Jade smiled. "It is scenic here."

"It is," Tony agreed.

"So, are you going to tell me about this case, or what? As the Supernatural Detective Agency's CEO, I expect to be kept in the loop."

Tony stared at Jade. "CEO? When did you start calling yourself that, and why are you the CEO?"

Jade looked at Tony as if the reason was obvious. "You're the lead detective. I thought that was fair as you started the agency."

Tony humphed. She hadn't so much started the agency as started seeing ghosts and been dragged into the dubious and dangerous world of supernatural detection.

"And I'm the co-detective, but my contribution is so much greater than that. Calling me chief executive officer is the least you can do." Jade looked down her nose at Tony, her expression daring Tony to disagree.

Jade really was a beautiful woman. And a fabulous friend, chasing after Tony at a moment's notice to make sure Tony was safe.

"And Maya was an associate..." Jade looked at Tony and tailed off. "Oh, shit. Sorry."

And there it was, that sick, humiliated, horrible feeling. You didn't just stop loving someone. Even when they so publicly stopped loving you. Jade wrapped her arms around Tony and pulled her into a soft, warm embrace.

"There is money in this case, right?" Jade mumbled into Tony's hair.

Tony sat up. "Five hundred pounds."

"That's good because we're both resting at the moment." Jade shifted awkwardly.

"*You* are," Tony said. "I was fired."

"They were so unsympathetic." Jade pressed her lips together. She'd already mentioned Maya. Tony guessed she was trying to make sure she didn't talk about Louise as well.

The names were two elephants in the room. Maya's conjured shame and hurt and betrayal. But Louise's...well, that was just pain. It hurt all the more because Tony had settled into the joy of being Louise's parent every day and not every once in a while when Amy felt like facilitating a visit.

There was a knock at the door.

"Fancy a nightcap, Jade?" Red called from the hall. "You too, Tony. If you want."

"Okay," Jade called back. "Thanks."

"Come down when you're ready then." Red's voice got fainter as they went back downstairs.

"I hope Red means a drink. Though an actual Wee Willie Winkie nightcap wouldn't go amiss in this room. It's freezing. And I don't get it. It's still summer, right? I haven't traveled forward in time?"

"I know!" Tony said. And she'd been feeling such a wimp with no one else complaining of the cold.

"Coming?"

"You go ahead. I'm done with this day, I think," Tony said.

Jade put her arm around Tony's shoulder. "Are you okay?"

Tony nodded. "Just exhausted."

Though after Jade left, Tony lay staring up at the ceiling for a long time. It was good to see her, but Tony had fudged Jade's question about payment. Tony hadn't found the necklace. And what on earth would Jade think if she found out about Raymond Walker? Tony was already an accessory after the fact or whatever the expression was. She didn't want to implicate Jade as well.

Tony turned the situation over in her mind until, at last, she drifted off, no nearer to finding a solution.

❖

Jade stared at the rows of wilting potato leaves and finely-fringed carrot tops. "Veg patch," she squawked.

Tony leaned on her spade, biting her lip so as not to laugh. "This is what farmers up here call it."

"It's a field. A real muddy one," Jade said, frowning angrily at the ground as if it had mired itself to spite her. No boots fitted Jade, so they'd stuffed the ends, and she was bundled up in a three-sizes-too-big old coat of Red's. She'd had to roll back the sleeves to get her hands out to hold a spade.

Tony sliced through the earth and turned it over with a fork pulling out ten or more good-sized potatoes.

"Thank you," she muttered to the potato stem trailing across the soil. It had done its job. It could rest now.

Jade eyed her suspiciously. "When did you start talking to plants?"

Like that was a bad thing for a lesbian that conversed with ghosts?

The clouds parted, and the sun gilded the field in late afternoon sunshine. It was warm, and the air was fresh. Tony slid her fork under another bunch of potato stems and lifted a bunch of smaller spuds.

Walking awkwardly in the too-big boots, Jade picked a spot farther along the row. She pushed her shovel into the ground only for it to stick a few inches in. She put one foot on the step where the handle met the blade and pressed down. The shovel sank another inch. Jade huffed, squared her shoulders, gripped the handle hard, and kicked down like a mule.

The spade shot down, throwing Jade off balance. She sailed forward, flipped through the air gracefully, and landed face-first in the mud.

Tony burst out laughing. Jade glowered as Tony pulled her to her feet.

"It gets easier, I promise you," Tony said.

"I've never liked potatoes," Jade said bitterly.

"Why don't you collect the other veg?" Tony suggested, waving toward the section of legumes, brassicas, and squash.

Jade scooped up a large trug decorated with double-sided axes and walked over to the bamboo poles covered with the winding stems of French and runner beans.

Tony spent a cheerful hour digging up potatoes, carrots, and sweet potatoes. She gulped down lungfuls of clean air and felt a gentle burn in her muscles. She loaded spuds into the wheelbarrow as Jade wandered over. The trug was piled high with beans, corn, courgettes, and a small pumpkin. The frown had gone, and Jade radiated her characteristic warmth.

"So, are you going to tell me about this case or what?" she asked.

Tony opened her mouth to tell Jade everything and felt suddenly, horribly cold. Sweat trickled down her spine as she felt a presence behind her. She turned around.

A man stood by the wheelbarrow. He was white with wavy, light brown hair and a thick mustache. He had heavy lidded, wide-set, pale blue eyes with dark shadows beneath them. He had a gash on his forehead and stubble on his chin. He looked in his forties. He wore a black leather jacket over a dark shirt and trousers cinched with a thick belt. He had the kind of mouth that only smiled at someone else's misfortune. He was of medium height and build, and wore an expression that lay somewhere between surprise and triumph.

"You see me, don't you?" His accent was Yorkshire, and his tone was sly and mocking.

Tony didn't answer. Jade snapped her head in the ghost's direction.

"Two psychic dykes." The ghost laughed nastily. "How queer."

His wickedness washed over her in a wave of rage and hatred with the threat of violence. He stepped closer, bringing the stink of stale beer and staler tobacco, earth, and the rusty smell of blood.

He pointed a finger at Tony. "You disturbed my grave," he said.

His eyes drilled into hers for several terrifying minutes. When Raymond Walker turned away, she saw the back of his head had caved in. Tony wrenched her eyes from the inky red, matted blood, the pulped flesh, and the ivory flash of splintered bone. When she opened them, he had disappeared.

Jade was staring after him. "Who are you?" she said sharply.

"He's gone," Tony told her.

The color had drained from Jade's face. "Who the hell was that? What was he talking about?

Tony took the trug from Jade's shaking hand. "There's something I need to catch you up on," she said.

❖

"You came all the way from London to Derbyshire to dig up a necklace?" Jade asked, stirring the saucepan on the stove. A head of steam fragrant with spices rose from it.

They'd returned to find Red cooking dinner. Jade had sniffed, frowned, tasted from the pot, and banished Red from their own kitchen. She'd told Tony to sit at the table and chop vegetables while she scoured the cupboards.

Tony didn't mind. Jade had ordered her around long before Tony had met Maya. And during the many previous painful absences of Louise. It was comforting. She nodded to confirm that she had traveled two hundred miles to retrieve a piece of jewelry.

"Even though you've little money and no work?"

Tony sighed. "This is work. You're always saying we should take the Supernatural Detective Agency seriously. Anyway, Bryony said it was likely there would be a finder's fee. The figure of five hundred pounds was suggested," Tony said, slicing corn on the cob to Jade's micro-instructions.

"She can suggest what she likes. It's what Red and Chris decide that counts," Jade observed. "Bryony told you she'd buried a necklace given by her ex-girlfriend?" She tasted the stew and added a splash of hot sauce.

Tony sipped her tea. The milk was creamy and delicious. It would be hard to go back to the ordinary stuff after tasting this. "Huh? Yes. She went on and on about it. They were all non-monogamous, with lovers coming out of the yin-yang. One of them gave Bryony a valuable necklace. Worth thousands, apparently. She couldn't wear it because Chris didn't like how close they were getting, so Joan buried it in the copse for her. She left her a map and everything."

Jade turned from the stove. "You're unbelievable. Map? Buried treasure? That didn't remind you of anything?"

Tony looked at Jade blankly.

"The plot to *Treasure Island*? How come you didn't recognize it?" Jade said, shaking her head.

"I haven't read it. Or seen the film." Tony stopped chopping. It had seemed an odd, even potentially ridiculous story, but Bryony had been so convincing. She thought about the details. "Oh. Do you think Bryony didn't have a girlfriend called Joan De Silva, who was very tall?"

Jade's eyebrows shot to the top of her head. "Her nickname Long Joan de Silva, by any chance?"

Tony swallowed. "Possibly. Do you think there isn't a necklace?"

"I seriously doubt it." Jade swept the corn into the pot along with chunks of pumpkin and came to sit at the table. "What happened when you started digging?"

"Raymond Walker's ghost appeared." Tony shivered. She caught Jade up on Bryony's version of the night Walker died. "Bryony said not to go to the police," Tony finished.

Jade glanced at the door to the sitting room. "And you can't," she said quietly. "Red's Black, they're both lesbians, and Walker's one of their own."

With a sinking feeling, Tony realized how right Jade was. She wished they lived in a world where a young Black man, or an older Black butch for that matter, could go to the police for help and not end up the object of suspicion.

"What about Sergeant Lewis?" Tony asked. Carol had helped them before. She was a lesbian and had proven she could be trusted.

"This is a serious crime," Jade said. "Sergeant Lewis would have to act on our information, and we might not come out of it real well. Anyway, one thing is sure, we can't move the body. We'd incriminate ourselves."

"That's what I thought," Tony said. "I suppose there is a body there. I only found a bit of a bone, and it was dark."

"He said you disturbed his grave," Jade pointed out. "You'll have to go back and check the site but don't dig any further. I'm going to avoid the copse and the corpse altogether."

Tony didn't want to go back. She sighed.

"Maybe you got it wrong?" Jade said hopefully. "A Halloween joke, you think? One of Bryony's lovers playing a trick on her many moons ago?"

Jade didn't look like she believed that for a minute. And Tony didn't either. Raymond Walker was too convincing, too full of hate. "And what do we do if a body is buried there?"

Jade wrinkled her forehead thinking hard. "He's been there over three decades. We can give it a couple of days to find this Lisa Walker."

"Do you think we should?" It was a horrible problem, but not exactly their problem. The sensible thing to do would be to get as far away from it as they could.

"We are the Supernatural Detective Agency, dedicated to helping ghosts," Jade said, tasting her concoction and smacking her lips. "And, seeing as we're up here, we could go and see Amy's parents."

Louise's grandparents lived a short train ride away in Manchester. Tony's heart flickered cautiously. Amy's mum had always liked her. She hadn't responded to the messages Tony had left, but maybe if Tony saw her in person, she might tell Tony where Amy was.

"But if we don't find Lisa Walker, we tell Red and Chris. And then we leave." Jade stabbed a piece of pumpkin, testing its rigidity.

"Okay," Tony said, pulling out of her reverie about Louise. "That's better than my plan."

"Which was?"

"To leave. And then to tell the police."

Jade exhaled slowly. "It may come to that. But then we tell Red. It's nothing to do with Red or Chris."

Tony thought of how the ghost had lied to get Tony up there. She didn't want to freak Jade out any further, but it occurred to her:

They only had Bryony's word for that.

❖

They were all sitting at the table drinking tea when Chris returned, bringing a breath of sweet air into the steamy kitchen. The climate apparently varied daily in Derbyshire, and this evening felt more summer than autumn. Chris prised off her boots, kicked them to one side, and straightened. She ignored Jade, nodded at Tony without smiling, and said, "Your friend's still here, I see."

Tony opened her mouth to speak, but Red cleared her throat. "Wash up, Chris. Dinner's ready."

Frowning, Chris took a long sniff, and her shoulders relaxed a little. She scrubbed her hands in the sink while Jade ladled out bowlfuls of stew and Red carved thick slices from Nick's loaf. Tony buttered the bread. The atmosphere was awkward, and no one broke the strained silence.

Chris sat in her place, looking at the bowl in front of her. Chunks of corn, potatoes, carrots, and pumpkin sat in a spicy, fragrant broth. Chris took a spoonful. Then she looked at Red in astonishment and scooped up another spoonful.

"Red," she said. "This is fantastic. It's delicious."

"Isn't it?" Red bit down happily on a piece of pumpkin. "Jade cooked it."

Chris opened her mouth. Closed it. Turned to Jade. "What is this dish?" she asked.

"Pepperpot stew, a vegetarian version." Jade tossed Chris one of her winning smiles.

Chris's face softened. "I've never...well, not for a long time. How did you...I mean, did you go shopping for the ingredients?"

"Not at all. All your own vegetables. I had to root around in your cupboards. The spices are a bit old, which is okay. I just added more of them."

"Amazing," Chris said, looking around the kitchen. "Something's different in here."

"We cleaned, Tony and I," Jade said. "Need clean surfaces to cook."

"Happen you do." Chris swallowed a mouthful. "We've let ourselves go since Bryony..." She didn't finish the sentence.

"That's understandable," Jade said gently, and Chris smiled.

They ate in a companionable silence. It was near sunset, and fiery fingers of orange light fell through the window onto the tiled red floor.

"Tony cleaned," Chris said suddenly with a chuckle and then a guffaw.

Red joined in the laughter.

Tony frowned. Why was that funny? Why wasn't it funny that Jade, who they'd known for five minutes, had cleaned?

She ignored them, biting down on pumpkin and letting scotch bonnet, garlic, and thyme tingle on her tongue.

CHAPTER FOUR

The chickens in the barn gawked at Jade in much the same way as they had Tony. Chris had sent them to collect eggs, and Jade had insisted on bringing the trug. If it hadn't been for the ridiculously large Wellington boots and a too-long and, frankly, fraying cardigan she'd found, Jade might have passed for a farmer. In a bad light.

Roosting hens scattered nervously when Jade loomed at them, her boots slapping on the bare concrete floor. She beamed at five dusky brown eggs left behind on the low ledge.

Tony inspected the nesting boxes keeping an eye out for Toxic Harvey. She had just spotted a large speckled egg in a corner when she was startled by a scream, a splat, and a triumphant crow.

Harvey glared up at Jade, who had jumped onto the ledge and was trying to stop the remaining eggs from rolling out of her swinging trug.

"Getoffoutofit!" Tony growled at Harvey in her best threatening London manner.

Harvey assessed her with one eye, found her wanting, turned his back, and advanced on Jade.

"Why do they keep this dangerous bird?" Jade shrieked, shrinking back and losing an egg in the process.

"Foxes? Fertilization? Suspicious musical theater actors?" Tony suggested. She pulled the pitchfork from the hay bale.

"Don't kill it," Jade said.

"Wasn't going to. I'm kind to animals," Tony muttered, wafting the spines firmly but carefully in Harvey's direction.

He puffed out his chest and sauntered away as if bored with the whole episode. Jade clambered down at the same moment Raymond Walker appeared by the hay.

"Great," Tony said. "We've just got rid of one nasty entity."

Walker looked at her with an expression to sour milk. "Why are you pratting about pretending to be farmers? I sussed out straight away you two are city dykes."

Tony twitched as she always did when the word dyke came out of a homophobe's mouth. Fine for lesbians to use it. Even allies at a pinch, though that made her uncomfortable. But when a bigot said it, it was meant as an insult of the worst kind.

"What do you want?" Jade asked abruptly.

"I want my body moving. They buried me on lesbian ground. It's disgusting, and I won't stand for it."

"Poetic justice for a homophobe." Jade rested her trug on the ground.

"And I want revenge. That bitch killed me. Tell her I want justice." Walker folded his arms.

"Self-defense was the way I heard it," Jade said.

Walker smiled unpleasantly. "Court won't see it that way. So what, I was handy with my fists? Women need keeping in their place. No judge is going to side with dykes running around behaving like men."

"Things have changed," Tony said quietly. Walker didn't seem to know that Bryony was dead, and Tony didn't want to enlighten him.

"You can't use this, so I'll tell you. What are you going to say? You heard it from a ghost? I enjoyed smacking them around. Lisa, her mother, that dyke bitch that was helping her get away. If I had my time over, I'd do it again. Only harder." Walker grinned as he melted away.

Jade sat on the ledge, looking as grim as Tony felt.

"Maybe we *should* tell the police," Tony said. "It could take ages to find Lisa Walker."

Jade frowned, thinking. "We can't move the body," she muttered a few minutes later.

"What is this, state the obvious moment?" Tony spluttered. "We've been over this. We'd get DNA all over it." What constituted DNA exactly? Body fluids? Tony tried to work out how much spit, tears, blood, sweat, or unmentionable fluids she might inadvertently spill moving a forty-year-old skeleton.

"You saw a finger? What if that's all it was?"

Tony thought about Walker's ghost. "He didn't have a hand missing."

"Who?"

"Walker. I think his whole body's up there. I can't tell without digging further, and I don't think I should. I might get sweat on something."

"More likely tears in this climate. Still, you're right. We should leave well alone. But it does mean we have no proof there is a body buried there, and if we go to the police, we could be throwing Chris and Red under the bus for no good reason."

Tony nodded. "And the only witness to his death being self-defense is a ghost."

Jade sighed, staring at the eggs as if for inspiration. "Which brings us back to Lisa Walker."

"We said we'd give it three days," Tony said tentatively.

Jade stood up. "Okay then. You need to push Bryony for info. And you need to return to Walker's grave."

Great. "And what are you going to do?" Tony asked.

Jade was peering at her hands with a horrified expression. "Scrub the chicken poo from under my nails. At least, I hope it's chicken poo."

"Fun jobs all around then," Tony said wryly.

❖

Tony had no idea how to summon a ghost. They came to her unbidden, usually at the most inconvenient of moments. Jade had promised to keep Chris and Red distracted while Tony wandered up to the copse to check the site in daylight.

Tony spotted the tallest tree but couldn't force herself into the wood. It looked benign with the sun shining on it. Branches stirred gently, fiery leaves fluttered down, and the air was fragrant with the smell of dark, wet compost. It wasn't such a bad place to lie. And yet Tony shivered. She didn't want to see Walker. Even in incorporeal form, the violence pulsed from him.

She thought of developers uprooting the trees and ripping through the land and felt sad. And then she imagined one of their machines turning up Walker's bones and officers arresting Chris and Red. She pushed her reluctance aside.

Her footsteps were light. Barely a twig snapped under her trainers. She found the rock, and the blunt spade was there to confirm she was in the right place. She'd forgotten it in her haste to get away. There were signs of digging, but the hole was shallow. Tony was shocked to see what little progress she'd made. Already leaves had settled over the depression as if the little wood was jealously hoarding Walker's remains.

She looked around to make sure there was no one in the vicinity. She pulled gloves from her jacket pocket, put them on, and pushed the leaves aside.

Rain had collected in the hole muddying the soil. She glimpsed yellowed ivory beneath it but didn't investigate further. It was the confirmation she needed. She lifted the spade and backfilled the small crater. She pressed the earth down with her shoe and then panicked. What was she thinking of, leaving a footprint?

She found a slim branch with many smaller branches coming off it and brushed the soil until the patterns of the underside of her trainer were blurred beyond recognition.

Bryony appeared then, looking quizzically down at Walker's grave. "I ask you for help, and apparently, you're doing the exact opposite," she said. Her accent softened the words, and Tony wondered if Chris had ever managed to stay cross with her for long.

"We're not touching the body," Tony said.

"We? Perhaps you haven't realized I'm not much help to you in the physical department. Not in my current state." Bryony tossed her head, a twinkle in her eye.

"My friend Jade and me. I don't want Jade anywhere near this grave."

The smile dropped from Bryony's lips. "Your friend's here? When did that happen?"

"Somewhere between the waste of a trip to Forest View and Walker's ghost viciously haunting us in the barn." Tony walked through the copse, making for a clearing beyond it. Roughly sawn logs were strewn across the area. Tony sat on one and let the sun play on her face, warming her.

Bryony sat beside her. "Why the barn?"

"We were there collecting eggs."

Bryony lifted an eyebrow. "And Walker hates chickens?"

"He wanted to talk to us. I think the poultry were incidental."

"What does he want?"

"Revenge. Justice. Oh, and I think he'd like to be moved too, so you're in agreement about that. He doesn't like being buried in sapphic soil."

Bryony swallowed. "Did he say that?"

"In between ranting about how he hates lesbians and loves to hit women."

Bryony grimaced. "I told you, didn't I?"

"You did. And you're right. He's horrible. No wonder Lisa wanted to get away from him."

Bryony played with her hair absently. "He was a monster."

"We need to find her, Bryony. We're giving it a few days, that's it. Forest View was a bust. What about Lisa's foster family in Brighton? Are they still in touch with her?"

"They can't help you. They emigrated, and I haven't a clue how to get in touch with them."

Tony sighed in frustration. She thought about Bryony's story. She'd implied several people were involved in getting young women away from abusive situations. "What about the rest of the network?"

"What are you talking about now?"

"Your rescue network. It must have been bigger than you and the people in Brighton."

"They wouldn't talk to you even if I had a way of contacting them. We had to shut the network down. We rescued a young woman like we did with Lisa. This young woman seemed to be settling into her new home. But a few months later, she returned to her abusive family. Her parents contacted the police. The two women who took her in and the woman who acted as her initial contact were charged. The three of them kept the rest of us out of it, explaining the whole thing away as an isolated, misguided incident. Fortunately, the police had no reason to think it was anything other than that. The women were given suspended sentences. The group broke up. We burnt address books, letters, and anything that would link us to each other. Lisa never mentioned her Brighton family after they emigrated. I'm as sure as I can be that they won't know where she is."

Tony grunted in frustration. "We've got limited time here, Bryony. I'm sorry, but if nothing pans out, we'll be heading back to London."

Bryony frowned. Then she turned her face up to the sun. Tony followed her gaze, and through the autumn leaves, she watched clouds scudding across the sky.

"I met Lisa in Hatherwell about a year ago. She was working as a home help for an elderly gentleman. I picked her up there. Gosh, now, it was just the once. It'll be a miracle if I can remember the old fella's address." Bryony drummed her fingers on the log. Or she would have if she could have. There was no sound, just her hand fading into and out of the ribbed bark. Then she sat bolt upright. "Fifty-seven Brook Street. How's that?" She beamed at Tony. "It's amazing what you can remember when you try."

Tony smiled back. It wasn't much, but it was a lead. Somewhere to start.

❖

There was a primary school opposite number fifty-seven, Brook Street. Tony arrived as the children were being dropped off. She blamed farm life for getting to Hatherwell by that time in the morning. Nine o'clock was practically late afternoon if you got up when Red and Chris told you to.

Tony watched a woman kiss her nine-year-old good-bye. Was Louise arriving at school right now? And where? Amy's number was dead. Or dead to Tony at least. Tony wrenched her eyes away. Jade was right. They should go to Amy's parents' house. Tony needed to do anything she could to get her daughter back.

Number fifty-seven looked like it had been recently renovated. The front door was new, with impeccable paintwork and polished chrome door furniture. A late-model compact car was parked on the neatly paved front drive. As Tony walked across the road to the house, she noticed an elderly man watching the comings and goings of the school. Tony nodded politely to him as she passed.

Tony pressed the video doorbell and stood back. It ding-donged reassuringly. Thankfully, it wasn't one of those silent doorbells. Tony supposed those bells did sound somewhere inside the buildings they were installed on, which was fine for the occupants. But inconsiderately anxious-making for callers.

A little voice came out of the doorbell. "Leave it on the doorstep."

"I haven't got anything for you. I need to ask you something," Tony shouted in the general direction of the bell.

The door opened so quickly Tony suspected the woman had been standing behind it. She was young and professional looking, wearing a tailored jacket and skirt. She eyed Tony cautiously. "I'm on my way to work," she said in a tone that suggested Tony was taking up her valuable time.

"I'm looking for Mr. Simmonds. Is he in?" Tony asked quickly.

The woman relaxed slightly. "Ah. I thought you were selling something or were one of those awful charity collectors. Mr. Simmonds has moved to Sunset Days Sheltered Accommodation. It's not far. Let me see." The woman stabbed her phone several times with neatly clipped fingernails. "Fifteen, Riverside Court."

Tony opened her mouth to say "thank you," but she was already looking at the smart blue paintwork of the closed front door.

❖

Access to the Sunset Days apartments was through a reception area. The middle-aged Caribbean receptionist smiled kindly when Tony indicated that she had come to visit Mr. Simmonds.

"Let me try him," she said, picking up the phone.

A moment later, she shook her head regretfully.

"Any idea when he'll be back?" Tony asked.

"No, my dear. They come and go as they please. We are here to take deliveries, and for emergencies, to tell them visitors have arrived, and sometimes for a bit of company if I'm honest."

"So, he could be out all night?"

The receptionist chuckled. "Indeed, he could. There's a side gate for residents. They all have fobs. Will you leave your name and number? I'm sure Mr. Simmonds will be sorry to miss you. He doesn't get many callers."

As Tony wrote down her details, it occurred to her that Lisa Walker might still be working for Mr. Simmonds.

"Actually, I'm trying to contact a former employee of his by the name of Lisa Walker," she said, handing back the message slip.

The smile disappeared from the receptionist's face. "Lisa Walker, you say?"

Tony nodded. "Does she work here?" Tony asked.

"She does not," the receptionist answered, taking the message slip firmly from Tony's fingers.

Tony was thinking of questions that might elicit more information when the receptionist pointed toward the entrance door. "I'm afraid I have to get on with my work now. The exit buzzer is just there on the right. Do you see it?" she said.

Puzzled, Tony left.

❖

Back at Oak Springs, Ed was bent over the truck's engine in the yard, tinkering away with what looked like a mallet and a blunt screwdriver. Red was perched on the rusting hulk of an old water tank with a bottle of beer.

"We don't want all that starting up again." Ed's voice came from under the bonnet.

"We certainly don't," Red replied, their back to Tony. "It was a nasty business. Is he trying to stir folk up in the village?"

"Happen he is, but I doubt he'll sway many to his point of view. We live in different times now, Red."

"Hope you're right, Eddie."

"Hi there," Tony called out.

Red turned and nodded a hello. "Ed, do you remember Tony?"

Ed popped his head out to look Tony up and down. "I remember. Are you the partner of the beautiful woman cooking up a storm in Chris's kitchen?"

He had to mean Jade. Red was looking at her intently. "No," Tony said.

"She's got someone at home, in London?" Red spoke as if the answer was barely of interest, looking down into the bottle.

"Nope." Tony narrowed her eyes at Red. She wasn't ready for anyone to mess with her best friend's heart either. Not when it was so fragile. Red shifted on the water tank and suddenly had reason to check their fingernails for dirt.

Ed chuckled. "Pass me that breaker bar, will you, Tony?" he said, nodding toward his large, battered, and very oily toolbox.

Tony peered into it, sensing some kind of test. What the hell was a breaker bar? Her hand hovered over a pitted and chipped crowbar, and a smug grin appeared on Ed's face. There was a long socket wrench lying in one of the trays. She pulled it out. "Is this what you want?"

"That's the one, luv, I mean, what do I mean, Red?" Ed turned to Red for help.

"You could use their name," Red suggested. "What pronouns do you use, Tony?"

"She, her," Tony said.

"But you're butch?" Red asked.

Jade bustled out into the yard with a plate of saltfish fritters. "She's working around to embracing it, I think."

It wasn't the first time someone had asked. Tony was always being mistaken for a man. She appraised Red, admiring the way Red stood in her skin, oozing female masculinity.

Ed walked to the cab and turned the ignition. Emily P purred to life to applause from Jade and a whoop from Tony.

"Thank you, Ed. How much do we owe you?" Red asked, reaching into the back pocket of their jeans and pulling out a well-worn, brown leather wallet.

Ed shook his head. "Nothing. I was right embarrassed by the way Arnie treated you. All the business you've given the garage over the years."

"You sure?" Red asked. "I should pay you for the part, at least."

"Arnie won't know it exists, let alone it's gone. There's not much call for spares for 1981 Bedford trucks around here. It's been sitting on that shelf probably as long as you've had Emily P." Ed wiped his hands on a rag.

"Stay for dinner then," Red said.

"Smells fantastic, but I can't. Meeting the lads for a drink."

"How about tomorrow?" Red suggested.

"I'll cook," Jade said. "Here, take another saltfish accra."

"Don't mind if I do. Coming for dinner will be a right treat," he said, biting happily down on the warm fritter.

CHAPTER FIVE

Nick arrived promptly at seven thirty with more milk, a pack of foil-wrapped butter, a tub of creamy soft cheese, and another loaf.

Red put the loaf in the bread bin while Tony put the dairy goods in the fridge, narrowly avoiding colliding with Jade as she tore out of the pantry to attend to a saucepan boiling over on the range.

"It's good to be here," Nick said, not sounding like it was good to be there at all.

"Delighted to meet you, Nick." Jade greeted him warmly. "Now, go with Tony to the dining room and relax."

"Don't you need me to do stuff here?" Tony asked.

"Nope," Jade said. "Red's all the help I need."

Tony frowned while Red smiled, their chest swelling with pride. Pride at muscling in on what was usually Tony's job. A job that Tony often moaned about doing, but that wasn't the point.

"Off you go. Your damn yam feet are getting in my way and on my nerves." Jade plonked napkins in Tony's hand and prodded her firmly through the door. "Put these on the table and fold them nicely."

Jade had spent much of the day reclaiming the dining room from dust, cobwebs, and ancient mending projects resting on yellowing newspaper. The room smelled of furniture polish and something Jade called room freshener that Tony suspected was pine disinfectant and washing-up liquid.

Nick pulled out an oak chair as polished and dark as the table and sat in it.

Tony stared at the napkins, wondering what version of folding nicely Jade wanted. She liked the one with a pointed top and the bottom folded under and tucked in so that it stood up. No matter how often Jade showed her, Tony never remembered the complicated one with three pockets to put cutlery in. Pointy top folded bottom, it was.

Tony glanced over to find Nick as stiff-backed as the chair.

"How are you doing?" she asked, sitting beside him.

"Feels strange," he said. "Haven't been out much. Or around folks." He looked at her hopefully. "I don't suppose, have you seen Mum at all?"

Tony shook her head. "Nick, I'm not sure we should talk about ghosts tonight. Chris and Red don't know I'm psychic, and I don't know how they'll react."

"You're probably right with Bryony gone. Hey, has Bryony been to see you?"

Tony was pleased when the kitchen door opened, and she didn't have to answer.

Ed stood in the doorway, shocked and bewildered. "Arnie sacked me."

❖

Even Jade's stew chicken with glazed sweet potatoes, macaroni pie, and salad couldn't tempt Ed away from the beer he was nursing between his large, grimy hands. He picked at his plate, pushing chicken and macaroni around without eating. He was different from the person who had chomped down three saltfish accra the day before. Nick glanced at Ed regularly with concern but ate heartily, sitting taller and gaining color with every bite.

Red was enthusiastic enough for everyone. They had lost the power of words except to say, "Your hand sweet, Jade. Boy, your food is the lick."

Jade was a star in the kitchen, and it was good to see her in her element. "You're showing your Bajan roots." She teased Red.

"Red's home brew's got a kick, Eddie," Chris said as Ed took the Sappho bottle opener and popped the top from a third bottle.

"Put some of this good food in your belly, old friend," Red said. "Don't waste that rice either."

"You eat it." Ed pushed his plate in Red's direction. "I'm too upset. I've worked at A1 Autos for twenty years. What am I going to do?"

Chris sighed. "Tell us what happened, Eddie. For goodness' sake, get it out of you. We're fed and watered. You can take the time you need."

Ed had clammed up after his big announcement. Now his face was flushed, his fists were clenched, and his shoulders tight. Maybe it would do him good to talk it out.

"He put cameras in the garage. Can you believe that?" Ed blurted out indignantly.

Jade leaned forward. "What kind of camera was it? Was it disguised as something else?"

Tony nudged Jade as Ed threw her a look to wither plants. Clearly, he wasn't in the mood to indulge Jade's interest in, some might say, her obsession with, surveillance gadgets.

"What does that say about trust?" Ed said.

Tony didn't like to point out that Ed probably broke trust when he took the part without asking.

"He asked me if I'd worked on your truck, Chris, and I said, happen I had. In my own time, of course. He was furious. 'Right then,' he said, 'you were caught on camera taking something off the shelf and putting it in your bag. I've got footage.' He's got footage! Who does he think he is, Steven Spielberg? 'I can't keep you on, not after this. Now I could go to the police, I'd be within my rights. But for old times' sake, I won't. Get your things, Ed, and go. You don't work here anymore.' You don't work here anymore! That snot rag of a man. He's been in charge five minutes, and he's upset one of our best customers." Ed gestured toward Chris. "Well, one of our oldest customers. And he's sacked me. What next?" Ed exhaled slowly, then finished his beer. "I'll take another," he said to Red.

Red and Chris shared a look. They must have come to one of their wordless agreements because Chris passed Ed another bottle.

"She makes a good homebrew, your lass." Ed nodded toward Red.

"Not my lass. That was Bryony." Chris closed her eyes briefly at Bryony's name. "Red does make good ale, though. But Red's not she, Red's they now, remember?"

Ed blinked at her. "That doesn't make sense, Chris. I'm just an ordinary, Northern bloke. This is Derbyshire. We're not ready for theys. What does it mean, anyway?"

"People that don't identify as he or she," Red told him. "Non-binary people."

"What happened to men being men and women being women?" Ed slurred his words slightly.

"Nothing's happened to them. We're talking about the world of people in between," Tony said.

Ed turned to her. "Are you a they too? You could pass for a man in the right light. When you turned up at the garage, I wasn't sure."

Tony didn't answer. She was used to being mistaken for a man in the binary world, and butch was starting to feel right as an identity. She hadn't even considered whether she was non-binary.

"It's too much for me. Words are changing too fast." Eddie stared morosely at the tablecloth.

Red patted his shoulder. "You don't have to understand, Eddie. You have to want to try."

Tony decided it was time to collect the empty plates. "I'll wash up," she said.

"Give you a hand." Nick stood up with her.

The kitchen looked like a bomb of tomato and jerk sauce had exploded in it.

Nick stopped in the doorway. "Wow. Your friend is one hell of a cook. She could also get a job turning ordinary rooms into splatter art."

Tony smiled, liking Nick more and catching glimpses of the man he was beneath his grief.

They washed and dried plates in a companionable silence while Tony worked around to subtly pumping Nick for information.

"I wanted to ask you something," Tony said when all the plates were neatly stacked on the draining board. "You've known Red and Chris a long time."

"Since I was ten." Nick brought more pots to the sink, took a sponge, and began to clean the table.

"I gather there have been a lot of women living here over the years."

Nick nodded, his attention on a particularly stubborn splash of tamarind paste.

"Have you ever come across someone called Lisa Walker?"

Nick stopped to think. "There was a Lisa around for a while."

"In the late 1980s?"

"No. It was in the early 2000s. She was close to Star. Star lived up here at Oak Springs for a good few years and was in the coven. They were partners, I think. I didn't get to know Lisa, and I don't know her second name. Star was a good sort. Very powerful in the coven, but she'd had a difficult past. We did a healing ritual for her."

"A healing ritual?"

Nick nodded. "The coven was all female apart from me. I was an honorary member. A few years before that, they'd never have welcomed a male practitioner. Some of the original Oak Springs women didn't like men coming onto the farm at all."

"Are you talking about the eighties now?"

"Yes. When Oak Springs became women's land."

"Separatism was common then," Tony said. "When I came out in the nineties, there were lots of lesbian separatists. Some of the clubs were mixed, but many were women-only. So, you are pagan?"

"I am, thanks to Oak Springs. I'm quite ashamed to say it all started when I crept across one night to see if the rumors of witches dancing naked on the full moon were true."

Tony gave Nick a questioning look, and his face flushed with embarrassment.

"It's no excuse, but I was sixteen. My friends at school dared me, and to be honest, I was mostly scared." Nick sat down at the kitchen table. "Let me explain what happened."

❖

Oak Springs Farm, July 1991

It was July, when the days are long, and the meadows alive with wood anemone and buttercup. The moon was shining from a deep purple sky with a scattering of clouds across it. Nick hadn't yet grown to appreciate the moon in all her glory, but he felt the pull of her as he jumped the fencing between the two farms. His feet were light on the damp grass. Sheep dozed at the other end of the field. He breathed in the sweet scent of barley cooling from the heat of the day, grass underfoot, and farm animals bedding down for the night.

He kept off the track. If he were caught on Oak Springs property, Chris and Bryony probably wouldn't call the police, but they would be angry. And they would tell his mum. He stopped mid-step to consider what he was doing. Mum would be upset if she knew. But he couldn't go to school tomorrow and admit he'd wimped out. He kept going, sure it was a load of old rubbish anyway.

He walked toward the farmhouse, unsure where the Oak Springs women danced in the moonlight. A fallow field, maybe.

He didn't know how much space they needed for that kind of thing.

As the farmhouse loomed nearer, he didn't feel so sure of himself. He'd laughed when his mates had called them witches. Suddenly it wasn't so funny. People said witches were evil. What if they did exist, and what if they could make bad things happen?

Moments ago, he'd been enjoying the warm summer night, but now he shivered. The barn owl's soft call turned sinister. Something rustled in the hedgerow, and he jumped half out of his skin. He knew it was only a sheep, but he felt it watching him.

He started to walk faster.

Hearing voices ahead, Nick slowed, trying not to make a sound. A low hum in the next field quickened his heartbeat. His breath came fast and shallow.

He stopped at the hedgerow separating the two fields. Little spots of light flickered beyond the hedge, outlining people standing in a circle.

He crept closer, peering through the twigs and leaves.

The women were humming. The sounds were weird and discordant but so melodic his breathing slowed. The voices seeped through him like sweet water, warm and pure. The women were spaced a step apart, holding hands in an unusual way. Their left hands were palm open to the right hand of the person on their left. The music grew louder. A thrum pulsed through the earth, and he felt its energy grow stronger. Women called out names. Isis, Astarte, Diana, Hecate, Demeter, Kali. He caught other words: goddess and lady and shining in the night, and for some strange, silly reason, he was suddenly holding back tears.

He felt so perfectly safe and humble. He closed his eyes, letting the words wash over him. His hands rested on the hedge. The green, growing leaf sparked beneath his fingertips, and he knew this was the deep connection to the earth he had always felt. This was the smell of apples ripening in the sun. Earth after rain. Hay in the barn. This was Derbyshire, his Derbyshire. And the life he knew, growing and farming, with each season playing its part.

Humans were a fraction of the whole. And he was an even smaller element within it. A drop of water in a river flowing to the sea.

❖

"I don't think they ever knew I was there," Nick said. "I crept away before the end of the ritual. Nobody asked me to become pagan. I found my own way to the goddess."

"You mentioned a healing ritual?" Tony asked. "When was that?"

"That was not long after the millennium. I was a member of the coven by then. Star was dealing with personal issues from her childhood. We did a ritual in the waning moon to help Star to ground her pain. It's not for me to reveal what she'd been through, but it was bad. I'm a gentle man, but it made me want to find her parents and...well..." He shook his head. "Never mind what I wanted to do. Some people should never have kids."

Abuse again. Tony felt unsettled. Lisa and Star were both survivors. Was that what drew them together? And Bryony was part of a network set up to help survivors. Abuse was a seam running through this case.

Was that important? If so, how?

❖

The conversation with Nick got Tony thinking.

Next day, at the crack of Harvey's squawk, Tony trotted downstairs to the sitting room to the shelf of old photo albums in the bookcase.

Somebody had labeled the spines. She pulled out one entitled *2000*. The photos were dreadful. They had faded, and the album had been damaged by water at some point. The first pages were snapshots of people sitting around a campfire in a field and then of a group gathering in the harvest. A younger Red waved from the tractor.

Tony leafed through the album, hoping to find a picture of Lisa Walker or, failing that, one of her girlfriend, Star. But there were only a few images where she could make out the faces of the subjects, and none of the pictures were labeled.

She turned the page, and there was a close-up of a younger Bryony and Chris. Chris smiled at the camera. Bryony was in profile, gazing lovingly at Chris. She was laughing at something and had been caught with her mouth open, head thrown back, and her long, dark hair trailing down to the center of her back. They both looked happy. The light in Chris's eyes was vital, hopeful.

Tony felt breath on the back of her neck. She turned to find Bryony smiling down at the photo. It couldn't have been breath then, even though the impression of it had been so strong.

"That was a good day," Bryony said. "Our fifteenth anniversary. Women were still living here. Not the numbers we had in the beginning. Mostly we were a retreat by then, a place to get back to nature and recover from whatever made the women seek us out."

A piece of paper fluttered from between the last page and the hardcover of the album. Tony retrieved it from the carpet.

It was a letter with tidy handwriting written in ink. There was an address on the top left corner: Sixty Ripley Street, Walkley, Sheffield.

Dear ReSisters,

Please help me. My father loses his temper all the time, and I don't know what to do. He hits me. It's just him and me, and there's no one to turn to. There's a playground next to Sandy Hill Secondary School. I'll be there after school every day for a week.

"It's from Lisa," Tony said.

Bryony looked upset.

"How did she know who to write to?" Tony asked.

"We had a PO Box," Bryony said. "We put adverts, well, it doesn't matter where now. I thought we'd gotten rid of that letter years ago. It could have implicated us. It still could." She put her hand out to snatch it and grunted in frustration when her fingers shot straight through the paper. "You have to burn that. Right now."

Tony memorized the address at the top of the letter.

"I should go there," she said.

"Why? Lisa hated that place. She'd never go back. It meant nothing but heartache and pain." Bryony folded her arms, her attention firmly on the scrap of paper in Tony's hand. "Get rid of it, Tony."

"There you are. What, not dressed yet?" Jade strode into the room and then stopped, her brow furrowing. "Is someone else here?"

"Your senses are improving," Tony said.

"Learning to distinguish, I think. Before our spooktastic life, I dismissed my instincts."

"Probably wise," Bryony said, a step to Jade's right making her jump.

Tony studied Bryony. There was an edge to her Tony hadn't seen before. Tony assessed her, trying to work out if she'd deliberately startled Jade. Bryony noticed Tony watching and shifted.

"Please, Tony," she said, her voice softening, the substance of her body already fading, "dispose of it and soon."

"She's gone," Tony told Jade. "I found this. What do you think?"

Jade skimmed the letter. "You going to check out the address?"

Tony nodded. See, Jade thought like an investigator. It was why she was so good at running the agency. It wasn't like they had a hundred hotter leads demanding their attention.

Jade clapped her hands. "Good because I've got a present for you. Come with me."

Tony followed Jade through the dining room into the kitchen.

"I can't wait to show you. It's perfect for getting around while we're here." Jade smiled brightly, opening the door into the yard.

"What is it?" Tony asked, caught up in Jade's excitement.

The day was fresh, and the sun was shining. Tony dutifully stuck her feet into Wellies and hurried to catch up as Jade disappeared around the side of the barn.

"Transport is all I'm going to say." Jade's voice drifted back teasingly.

Tony smiled. What could it be? Another vehicle? Tony didn't mind if it was old like Emily P. She paused, picturing cool, vintage cars. What if it was a Mini Cooper? Or even better, an MG? *Oh, my.* Tony saw herself in a racing green MG, the top down as she sped along the country lanes.

She turned the corner, and the vision of herself in the supercool convertible popped like a balloon.

The transport was vintage, all right. An old bicycle in a terrible state of repair rested against the barn wall. The paint was so chipped, and there was so much rust Tony couldn't tell what color it had once been. The wheels were covered in cobwebs and mud, and the leather on the seat was cracked. The only thing that looked reasonably intact was the crossbar.

"Try it. Go on," Jade said enthusiastically.

Tony blinked at her. Had Jade lost her mind? Tony walked closer to the bike and squeezed one of the brakes.

The bike responded with a groan as the brake pads dislodged a decade of dust from the tire rim.

"Is it even safe?" Tony asked.

Jade nudged her. "Where's your sense of adventure? It's sweet, no? I was worried about that long walk to the village. Now you can cycle all the way to Hatherwell if you want to."

"What if I don't want to?"

"For goodness' sake, Tony. Don't look a gift bike in the mouth. Have a shower, get dressed." Jade was beginning to get annoyed.

"Is there any point? Chris has surely got all kinds of farming delights lined up for me. I'll be covered in ten types of crud before lunchtime."

"I'll square things with Red and Chris. You follow up on that lead and go to Sheffield. And yes, you do need to shower. It's a slippery slope to anti-social body odor. You're a detective, not a farmer. People won't talk to you if you smell of dung."

"You've got a point there, Miss Marple. Although I'm not a detective or a farmer, I'm a lighting technician playing at being an investigator."

"Tomatoes, to-ma-toes," Jade muttered under her breath. "You can cycle to Hatherwell and take the train to Sheffield."

"And if I accidentally leave that thing on the train, I'll be doing Chris and Red a favor, right?" Tony said.

"Don't you dare." Jade narrowed her eyes at Tony. "Get showered and make it real quick. I'm cooking pancakes for breakfast."

Tony brightened up. That was a prospect worth showering for.

❖

By the time Tony reached Lisa Walker's old street, she was seriously considering dumping the ridiculous bike. She disapproved so strongly of street tipping that she couldn't bring herself to, but with each rusty squeak, the temptation grew.

Lisa must have had good calf and thigh muscles. Her old street was on a steep hill. Halfway up, Tony got off and pushed the bike, sweating in the late afternoon sunshine. The row of buff-colored brick, terraced houses snuggled up to the pavement. Maybe front paths were a step too far after struggling up that slope. The houses looked Victorian, with slate roofs and sash windows.

Tony rang the bell at number sixty. A minute later, a middle-aged white man opened the door.

"How do," he said in a not friendly, not hostile, neutral way. "What can I do for you?"

"I'm sorry to disturb you," Tony said, feeling awkward now that she was standing at the door. "I'm asking about someone who used to live in your house called Lisa Walker. I don't suppose you've had any contact with her?"

The man looked at her curiously, knitting his bushy eyebrows together and furrowing his forehead. "You do know the Walkers disappeared a long ago?"

Tony swallowed. It seemed a stupid question when you put it like that.

"We heard about it when we moved in ten years ago, but it was all well before our time."

"What about any of your neighbors? Would you happen to know if they've been in touch with Lisa?"

"In touch with a young girl that went missing donkey's years ago? Can't say I've heard owt like that. You'll want Mrs. Mackey at number sixty-three. She's lived on this street for over forty years. I believe she knew the Walkers."

"Thank you."

The man stared after her as Tony wheeled the bike along the pavement and scanned the house numbers on the other side of the street.

"You want to give that poor bike a drop of oil," he called after her. "Crying out for it." He laughed at his joke and shut the door.

Tony crossed the street to number sixty-three opposite. The front of the house was well-kept, and the doorstep was clean and polished. Tony rapped the brass, urn-shaped door knocker.

A lady in her eighties came to the door. She looked Tony over before smiling hesitantly. She had a coppery tint to her hair, a light olive complexion, oval shaped deep brown eyes, and strong features in a face that had weathered well.

"Hello. Are you collecting?" the lady asked. Her voice was firm with a Yorkshire accent. "Only I never give at the door."

Tony shook her head. "I'm not from a charity. Are you Mrs. Mackey?"

The woman nodded. "I am, luv. What can I do for you?"

Tony smiled. Mrs. Mackey had recognized Tony's assigned gender at birth. "I'm asking after someone who used to live at number sixty, Lisa Walker. I'm trying to find her."

Mrs. Mackey looked at Tony in astonishment. "Trying to find her? After all this time?"

"Well, yes. Has Lisa ever been in touch with you?"

Mrs. Mackey put a hand over her mouth, looking upset. "Have you, I mean, do you have reason to think she's alive?"

Tony blinked. "Oh yes, Mrs. Mackey. Yes, I do."

Mrs. Mackey's eyes filled with tears. She pulled a handkerchief from her pocket and dabbed at her cheeks, trembling. "You can't know how happy I am to hear you say that." She took several deep breaths. "You'd better come in." She eyed the bike. "You can prop that up against the wall. It'll be safe enough."

Tony followed Mrs. Mackey into a clean and tidy living room. The 1970s suite was comfortable and had been impeccably preserved. Tony sat on a burnt orange wing-backed armchair and waited while Mrs. Mackey made tea. There were framed photos of a boy at different ages, growing into a young man, and a more recent one considerably older.

Mrs. Mackey had a bit more color in her cheeks when she returned with two cups and saucers. She put Tony's cup on a small side table, carefully placing it on a coaster featuring Blackpool seafront and promenade.

"So," Mrs. Mackey said a little breathlessly when she had seated herself opposite Tony. "I still can't believe I heard you right. You've come to ask me about that poor girl, Lisa Walker?"

"Poor girl?"

"Well, yes. I'm assuming you know about the father, Raymond Walker." Mrs. Mackey rolled Walker's name around her tongue as if it were an unpleasant taste.

"I heard he was strict," Tony said carefully.

"Strict is one word for it. Parents were strict in those days. We're talking about the seventies and the early eighties. Attitudes have changed. For the better, in my opinion. Walker was a brute. He beat his wife, you know. She put up with it for a while and tried to leave once when Lisa was little. But he found them at her sister's and convinced her to return. She stuck it out until Lisa was ten. But she left one day while Lisa was at school."

Mrs. Mackey took a sip of her tea, staring at the net curtain on the window overlooking the street. "He took it out on Lisa after that. Lisa was a lovely child, kind and helpful. How he ever had cause to lose his temper with her, I don't know. Not that that's an excuse, even if she had been naughty. I'd hear him start on the child when he was drunk. I went over to intervene one night, and he told me to keep out of it, or he'd make my life a misery. He was a policeman, you know. He said he'd fix it so it looked like I was guilty of something, you know, frame me, and put me inside. I couldn't risk that. I had my boy to look after.

"It was agony hearing him hurt the child and not being able to do a thing about it. When Lisa was eleven, I reported him to the NSPCC, and someone came to talk to him. But Lisa said everything was all right. She was terrified of him, I suppose. He guessed it was me. Came over in a drunken rage and said if I didn't keep my trap shut, he'd make sure something happened to my lad. After that, I did everything I could for her, but I'm ashamed to say I gave up reporting him. Lisa was friends with my son. He was a gentle boy, and bullies picked on him in the playground, but Lisa stuck up for him. She came to me after school and stayed as late as she dared. I fed her and was happy to. She was so sweet-natured. I don't know if you know both Walkers disappeared on the same day? I was sure he'd killed her and then himself. But no bodies were ever found. I blamed myself for years. I'd close my eyes and see her face." Mrs. Mackey took a deep breath. She remembered the cup and saucer in her lap and drank her tea, slowly studying Tony. "But now you're telling me she isn't dead."

"Well, I'm pretty sure. I'm looking for her on behalf of a friend." Bryony wasn't exactly a friend. She was barely an acquaintance, but Mrs. Mackey didn't need to know that. "My friend saw Lisa as recently as a year ago."

Mrs. Mackey's shoulders relaxed, and her eyes filled with tears again. "I'd love to see that girl again. Well, she'll be a woman now, I suppose. I'd like to thank her for everything she did for my lad. He's doing well, works in finance over in Manchester. He stood up to those bullies, you know, after Lisa disappeared. He was brokenhearted she'd gone, and he said he owed it to her. They left him alone, which was some small comfort. What about *him*?"

Tony raised her eyebrows. "Him?"

"Walker. Is he dead?"

Tony sipped her tea carefully, keeping her expression neutral. "I don't know," she lied. She had to, even though she would have liked to give Mrs. Mackey the satisfaction of knowing Walker couldn't hurt anyone anymore.

"Well, I bloody hope so." Mrs. Mackey put her cup firmly back on the saucer and put the saucer on the side table. "She's not been to see me, or been in contact, ever. Everyone's moved away that knew her. I'll check with my lad, but I think he'd have told me if Lisa had been in touch. I don't know how she'd find him anyway."

"Social media?"

Mrs. Mackey looked at Tony as if she'd broken into fluent Slovak. Then her eyes drifted back to the window. "She was only thirteen when she disappeared. A lass. How did she manage?"

That didn't sound right. Tony was sure Bryony had said Lisa had been fifteen. "Thirteen? I thought she was older?"

"No, definitely thirteen. Nearly fourteen. I'm sure because her birthday and my son's are just a few days apart. She disappeared in November, and their birthdays are in December. So how did she look after herself? She wasn't on the street, I hope?"

"I don't know." Tony didn't want to admit to having any information that could implicate the rescue group, ReSisters.

"Well, I'm sorry I couldn't help you, love. But you've helped me." Mrs. Mackey leaned forward. "If you find her, will you ask her to visit me? Will you tell her I'm sorry I didn't do more for her?"

The old woman looked full of regret. On impulse, Tony reached over and patted her hand.

Mrs. Mackey saw Tony out. Tony wheeled the bike away from number sixty-three turning to wave. It had been a waste of a journey for Tony, but, for Lisa's neighbor at least, it had been a trip worth making.

❖

As Tony approached Wooly Mill, the unholy squeak of the old bike was getting on her last nerve. It spoilt her enjoyment of the dusky clouds above. Not for the first time, Tony marveled at the sheer space out in the countryside. Buildings claimed London, devouring the ground and climbing up to take over the sky. She slowed as she reached the high street. The clouds glowed scarlet with the last of the sunset. Tony drank in the beauty of it, letting the irritating sound fade from her consciousness.

Suddenly, a man staggered into her path. Tony slammed on the brakes. They responded with an earsplitting screech.

The man snapped upright, angry and aggressive. "Look where the fuck you're going." Arnie Rawlings was stocky and tall, and even weaving drunkenly, he was scary. He gawped at her before recognition clicked in, and he squared his shoulders back. "Trying to run me down?" He snarled the words, shortening the distance between them.

Sensing the violence in him, Tony put a foot back on a pedal, thinking to get around him. But he blocked the way, and his fist went back. Tony let the bike drop, ready to fight. From bitter experience, she knew to get the first punch in if she didn't want to be the one bleeding on the ground.

"Arnie, Arnie, stop this now." Nick appeared out of nowhere, tapping Rawlings on the arm to get his attention.

"Tried to kill me," Rawlings slurred.

"You walked out in front of Tony," Nick said gently.

Tony eyed them warily. Adrenaline surged through her bloodstream. She was angry now, not scared, and sick of homophobes deciding her existence alone was a reason to lay into her with fists and boots.

"Might have known you'd take the lesbian's side over me. Don't know why you bothered to meet me in the first place." Rawlings shoved Nick aside, advancing on Tony.

Tony held her ground. She squared back and pulled up, aware of his six-inch advantage and likely four stones in body weight.

"I'm the decent man here." Rawlings stabbed a finger toward her.

She resisted the urge to snap it in two.

"A normal bloke. Law-abiding. You've wormed your way into this village. Sooner or later, they'll see you're not like us. And you never will be."

"Stop it, Arnie." Nick tugged on Rawlings's sleeve.

Vera appeared as Arnie brushed Nick roughly away. She looked at Rawlings with disgust. "Keep my Nick away from that man," she said. "Don't let him draw Nick into his troublemaking again."

Oblivious to his mother standing next to him, Nick stepped in front of Arnie. "Go, Tony. He's drunk. He'll not listen to reason."

Tony glanced at Nick, remembering Arnie had said Nick had asked to meet him. She'd liked Nick. Considered him an ally. But here he was, drinking with a homophobe. She picked up the rusty, old bike and mounted it without a word.

She felt Rawlings's hatred on her back as she squeak-squeak-squeaked away. His laughter sailed after her, compounding her humiliation.

CHAPTER SIX

Tony liked feeding the chickens and collecting their eggs. The hens came bustling to meet her. Now that she was used to the speed at which they came toward the feed, she wasn't alarmed by it. She could see how gentle they were beneath all the pecking and flapping. Harvey was always within charging distance, so she kept him within her sight at all times.

She put the eggs in her basket, admiring the different colors and markings. She held a pale creamy one in her palm, marveling at the pattern of the light brown speckles.

"You look like you've settled into farm life."

Tony turned to find Vera sitting on a bale of straw.

"I wouldn't go that far. I'm happy with the chickens, though." Tony walked over and settled herself on a crate near Vera. Interestingly, Harvey watched them but didn't sneak closer. "You'll have to come and visit more often if you keep that rooster away from me."

Vera laughed. "Don't be intimidated. It's what he wants. He's just a chicken, you know."

A chicken that has a pact with the devil, maybe.

"Did you have a word with Nick last night?" Vera asked.

Tony frowned, remembering Arnie Rawlings's aggression. He and Harvey had a lot in common, bar the homophobia. Prejudice was surely a human invention. "No," she answered Vera. "It was better I left. Rawlings looked about to hit me."

"And you looked about to stand up to him if he did," Vera said with admiration. "Brave. He's always been a vicious bugger. Not sure how you would have come off, if you don't mind me saying."

Tony was aware she'd likely have come off worse, and it irked her. Men like Rawlings relied on people's decency and gentleness to get away with their intimidating tactics.

"So, will you talk to Nick, go see him, maybe?" Vera leaned back against a bale set at a right angle to the one she was sitting on.

"Why was Nick meeting Rawlings, do you know?"

"He doesn't agree with Arnie Rawlings's attitudes. Nick doesn't have a hateful bone in his body. Never has had. He'll be feeling sorry for Arnie, perhaps. And I'll warrant he was trying to talk Arnie around."

Tony considered Vera's suggestion. "You said you didn't want Rawlings dragging Nick into his troublemaking again. Has it happened before?"

"When Arnie was a teenager, and Nick was still a boy. Back when Oak Springs was full to bursting with lesbians. I think that was part of the trouble. If it had just been two or three, the village wouldn't have got so up in arms."

Tony shifted uncomfortably. She'd liked Vera, warmed to her. Suddenly Tony was worried what Vera might say.

Maybe Vera felt Tony's discomfort because she frowned. "You have to remember, Tony, this was over forty years ago. Wooly Mill had barely heard of Women's Lib, let alone women's land, and lesbianism was outside most folk's comfort zone. We knew Chris. She was born here. She inherited the farm from her mother and father in her twenties. The others were strangers. I'm sorry I didn't do more, especially when things got out of hand. It came at a bad time for me. My husband had just died. The shock and the loss hit Nick and me hard, and we kept to ourselves. At least, I thought Nick was. They were different times, Tony, and the Oak Springs women were a bolshy lot. They weren't farming folk, and most weren't even from Derbyshire. The trouble really kicked off when they had what they called a Spring Equinox festival on Oak

Springs land. The authorities knew nothing about it, and neither did we, not till the Easter Fayre."

❖

Wooly Mill, April 1985

Vera took another tray of cups and saucers to the church hall kitchen. Everyone had turned out for the Fayre, and that was a good thing. It kept her busy, kept her from thinking about Jed.

Even thinking his name hurt. She swallowed, and the sage green earthenware cups rattled as she put the tray down by the sink. Dolores put them into the washing up bowl.

Vera picked up the tea towel. "What a turnout," she said.

"I'm pleased. I thought people might not come with all those, you know, those," Dolores lowered her voice to a whisper, "independent women running amok in the village."

Running amok? "Do you mean the Oak Springs women?" Vera asked. "What have they done now?"

Dolores stopped scrubbing at a coffee stain. "You mean you haven't heard? They're holding some kind of hippy festival. Chris didn't warn you?"

Vera shook her head, not at all happy to hear the news. There were already twenty or more lesbians living at Oak Springs. Chris's parents must be turning over in their graves. Sometimes the women strayed onto her land, and that was a problem right now when she wanted peace and quiet and needed to know her space was her own. She didn't mind what they got up to, not really. She couldn't see that they were hurting anyone. All she wanted to do was walk the fields and the places on the farm she'd walked with Jed.

"We called Hatherwell police station as soon as we heard," Dolores was saying, "but they were no help. Said they were short-handed, what with all the trouble at the pits with the end of the miners' strike. Said there wasn't much they could do, not if it's on Chris's land."

Vera loaded the tray with the clean crockery, not relishing the thought of having a difficult conversation with Chris. They were neighbors, and she'd always tried to get on with her neighbors, but Chris could be so defensive.

"You know Chris asked Roy if they could have a girls' night at the Plough," Dolores said.

"A girls' night?" Vera didn't know what that was.

"Women-only, she called it. But it wouldn't be for us, even though we're women, of course. It would be for them. For their kind. Roy told Chris to sling her hook, thank God." Dolores spoke as if the village had been saved from the plague. "The men were up in arms. Being kept out of their own pub? The idea of it!"

When the tray was full, Dolores elected to come through to the tea stall, too, as it was nearly their turn to take over.

The hall was bustling with villagers scouring the stalls for Easter gifts. Cakes were popular, as always. Mrs. Jessop's hot cross buns had almost gone, and her simnel cake, rich with fruit and nuts, was proudly displayed on a glass cake plate with a small sign announcing it was the star prize in the raffle. A hush fell across the hall. Vera turned and saw a young couple standing alone in a clearing made by villagers stepping away from them. A white woman with blond hair streaked with blue walked calmly to the cake stall. If she was aware of the open staring from the villagers, she didn't show it.

"Could I please have a slice of coffee-and-walnut cake?" she asked pleasantly.

Mrs. Jessop flinched. Whether that was because of the young woman's southern accent or her hair, Vera didn't know. Mrs. Jessop was reaching for the cake knife when the woman's friend joined her. The second woman looked militant with DM boots, patched jeans, a man's vest, and no bra underneath it.

"Are there any meat products in that?" she demanded.

Mrs. Jessop appraised the second woman in a way that suggested she didn't like what she saw. "It's cake."

"I want to know if there's lard in it," the angry woman said, tossing her head hard enough to shake a tiny silver axe earring in her right ear.

Mrs. Jessop's intake of breath could be heard all the way to the tea stall. "Never. Not even in the war years have my family resorted to baking cakes with lard, young lady."

The young woman huffed. "I'm not a lady. I'm a woman."

"Leslie, please, there's no need. I mean, let's be nice," the woman with blue hair murmured in a pacifying tone.

Mrs. Jessop let the cake knife drop from her hand. "Actually, that cake's reserved," she said.

"Oh…" The blue-streaked hair woman ran her eyes over the other cakes and pastries.

"They all are," Mrs. Jessop said quickly. "I was just about to put the tickets on." She stood back, folding her arms, and anyone who knew Mrs. Jessop would know that was the end of that.

The blue-haired woman swallowed and took a step toward the sweet stall.

"I'm all sold out, duck," Mrs. Grey said, screwing the lid down on a jar of sherbet lemons.

"Nothing for you here, either," the postman's wife called out from the bric-a-brac stall.

"We're finished with tea and coffee as well," Dolores shouted for good measure.

The blue-haired woman caught Vera's eye. Vera saw she was young and vulnerable and hurt, but her angry friend pulled her away, and Vera wished she'd said something, offered her a cup of tea at least. It felt wrong. Still, she did nothing as the two lesbians left the church hall to a low hiss of complaints from the villagers.

"Mum. Mum."

Nick was tugging at her arm. He looked up at her with all the anxiety and confidence of a nine-year-old. "You've got to come. There's trouble on the hill. Old Mr. Grey has got his tractor out. He says he's going to mow down those ladies at Oak Springs."

❖

Behind the wheel of her Ford Escort with Nick in the back hanging out the window, Vera was shocked to see the number of lesbians walking on both sides of the road. They all looked to be heading for Chris's place. They had backpacks, some with tents strapped to them. Some were in flowing, hippy clothing. Others looked like the angry woman from the church hall wearing men's boots, jeans, and T-shirts. There was a lot of short hair and little or no makeup. It wasn't just the clothing that was different about these women. They were confident, Vera realized. Sure of themselves. They had their arms around each other and held hands openly. Vera didn't know what she thought about that. A large group of women walked together, some wearing leather jackets and studded belts over jeans, others with hippy clothes with scarves tied around their heads. A pack of dogs ran alongside them.

Vera slowed the car. "Are those your dogs?" she asked one of the women. "Because you need to get them on leads."

The woman looked at Vera with disgust. "We're anarchists. We don't own these animals, and we don't put them on leashes either."

"You'd better. There are sheep in these fields," Vera said, angry at the stupidity of it.

She was still shaking her head as she turned onto her track. The Greys' farm bordered Oak Springs to the south and Vera's place, Willow Farm, had common hedges with both. She heard shouting as she got out of the car and followed the sound. Nick trotted beside her holding her hand tightly.

A campsite had sprung up in Chris's fallow field next to the Greys' farm. Tents were pegged to the ground, and makeshift shelters made from tarps were strung between trees or on top of a network of bent sticks. The tang of wood smoke and the scent of onions and tomatoes stewing down came from a large campfire. The fire pit had been sensibly placed over a foundation of stones and paving slabs. Tin mugs, plates of food, and cans of lager were abandoned around it. Three women were shepherding a group of small children to the side of the field farthest from the Greys' place. Some of the kids were crying.

The action was centered on the border between the two farms. The lesbians had interlinked elbows and formed a line looking like a scene from the telly about the Greenham Common nuclear plant. They were chanting something about a fish and a bicycle. Someone began a round of "She'll be coming round the mountain." When a chorus of "She'll be coming with a woman when she comes" rang out, Vera looked down at Nick and considered telling him to get back to the farmhouse. He looked like he didn't know what to think, which was pretty much how Vera felt herself.

The villagers on the Greys' land were mostly old man Grey's drinking buddies. Some of Mrs. Grey's WI pals had torn themselves from the Easter Fayre, bringing cakes and sausage rolls with them. They were handing them out along with cups of tea and bottles of beer as if this was a picnic on the village green. The Greys were retirement age, but none of their kids had stepped up to run the farm, and they refused to sell up and let it go. They believed in "the old ways" as Mrs. Grey was telling anyone who could hear her over the lesbian singing. She waved Vera over.

As angry as she was with Chris for having a festival on her land, Vera didn't want to publicly take sides. She sighed. If she didn't walk over to Mrs. Grey, that's what the village would decide she was doing anyway, so she went, taking Nick with her.

Ron Grey climbed into the cab of his tractor. He stared at the Oak Springs women for a moment, so red-faced Vera feared for his heart. He fired the tractor up and the singing disappeared under the engine's roar.

Everyone on the Greys' side fell silent as he drove straight at the women.

He turned at the last possible moment. A second later, screams and shouts came from Oak Springs. The muck spreader was hitched behind the tractor, and it was showering the women, their tents, and anything within range with slurry.

Applause went up from the villagers, but Vera felt sick. There were kids over there.

She began to walk back to Willow Farm, keeping Nick close.

"You don't approve?" Mrs. Grey stepped into her path.

Vera looked her in the eye. "Happen, I don't."

"Ron's only spreading a bit of muck their way. I'd be worried if I were you. I mean, where is all the crap going to go? I heard they've digging pits, and you're downhill, aren't you? More than we are. We just need a heavy downpour and all that will be washed onto your land. Human muck, Vera. You want to think about that before you go defending them."

Vera let the words settle. She nodded to show she'd heard Mrs. Grey and then turned. The tractor stopped. The silence was sudden and ominous.

Chris had driven all the other women out of range of the spreader and was standing alone, arms folded, eyes blazing. Vera blinked. Chris looked as solid and unmovable as the slab of the old Peak limestone her parents had used to build the front porch.

Old man Grey climbed down and stood to face Chris.

Mrs. Grey left Vera to put a mug of tea in her husband's hand.

Vera had just started off again when she noticed the young barmaid from the Plough hanging over the Greys' gate. She was staring at Chris along with everyone else, but her face wore a different expression. This was the girl Arnie was sweet on, and someone had said they'd been out once or twice. From the way young Bryony was looking at Chris, one day soon, Arnie was going to have a very broken heart.

❖

Jade swung open the door from the inside when Tony was a step away from entering. She nearly dropped the eggs.

"You were ages," Jade hissed, snatching the basket and pushing Tony back out into the yard.

Tony huffed. She had been looking forward to a hot cup of tea. And maybe a slice of whatever Jade was baking that smelled so good. "Vera told me about things that happened long ago. It was interesting, actually. Explained a few things—"

"You need to be worrying about things that aren't happening right now. Like us not getting any further in this case," Jade interrupted rudely.

Tony rubbed her hands together. It was cold in the open yard. "Can't we talk in the kitchen?" *Pressed up against the range cooker.*

"No. Red is cleaning a ferret cage on the dining room table," Jade said in a tone that defied further explanation.

Why does it need cleaning and where is the ferret were just two of the questions burning on Tony's lips. But the look on Jade's face commanded her to silence.

"Chop, chop. Time's a marching." Jade lapsed into trait expressionism. "The search for Lisa Walker, what do we know?"

"The woman at the care home wasn't any help. There's the unresolved lead with her former employer. No one's heard from Lisa at her childhood address. I spoke to a neighbor, called Mrs. Mackey, and she's lovely, but I didn't learn anything useful, I'm afraid. That's it."

Jade tapped her foot. "What about the woman in the care home? She mentioned a group."

"The Hackney Survivors Group."

"Circa when?"

"She didn't say when. It sounds like something from the nineties or noughties, but that's a guess."

Jade brightened. "I'll call Sergeant Carol. I mean Sergeant Lewis. Maybe she can point us in the right direction. And what about you?"

Tony flinched under Jade's scrutiny and came up with an idea. "I'll go back to Forest View," Tony said. "Maybe Sandra's having a better day today."

❖

Forest View Care Home looked much the same as the last time Tony had visited, except there was a splattering of weak sunshine that brightened up the grounds. Tony had liberally oiled the old bike before leaving Oak Springs. The treatment had dampened the terrible squeak but not eliminated it.

She looked around for a bike rack and then thought that bicycles were probably not the transport of choice for the majority of the residents. Or the staff, judging by the number of cars in the car park. She left the bike propped up against the only tree in the whole of Forest View. She couldn't contemplate a scenario in which it might be stolen. A passing bike thief was more likely to shudder than sneak off with it.

Bryony hadn't suggested it, but Sandra was Tony's only strong lead. She hoped that Sandra was having a good day and might have some useful info to impart.

There was a young South Asian woman on reception. Tony supposed people worked different shifts, but it would have been nice if she hadn't had to start from scratch. She smiled encouragingly, and the receptionist smiled back.

"I've come to see Sandra," Tony said.

The receptionist had impeccable hair and makeup and beautifully manicured, very long fingernails. "Sandra?" she repeated vaguely.

"It's okay, I know the way," Tony said, taking a step toward the ground floor bedrooms.

"Hold up, um…um…"

Tony suspected the receptionist was fumbling for a gender pronoun. "I know where her room is," she said quickly.

"But there isn't anyone here called Sandra."

Tony stopped. She turned back to the receptionist, who, according to her name badge, was called Aisha.

"I don't understand. I was here a few days ago, and there was a different receptionist." Tony cast her mind back. "Madeline."

Aisha crinkled her forehead in a confused, thoughtful way. Her fingers drummed on the countertop. "Are you sure you have the right care home?"

Tony scanned the green walls, the long staircase, and the padded armchairs. "Yes," she said.

"I'm very sorry," Aisha spoke slowly and carefully. "There are no residents at Forest View called Sandra, and the only Madeline on the staff team is our nurse. She doesn't carry out reception duties."

Tony felt uneasy. Something wasn't right here. Her gut told her whatever was amiss, Aisha wasn't a part of it.

"Maybe I have got the wrong place." Tony frowned.

Aisha lowered her voice. "Some of these places look very alike. I used to work in a home on the other side of town, and they get their furniture from the same supply depot."

Tony smiled politely. "Perhaps you're right. I'll go back and check my information." Not knowing what else to do, she turned around and left.

She walked to the bike and stood thinking. What was going on? And what should she do? She could hang about in the grounds, see if the other receptionist, or nurse, or whatever she was turned up at the end of Aisha's shift. That's if she wasn't being observed on CCTV lurking. Tony glanced up, looking for cameras.

The main doors swished apart. Out of the corner of her eye, Tony saw shoulder-length blond hair and the back of a navy blue tunic and trousers. Tony ducked back as the person swung a bag over their shoulder, giving Tony a side-view of their face.

It was Madeline.

And she was leaving.

Tony had a second to decide. Madeline might lead her to some answers.

The bike was totally inappropriate for a tail situation. Tony let Madeline get a little way ahead, and then she slipped after her leaving the bike to its own devices.

❖

Madeline walked to the bus stop a short distance from the care home and got on a number twenty-three bus. Tony let several people go in front of her so that she could board unobtrusively. She put her hood up and took a seat several rows behind Madeline.

The bus meandered in slow traffic through the town center. Most people got off at the high street, but to Tony's relief, others got on and filled the spaces between them. Tony looked at Madeline every time they neared a bus stop, but she appeared to be glued to her seat absorbed in her phone.

Then, as the bus headed out of town toward Bakewell, Madeline stood and pressed the stop button. Unfortunately, no one else did. The bus slowed, the doors opened, and there was no convenient throng for Tony to hide behind.

"Thank you, driver," Madeline called out, stepping onto the street.

Tony waited until the doors were closing before she jumped up, shouting, "Sorry, driver, I need to get off." Half the bus turned to stare at her, but by a stroke of luck, Madeline was out of earshot. She was already turning into a side road.

Tony hurried after her and then immediately hung back. Madeline had slowed almost to a stop to check her phone.

After a moment, Madeline continued. Tony waited until there was a good distance between them and followed.

Tailing people wasn't as easy as it looked in films. How much distance to leave? If Madeline turned, Tony needed to be far enough away not to be recognized. On the other hand, she didn't want to lose Madeline altogether.

An old lady walked toward Tony. She crossed the street timidly. And then, a middle-aged man walking in the opposite direction glanced at her then quickly away. He passed Tony, giving her a wide berth. Tony frowned. Maybe it was a dodgy neighborhood. The row of buff-brick terraced houses with their doors a stone's throw from the pavement looked charming enough, but those late-Victorian features could hide a multitude of modern day Peaky Blinders.

The middle-aged man had stopped to stare after her. Tony crossed the street and bent down as if to tie up her shoelace. He walked on.

Tony hurried along the street, arriving at a house several doors down in time to see Madeline disappearing inside.

Tony observed the house cautiously. It had graying net curtains at the windows. The white uPVC door and window frames were covered with a layer of grime. It wasn't in bad repair, but there was an uncared-for look to it.

What now? Was all this cloak-and-dagger stuff necessary? Maybe she should just confront Madeline. Someone had lied about Sandra, after all, and Tony's money was on Madeline. But if she was working, it would be better to wait until she left her client's house.

Then again, was confrontation a good idea? Tony remembered the way Madeline had smiled at her from the old man's room and shivered. Jade was always telling Tony to trust her instincts.

The old woman was back, from the corner shop, it looked like, going by the carrier bag clutched in her hand. Her eyes darted nervously to Tony.

Tony didn't normally frighten old ladies.

Then she remembered her hood was up. The fact that Tony was lurking on the street for no apparent reason could also have had something to do with it.

Tony pulled the hood down and smiled.

The woman backed away practically into the road.

Honestly, that was Tony's best smile, and if it didn't make her look approachable, there was really nothing more to be done.

The old woman was glaring now. She glued her eyes to Tony, risking a seriously cricked neck as she passed. So much for Tony not drawing attention to herself.

Tony looked at her watch, pretending she was waiting for somebody.

The old woman went inside her own house and slammed the door.

A minute later, the net in her window twitched.

Tony crossed the street to get out of the old woman's eye line. And then she realized there was an archway between number fifty-two and number fifty-four.

On an impulse, she slipped into the alley, feeling the presence of the walls on either side. They were cool and smelled of rainwater and damp brick. Sound was curiously dampened. At the other end was another alley at right angles running behind the terraced row and a low wall with a side gate to number fifty-two's backyard. There was an old shed and some pots with long-dead plants in them.

Voices floated out of the open back door. Tony crouched behind the low wall to listen.

"Really? That's disappointing." Madeline's voice was a little faint, but Tony recognized her West Country twang immediately.

"He must have been worth a bob or two. Local businessman and all that. The good councilor, as we know." The female-sounding person who replied had a Yorkshire accent and didn't sound like she liked the person she was talking about. "I was expecting more," she continued. "But I'm telling you, I've been through the place with a toothcomb. We could see if a collector's interested in those old bits of furniture, I suppose. That clock, maybe."

"Only if we know someone in the antique business. Not worth the risk, otherwise. Nothing to connect us, remember." Madeline's voice came nearer. Something was dragged outside. A lighter clicked, and the smell of cigarette smoke drifted over the wall.

Tony peered cautiously into the yard. Madeline was sitting on an old kitchen chair with her back to the wall near the back door, smoking.

Tony crouched back down.

"There was a wife, wasn't there, so where's her jewelry? They were well-off. She would have had some, surely?" The other woman sounded like they were standing in the kitchen doorway.

"He said she died in 2010. Maybe he got rid of it," Madeline said. "He talked about her endlessly. Missed her, I suppose. Not that I feel sorry for him."

"Shame we can't get our hands on the house. That would really sort us out."

"It would, wouldn't it?" Madeline said. There was the sound of a foot grinding on the paved ground. Madeline sighed. "But that's not going to happen."

Tony felt the buzz a second before "Ghost Town" by the Specials blasted from her pocket. Jade had decided it was the theme tune for their agency and set it as her ringtone on Tony's phone. Tony started to run, pulling the phone out of her jacket pocket and shutting it off. She was out the other side of the alley as the gate scraped behind her.

On the street, the only place to hide was the other side of a dirty white transit van. She crouched behind the wheels hoping Madeline or her friend didn't come into the road to investigate.

There were footsteps nearby. Tony didn't dare move, not even to peek around the vehicle.

A minute later, it went quiet.

Tony jumped out of her skin when a leg stepped around the side of the van.

A leg clothed in floral, viscose trousers on top of a slip-on shoe with a sensible heel. It was followed by the rest of the body of the old woman.

"Just what do you think you're playing at, young man?" she said, throwing off any fear she may once have had in favor of power and fury.

"I…I am, um, I'm looking for my contact lens?" Tony offered, making a half-hearted attempt at searching the ground by her feet.

The woman glared at her. Then she put two fingers to her own eyes and pointed the fingers at Tony before marching away.

Popular film has a lot to answer for, Tony decided.

❖

Jade picked up as soon as Tony returned her call. Tony didn't have a chance to tell her how close she'd come to being discovered and that Jade's obsession with the Specials was to blame.

"They trashed the veg field." Jade sounded tense.

"Who has?" Tony asked.

"We don't know for sure. The only person with a grudge is that Rawlings man. Red doesn't think he would do it himself, though."

Oh no. They could handle one homophobe. A fanatic with paid mercenaries or, even worse, other homophobes happy to commit acts of destruction was another matter. What was the collective noun for a group of homophobes anyway? A bigotry of homophobes? A discrimination? A spittle?

"You listening to me, Tony?" Jade interrupted Tony's musings.

"Yes," Tony said defensively, trying to sound as if she had been paying attention.

"Come home quick, babe. We need you here."

Tony ended the call. And then she wondered when had Jade started thinking of Oak Springs as home?

And what did that mean?

There were tire tracks up and down the veg patch. Craters had been furrowed into the tidy rows of root veg. Beans and sweetcorn had been reduced to pulp. Bamboo poles were split and broken, and the squash lived up to their name. Tomato plants lay in a heap of crushed stems and mashed fruit.

Someone on a dirt bike had gone to town on the place. It was sad to see the destruction of edible things. And horrible to know the person targeted the farm because lesbians owned it.

Red and Jade were sorting through the debris and collecting any usable legumes, corn, and tomatoes.

Chris stood in the middle of the field with her back to Tony. Her head was bent, and her shoulders hunched over. Tony went over to her.

"When did this happen?" she asked.

Chris looked like she'd aged ten years since breakfast.

"This afternoon. I was working in t'top field. I thought I heard a bike, but young 'uns are always tearing up and down the main road at stupid speeds. I was coming back for a cuppa when I saw all this."

Red appeared at Tony's shoulder, lugging a large sack crammed with the salvaged debris.

Chris sighed. "Now the tops have been destroyed, the root veg will need pulling, or they'll rot in the ground."

Tony's heart sank. And then her back joined in the pity party. It ached just thinking about the digging involved. "When are the police coming?"

Chris's expression soured. "What can they do?" She nodded off toward the destruction. "They'll trample on anything we haven't had a chance to salvage."

Red frowned, saying nothing.

Jade caught Tony's eye and shook her head.

Tony wouldn't have pushed the point anyway in the circumstances. But she did wonder why Chris was so reluctant to involve the authorities. Was she ignorant of the body in the copse, as Bryony believed? Or was there something else she wanted to keep hidden?

❖

Tony woke to the sound of her phone. She nearly let it ring out, but curiosity dragged her from sleep.

"Hello," she grunted, looking at her watch. Shit, it was seven thirty. She was surprised Red hadn't stomped in and thrown Harvey at her.

Nobody answered her.

"Hello," she said again, speaking louder. Then she wondered why everyone did that. Shouting wouldn't help if there was something wrong with the line. Which there wasn't because now she could hear labored breathing.

"Is there anyone there?" she asked sharply, fully aware of the irony of a psychic asking such a question. Could it be a ghost? Were ghosts capable of dialing cell phones now? She sincerely hoped not. She'd never get any peace. She'd have to give up her mobile phone altogether.

"Do you know where Lisa Walker is?" A husky voice broke into her thoughts.

Tony sat up in bed. "No. I'm trying to find her. Do you know where she is?" This was a new development. A good one. Except for the disturbingly heavy breathing on the other end of the line.

"Who is she to you?" the breathless, almost certainly, male person asked.

Tony was about to say that she didn't know Lisa, but the man's brusqueness was annoying. And the breathing was starting to creep her out.

She swung her feet out of bed. She felt better standing up. Braver.

"Who is this?" she said.

The phone went dead with a click.

Tony had scrambled into an old pair of Red's pajama bottoms and was staring idly out of the bedroom window, wondering about the phone call. It seemed someone else was looking for Lisa Walker. Or even better, perhaps knew where Lisa Walker was. She checked her phone for the number and saw it had been withheld.

Curious. She was contemplating darting about in the shower, which was likely to be lukewarm by now, when the phone rang again.

Tony snatched it up. "Who is this?" she said before anyone could speak.

"Nick," came the reply.

"Oh." Tony was annoyed. The last time she'd seen Nick was at his little tête–à–tête with the homophobe formally known as Arnie Rawlings. "What can I do for you?" she said in a cool tone, checking her watch. It was seven forty-five. The farming community didn't stand on ceremony when it came to early morning phone conversations.

"Sorry, did I wake you?" Nick asked.

"No. I was about to get into the shower."

"Oh." Nick sounded flustered and awkward.

Well, he should. Tony realized she'd developed a soft spot for Nick and felt let down.

"I want to ask you a favor," he said. "I'm telling you before I apologize, so you don't think I'm only apologizing because of it."

"Right."

"I'm apologizing, but mostly I'm explaining. We were friends a long time ago. When I saw him in the pub, I went over, hoping to get him to drop all this anti-gay nastiness. He wouldn't listen, though. When he left, I decided to go home too, and that's when I saw him having a go at you."

"I see." Tony softened. The explanation put a different, more flattering light on the situation. "Okay, thank you for explaining. I appreciate it. What's the favor?"

"I've been working with a medium called Miranda, and she and I would like you to come to a seance?"

Tony searched for a polite way to say *hell, no*. "I'm ever so busy for, well, ages," was the best she could come up with.

"Tony, please. I've known Miranda for a long time. Well, seven months, but we've got close during our psychic explorations. Something's wrong. She said she's having trouble from the other side."

The seconds ticked by while Tony considered how to react. "Okay," she said cautiously. "But only if I can bring Jade. She's psychic too."

"Great," Nick said cheerfully. "Can you come tonight at eight?"

"I'll check with Jade and text you later." Tony ended the call and walked to the window. The sky was shrouded in a thick, gray blanket high above the patchwork of fields. A low-lying mist rolled over them. The day hadn't even properly started, and she had two strange things to puzzle over.

❖

Miranda was sitting on a high stool at the breakfast bar in Nick's kitchen. Wisps of brown hair drifted from a headscarf decorated with astrological symbols. She wore a sea-green flowing, collarless shirt with sunburst patterns and multicolored cotton trousers with a drawstring waist.

"You're Tony," she said in a carefully calm voice. She sounded like a psychiatrist.

Something about Miranda set Tony's teeth on edge, and the woman had only said two words.

Miranda frowned sharply, and Tony panicked she actually could read minds. But Miranda was peering over Tony's shoulder. "I didn't know you were bringing a…friend," she muttered.

"I did mention it," Nick said tactfully. "Tony's a bit of a psychic herself, you know. They both are."

Which miffed Tony. She'd never wanted psychic powers, and, quite frankly, they got in the way a lot of the time, but one thing they were was just short of amazing. Saying she was a bit of a psychic was like saying Usain Bolt could manage a light jog.

Miranda looked like she was trying to pass gas. "It's best not to dabble in these matters without professional guidance. The spirit world can be problematic," she said in a clipped voice.

Jade raised her eyebrows. Tony tried to squelch the irritation Miranda brought out in her because the medium was as tense as a board.

"What's the problem?" Tony asked, pulling up a stool.

Miranda sighed. "It sounds ridiculous. I'm a medium, after all. I should be able to handle this kind of thing."

"Ghosts can be disturbing. We have some experience with this," Jade said.

Miranda turned to her. "That's what I say. The spirit world isn't to be trifled with. But that was something I said without knowing how unpleasant they can be."

"What's happening exactly?" Tony asked.

"I am being plagued by a spirit. He says awful things, horrible things." Miranda snatched Tony's hand in hers. "Let me show you." She clasped Jade's hand and nodded at Nick. "Join the circle, please."

A second later, they were all holding hands. "Tell them what you told me," she said urgently.

The temperature in the room plummeted. Tony felt a vibration, a strange change in the energy around them. Someone was materializing outside the circle. Tony smelled earth, damp leaves turning to mulch, and a vision played of worms turning in rich, dark soil.

"Bloody marvelous. Finally, someone does as I ask." Raymond Walker manifested in front of the range, his hands in the pockets of his leather jacket and a smug smile on his lips.

"He's here," Miranda whispered. "Can you hear him?"

"Yes," Tony and Jade said together.

"All these years, I had no idea psychics existed," Walker said. "And now look. Three of you. Whoever said good things come in threes hadn't met you three witches."

"No one says that." Jade spoke brusquely. "They say that things come in threes. Not necessarily good things."

"They got that right then, with you lot. Who's the bloke?"

"He's not a medium," Miranda said in a shaky voice.

"So, you can't bother him," Tony said quickly.

"Really? Not even if I do this?" Walker pursed his lips and blew.

A pencil shot across the top of the breakfast bar. The point stopped an inch from Tony's chest.

"I see you've learned a new trick," Tony said, trying to sound unnerved and calm and not at all shocked that a pencil had nearly stabbed her.

"I have. And I'm getting stronger. Ever since you disturbed my grave."

Tony blinked. This was a new and horrible turn of events. Nick couldn't hear Walker, but Miranda could. Walker could implicate Tony with Miranda as a witness to his claims.

"I'm glad you contacted us, Miranda." Tony's mind raced. "We've come across this troublesome spirit before."

"You've no idea how troublesome I can be, girly," Walker said slyly, and his smile turned sinister. "Shall I tell her where I'm buried?"

"I'm very sorry he's latched onto you, Miranda," Tony went on as if he hadn't spoken. "He likes to torment mediums."

Jade caught on immediately. "He's a real piece of work. Makes up wild claims to cause mischief."

Miranda leaned across to Tony and lowered her voice. "You really can see him?" she asked.

"Yes. Can you?"

"Not clearly. Usually, the voices come to me inside my head, but I've never heard them properly or seen even an outline of a person. And that's not all. It feels terribly cold in here and strange. I can only describe it as a disruption to the normal energy of the space." Miranda scanned Tony's face as if looking for answers there.

"Perhaps your powers are growing," Tony suggested.

"Or it could be the strength of our combined psychic ability," Jade added.

"I preferred it how it was. He's been whispering in my ear for hours. So, he's a meddlesome spirit? What do we do then?"

Tony saw her chance and took it. "For a start, you can't believe a word he says."

"People have taken his claims seriously, gone to the authorities, and made a fool of themselves." Jade gave Tony's hand a little squeeze. "Lots of people are only too happy to discredit mediums. Unfortunately, some of the people are ghosts."

Miranda inhaled deeply, nodding. "I see. You're right. There are plenty of skeptics out there."

Walker's smile twisted. He drifted to the breakfast bar and stood behind Nick. "Don't mind me, love. I wouldn't want to stop your silly seances. In fact, please carry on. I may come and visit you again."

Miranda shivered.

Walker snapped his fingers in Jade's face making her jump. Tony wanted to flatten him. Or vaporize him or whatever a person did to ghosts.

"You two know what I want. Get it for me, or I'll find someone who will." He smirked at Tony for a minute and then thankfully disappeared.

"He's gone," Tony told the others.

Miranda rubbed her bare arms. All the little hairs were standing on end. "Do you think he *will* come back?"

"I don't know," Jade said gently.

Tony felt sorry for Miranda. If Deirdre ever got in touch again, Tony could ask her what to do. Though from previous experience, she knew ghosts didn't go away until they got whatever they came for.

Walker was a ticking time bomb. Tony had no idea how many mediums and psychics there were in Derbyshire, or indeed within whatever range Walker possessed. But if he found one and told them he was buried at Oak Springs, Tony and Jade were in trouble. What if Tony had left DNA at the site? Scores of witnesses had seen Tony in Wooly Mill. Walker's new tactic had really put the cat among the pigeons.

❖

Jade dropped into Tony's room when Tony was getting changed for bed.

"Hey, some good news after our horrible evening. I heard back from Sergeant Lewis. She's got a lovely voice, hasn't she?" Jade sat on the bed, getting in the way of Tony putting on her nighttime T-shirt. Jade had washed some ancient lesbian leftover clothes she'd found somewhere in the farmhouse and had proudly presented Tony with a faded, marl gray T-shirt decorated with a screen-printed double women's symbol.

"Are your hormones rampaging or something?" Tony asked.

Jade grinned. "It's the fresh country air."

"You haven't stood downwind of the pig house, then," Tony grunted, struggling with a ridiculously tight armhole.

"Maybe you should put a foot back in the water. It's lesbian city around here," Jade said, looking thoughtful.

"In Wooly Mill?"

"Well, maybe not in the village. But Todmorden and Hebden Bridge are a stone's throw away. And they have a club night. You could strut your stuff on the dance floor."

Tony managed to get her other arm through the T-shirt and tried to pull it down. It grazed her belly and refused to go any further.

Jade squinted at her. "Though perhaps not in that T-shirt. I don't think that will bring the bees flooding to your honey."

Tony peeled off the ridiculously small T-shirt and tossed it at Jade.

She caught it, laughing. "That, though," she said, nodding toward Tony's bare torso, "would work. And when I say work, I mean werk, girlfriend…boyfriend…person friend. By the way, can I just add how much I love you embracing your butch identity?"

"Good to cover all bases," Tony said, pulling on her old T-shirt. It was a bit sweaty, but she could breathe, and honestly, she didn't think the empty room would complain. Jade's words landed, and she thought about them for a moment. "Thank you. I'm trying butch on for size. Hopefully, it will fit better than that T-shirt. And, I don't think so about dipping a toe in the sapphic pool. If I imagine flirting with someone, I think about Maya and what she did. I need to heal some more. Now, you mentioned something about Sergeant Lewis?"

"Oh yes." Jade snapped to attention. "But before we leave the last topic of discussion, don't forget how attractive you are."

"Thank you." Tony sat next to Jade and rested her head on Jade's shoulder. Jade was sassy and sexy and her very best friend in all the world. Tony was lucky to have her.

"Sergeant Sweet Tones tracked down the person who used to lead the Hackney Survivors Group. He wasn't in touch with Lisa Walker, but he contacted a friend of Lisa's from the group," Jade said.

"Star?"

"No. A woman called Helen. She called five minutes ago, and she's happy to meet up tomorrow. She lives in Manchester."

"Manchester," Tony repeated. "That's where Amy's parents live."

"I know." Jade squeezed Tony's hand. "Shall we go tomorrow?"

Jade offering to come with her made Tony feel all warm inside. "Maybe we'll get answers from both meetings," she said with a cautious flicker of hope.

CHAPTER SEVEN

Amy's parents lived in a nice semi-detached house on the outskirts of Manchester. Tony took a deep breath as she and Jade walked from the bus stop along the street where Amy grew up. Mr. and Mrs. Delaware were great parents. They had supported Amy's sexuality and her relationship with Tony. Amy's mum had encouraged them when they talked about having a baby. It was Amy who'd wanted one. Tony had been, frankly, terrified.

The terror disappeared a few weeks after Louise was born. To be replaced by exhaustion and a kind of love Tony had never known before or since. One night she held Louise to her shoulder, tiny and warm, and rocked her until she fell asleep in Tony's arms. Everything changed in that moment, and Tony would never stop being Louise's parent, no matter what.

Tony took a deep breath standing now before the Delawares' blue timber door. She glanced at Jade, who squeezed Tony's hand.

Tony rang the bell.

Mrs. Delaware opened the door, all smiles. She saw Tony, took a step back, and started to shut the door.

"Mrs. Delaware," Tony said. "Please. I want to talk to you about Louise. You remember my friend Jade?"

Amy's mum looked at Jade, gave her a crisp nod, and turned back to Tony.

"I can't see what we've got to talk about, Tony," she said. "I tried to let you down gently by ignoring your messages. I never thought you'd come all the way up here. But seeing as you did, I can say to your face I won't be telling you where Amy is. And I don't think you should see Louise."

Tony stared at Mrs. Delaware, perplexed. She'd always been so friendly. Now she was angry and hostile. But amid her confusion, Tony realized Mrs. Delaware knew where Amy was.

"I don't understand, Mrs. Delaware," Jade said. "Amy left Louise with Tony with no prior arrangement."

Amy's mum nodded. "I appreciate that, Jade. And you won't have had childcare set up, Tony. I know you work full-time. I realize Amy turned up unexpectedly. She said as much. She was, well, she needed to sort herself out. But it wasn't all right, what happened. You should have phoned Amy to say you weren't coping. Phoned me even."

Mrs. Delaware wasn't making sense. "But I was coping," Tony told her. "Okay, it was hard at first, but it got easier. Louise was brilliant, and we worked it out. She'd started school, Mrs. Delaware. She'd just settled."

Mrs. Delaware tensed. "And what about the nights you left her?"

Tony blinked. What was Mrs. Delaware talking about?

"Amy got a letter, Tony. Thank God someone cared enough about the poor mite to tell us you were leaving her alone to go to work. And to go out to bars with women."

Tony opened her mouth to speak, shut it, and sucked in air like she was running out of oxygen. "Rubbish," she said finally. It wasn't her most eloquent moment.

"That didn't happen, Mrs. Delaware," Jade said.

Amy's mum looked from Jade to Tony in confusion.

"I was with Louise every night. There was no one I'd trust, not my girlfriend, not even Jade, to be with Louise. Not when she was missing Amy so much. She cried every night at first, Mrs.

Delaware. There is no way I would leave my child with anybody when she was like that." Tony was shocked to the core.

"But that's why Amy came to get Louise," Mrs. Delaware said uncertainly. "She wasn't ready, not really. That's why she told me not to talk to you if you called."

"You said there was a letter? Did you see it?" Jade asked.

"Yes. I've got it here." Amy's mum stepped away from the door. She returned a moment later and pushed a white envelope toward Jade.

The envelope was addressed to Amy by hand in blue pen. There was a post office franking stamp with no date. The letter inside was on old-fashioned writing paper, written by hand in neat, rounded script as if the sender wanted their words to be very clear.

Tony Carson is leaving your daughter alone in her Poplar flat. I've seen your daughter letting herself in after school when Tony Carson is at work or out with women. Sometimes she doesn't get home till the next morning. I thought you should know. A friend.

Tony read it twice while Jade photographed the short note and handed it back to Mrs. Delaware.

"It's just not true," she said, her voice shaking.

"But why would someone make it up?" Mrs. Delaware asked.

Tony couldn't think of anyone who hated her enough to send the letter. Whoever it was was no friend of Tony's and no friend of Amy's either.

"I don't know," Tony said. "It reads like a neighbor wrote it, but none of them would have your address."

That was another strange thing. Tony would have had to look it up herself.

"Well, I don't know what to say." Amy's mum shifted uncomfortably.

"I do," Jade said, pulling herself up to her full five foot three inches and looking Mrs. Delaware firmly in the eye. "That," she stabbed a finger toward the offending envelope, "is a pack of lies. I know that, Mrs. Delaware, because I was either with Tony and Louise or I phoned Tony every evening to check in with her. It was one heck of a change in circumstances when Amy turned up with Louise. I don't think I missed a day, did I, Tony?"

Tony shook her head. Jade had been a lifeline.

"I called from Lesbos for a week. I video-called, Mrs. Delaware, so I know exactly where Tony was, and I spoke to Louise most days too. I can show you my phone records if you like."

Mrs. Delaware blinked. "Oh, I'm sure that won't be necessary."

"Ah, yes," Jade said, remembering something. "You sent me videos sometimes, didn't you, Tony, on the days I couldn't come round. Tony can show you those."

"They sacked me," Tony said.

"I beg your pardon?" Mrs. Delaware, looked startled.

"I canceled so many shifts at the theater they fired me. I'd never leave Louise alone. She's my child." Tony's voice broke, and she swallowed hard.

Mrs. Delaware's face softened. "I know she is, Tony. I'm not one of these people who think biology is everything. Mr. Delaware and I will talk to Amy, okay?"

Tony nodded, her head spinning.

"So, when will you be in touch with Tony?" Jade was politely formal.

"Do you believe me?" Tony blurted out. She knew it was ridiculous, but a part of her needed to know Amy's mum hadn't swallowed the lies in the letter.

"Actually, Tony, I do," Mrs. Delaware said, then she glanced at the envelope still in her hand. "But…"

"Ask Louise," Jade said. "You don't have to accept our word. Though don't forget we have video evidence if you need it. Let me send it to you anyway. You'll see how happy Louise was with Tony, how much she loves Tony. Tony's a good parent."

Mrs. Delaware nodded. Jade took her phone number, and they left.

Tony felt numb. She barely registered their walk back to the bus stop. She had no clue how to start processing what she had just discovered. And the worst thing was she couldn't imagine who would send the letter. Or what they would gain from doing so.

❖

The bar in Canal Street was quiet at two in the afternoon. Jade walked confidently in, scanning the tables for the woman they were to meet. A lesbian couple was sitting near a winding iron staircase that led to an upper level, and a man nursed a pint at the bar. Helen had pinged Jade a pic of herself which resembled no one in the immediate vicinity.

Tony breathed in the scent of yesterday's beer and today's polish and relaxed. The exposed brick walls and wrought iron pillars were typically Mancunian. Wooden floors, tables, and the L-shaped bar counter softened the industrial look. Rainbows of light theatrically dressed the ceiling.

Jade's phone tinged. "Helen's upstairs," she said. They got coffee and went to the upper level. A woman sat in a low armchair next to a small table in the otherwise empty gallery space overlooking the bar below.

"Jade?" she asked as they approached.

"Yes. This is Tony," Jade said. "Thanks for meeting us."

Helen was a light-skinned South Asian woman with short blue-black hair, a small nose, and very defined, very dark eyebrows with a sweep of thick eyelashes framing her brown eyes. It was hard to tell her age. She didn't have many lines and no sign of gray in her hair, but her face looked lived in. Tony got the feeling that life had happened to Helen, and not all of it good. Or maybe she'd just had a late night, and Tony was letting the woman's membership of the former Hackney Survivors Group color her judgment.

"That's okay. It's my day off," Helen said. "Have you come over from Derbyshire?"

Jade nodded, stirring the multicolored miniature marshmallows floating in the foam of her Pride latte. Pride extended into September in Manchester, apparently, and Tony approved. Why should pride be restricted to a month? Were gays expected to be ashamed for the other eleven?

"Are you living on the women's land farm?" Helen smiled at them over her tall glass of something clear and sparkling.

"Yes. Except, it's not women's land anymore," Tony said.

"Are they still doing their good work?" Helen asked.

Tony and Jade exchanged a glance.

"Lisa told me. Don't worry, I've never said anything."

"No," Tony said. She had no idea what Helen was referring to, but she instinctively protected Red and Chris.

"Shame," Helen said. "Well, what do you want to know?"

"We're looking for Lisa Walker," Tony said.

"Do you mind telling me why?" Helen pushed her straw around in the glass.

"One of the women at the farm needs her help," Jade said. It wasn't a lie, and Helen didn't need to know the woman was a ghost.

"I lost touch with Lisa about three years ago," Helen said.

Tony sighed, anticipating another wasted trip.

"Were you good friends?" Jade asked.

"We were close for a while. Not as close as she was with Star, of course."

Tony perked up. "Star was in your group as well?"

"Yes. Do you know her?" Helen asked.

"Not directly. I'm friends with someone who was in a coven with her when she lived at the farm," Tony said. "Lisa was her partner, wasn't she?"

"They'd broken up by the time I met them. But they were tight. Very good friends." Helen turned her head away, looking reflective. "The group was good. We shared a lot of stuff. But the social in the pub afterward was even better. That's when we could be ourselves."

"What do you mean?" Jade asked.

Helen settled back in her chair, ready to explain.

❖

The Oak Bar, Stoke Newington, London, 2008

Helen took a drag on her cigarette, huddling as close to the doorway as she dared, attempting to stay out of the February drizzle. It had been over six months since the smoking ban in pubs had come in, and still Helen couldn't get used to having to go outside. Pints just weren't the same without the nicotine kick. Star was next to her, tucked inside the arched porch squeezing strands of tobacco into a rolling paper from the blue packet poking out of her breast pocket. Helen watched Star's fingers as they effortlessly created a slim cigarette and wondered what it would be like to feel those fingers on her skin. She felt a blush start to work its way up her neck to her face and hoped Star wouldn't notice. Fortunately, Star was concentrating on her roll-up. She licked the edge of the paper, sealed it, and whipped her Zippo out of her back pocket. The lighter flared, throwing a flattering light on Star's cheekbones and blue eyes.

Star looked over and smiled. Not the sultry, come-to-bed smile Helen dreamt of but a kind, big sister smile. "You were very brave tonight. Sharing isn't easy. I know."

Helen tensed, feeling guilty and hating feeling it. Everyone in the group was a survivor, but she still felt disloyal to her mum telling people about *him*. She'd hated him and what he did so much she'd run away. Now she was far from Mum and couldn't phone her. Some nights she missed her so badly she cried. She never told anyone that. Not even Star. The group was angry. They wouldn't understand. She didn't blame them. She was angry too. He should be in prison for what he did.

"You okay, Helen?" Star was looking at Helen with a worried expression.

Helen took another drag and nodded.

"Feeling vulnerable?" Star asked.

Helen swallowed and nodded again.

"Can I give you a hug?"

Helen relaxed into Star's arms, breathing in her clean, sporty scent. She had a strong word with her heart and with the even more traitorous throb between her legs. She knew Star wouldn't consider a relationship with Helen. She must be ten years older, not that Helen cared. Helen was eighteen, an adult. But, even if there wasn't an age difference, Helen was new to the group, and Star mentioned Helen's vulnerability a lot.

"Come on, let's go back to our drinks," Star said, pulling away.

In the warm interior of the pub, Lisa was alone at their table. She glanced up with a worried expression. Lisa was very vocal. She was around the same age as Star, and she was a good laugh, but she didn't have Star's gentleness. Lisa was tough. She went on marches and demonstrations every week, and Star went too. They'd asked Helen, but she didn't want to be on the street surrounded by angry, shouting people, even if they were shouting for justice. Lisa came from the south coast, but she had a northern accent. Helen hadn't asked. You didn't ask. It was an unspoken rule.

"The others have gone, and I've just got off the phone with my head of department. We were discussing the case, you know, the one I was telling you about, Star," Lisa said.

"Has something else happened?" Star pulled up a chair.

"No. I was voicing my fears, that's all. Department head says there's not enough to go on."

Helen sipped her pint, listening. Lisa had been unhappy with her job for some time. She worked long hours as a junior social worker for child protective services. Helen didn't know how she did it, how she surrounded herself with all that misery with the background she had. But thank God she did. The children under her watch were lucky to have her.

Lisa turned to Helen. "Tell me this," she said. "What do you think about a child who is super-obedient? Whenever she's asked to do something, she jumps to it. If I ask her a question, she looks to her father. Flinched when the father leaned over her to pass me a cup of tea?"

Helen went cold. "I'd say she's being hit or verbally abused, controlled."

Lisa nodded. "The father is charming, and he knows which buttons to push. He complained about the last social worker until she got taken off the case." Lisa swigged her bottle of cider. "That little girl, if something's going on, and I feel in my bones it is, what is her life like? She doesn't hold eye contact with me for longer than a second."

Helen ran her hand along the side of her chair seat repeatedly. The movement calmed her. She had started doing it sometime after her real dad died and Mum remarried. She tried not to think about the little girl, and especially about how alone she might be. Helen knew what it was like to cry at night and know no one was coming to help.

Lisa opened a packet of cheese and onion crisps, offering them around. "Even after what happened to that poor baby in Haringey last year, they're still scared of removing kids unnecessarily. Cleveland has a long legacy. You'd think they'd be worried about missing something. Look at those social workers in Haringey, facing a witch trial. Sorry, Star."

Star smiled. She was proud of her religion. "No offense taken, Lisa. It is a witch trial."

"When will this country stop blaming social workers for parental abuse? Our hands are tied a lot of the time. The abusers are the ones who should be punished. Even survivors can't always recognize signs of abuse when people are working hard to cover it up. The weight of the whole system's against us. It wears me out. It really does." Lisa scrunched up the crisp packet and dropped it on the table.

Star moved her chair closer to Lisa and put an arm around her. "Hey, you do a lot. You're making a difference."

"Am I, though?" Lisa had tears in her eyes.

Helen wanted to put an arm around Lisa too. She seemed so little and sad, and Helen knew what Lisa had been through. Right now, Lisa looked like she was carrying all the pain in the world.

"It should be survivors in charge of making those decisions," Helen said.

Lisa nodded. "As long as the survivors are worked out. The joke is, people say survivors see abuse everywhere. But actually, those people don't want to see how much abuse there really is. And even when a child dies, the sentences being handed out..." Lisa tailed off, staring at the table.

Helen felt exhausted with the weight of it all. "Time I was going," she said.

Lisa looked up. "I haven't messed with your head, have I, talking about all this stuff? It's a lot, I know."

"It's okay," Helen lied.

Helen wanted to believe there were people like Lisa, stopping the abuse. She didn't want to hear that kids were being left in bad situations because good people weren't being listened to.

"See you next week, though, yeah?" Star got up to give Helen a hug.

"Sure." Helen nodded. She pulled herself from Star's arms and walked out into the cold night.

❖

"I lost touch with Lisa about three years ago when they moved out of London," Helen said. "I don't know if this has helped at all, but I hope so." She sucked up the last of her drink and let the straw fall back into the glass.

"Do you remember a woman from the group called Sandra?" Tony asked.

Helen shook her head. "No, but I moved back up north two years later. The group was still active. Lisa and Star would talk about it."

"Okay, well, thank you for meeting us," Jade said.

"I hope you find them, and if you do, will you please give my number to Star? I'd love to see her again." Helen smiled hopefully.

Tony guessed that Helen was still carrying a torch for Star. She hated being cynical, but maybe that was why Helen had agreed to talk to them.

Jade stood up. Tony was a second behind her.

"Thank you," Tony said. "Call us if you think of anything else."

❖

A breeze rolled up from the valley bringing the scent of ripe apples. Tony sat on a weathered stool and closed her eyes. The sun was hot, but wispy clouds drew a thin veil across the sky, tempering its heat. A blackbird sang sweetly in the small pear tree on the edge of the vegetable patch. The bird sang and sang, filling the orchard with joy.

Like a child. Happy in the moment. Looking forward, full of excitement. Carrying no regrets about what has gone before.

Oh, why did she have to go and think of children? Of Louise? The pain of missing her stabbed through Tony so acutely she bent forward, breathing in and easing the air out.

"Tony?" Jade's voice, gentle and concerned, interrupted Tony's vision of Louise in the back of the car as Amy drove away. Louise screaming at her mother, angry and frightened, tears rolling down her cheeks.

Tony hadn't realized then that Amy was taking Louise away and breaking all contact. Tony had called the next day and the day after that, and then she'd got a dead tone when she phoned. Mrs. Delaware had told her Amy had gone away. And then Bryony had turned up.

Tony blinked as Jade's arms wrapped her up. She leaned into Jade's warmth. There was hope now. Maybe Amy's mum would talk Amy around. "Vegetables," she said, pulling away. "Which ones do you want?"

Jade looked as if she wanted to say something, but she kissed Tony on the forehead. "Come on then. I can't trust you to choose them. You're not nearly picky enough."

As Tony stood up, she could have sworn Jade muttered, "Given your past lovers." But when she looked at Jade, she was striding toward the onions with an innocent expression.

A section of veg in raised beds had escaped the worst of the damage. Tony snapped a fat ear of sweetcorn from a plant leaning wearily toward her. She took a bite.

"Hmmm." Jade was on her knees inspecting onion tops. "That one. That one. Not that one." She stood up and raised her voice. "Tony! Are you paying attention?"

"Of course I am," Tony lied.

Jade narrowed her eyes and waved a purple-painted nail at the courgettes. "That small one, the fresh-looking one next to it, and, oh, yes, that firm pair further back."

"Which pear?" Tony turned to the fruit tree. "There's so many." She bit into the corn again.

"Tony Carson, you have the attention of a goldfish. And that's being generous. I'm still talking about courgettes."

Tony frowned. "Are you? Why?"

"Don't test me. I also need four firm, sweet corn cobs. Now then, how about—"

"You don't need to micro-manage me," Tony complained. She picked several cobs. Their green husks had peeled back to reveal tightly packed, bright yellow kernels. She stuck them in the oversized pockets of her borrowed cargo pants.

"It's my prerogative. I'm the chef. You're the vegetable purveyor."

"Purveyor isn't the right word. I'm the vegetable producer."

"Chris and Red produced them."

"Selector?"

"Not without my help."

"Gatherer?"

"Barely."

"Oh, for goodness' sake, Jade, I'm capable of picking a few vegetables." Tony put her hand on one hip and waved the corn cob at Jade with the other.

"Only if I want a side order of insects," Jade said at the same moment that Tony registered a tickling sensation.

A trail of ants was walking up the cargo pants and disappearing under Tony's T-shirt. She threw the corn on the ground and flapped at her trousers. She shuddered, imagining ants in places ants should never be.

Jade stepped forward and, with one mistressful stroke, swept Tony's midriff clean of insects.

Tony gazed into Jade's eyes. "Your quick thinking and decisiveness are why I almost fell madly in love with you when we worked together on *Les Mis*."

Jade smiled.

"Of course, that was before I saw you in the East Wittering End of the Pier Society's production of *Cats*. Your outfit was a passion killer. Baggy, puce, and furry," Tony added.

Jade winced. "The costume designer hated me."

"The costume designer hated life, to be fair." Tony flicked away something crawling down her back and froze.

"They said you were a detective. Happen, they were mistaken or joking or lying, because from where I'm standing, you're an insult to the name."

Raymond Walker stood next to the wheelbarrow. His arms were folded, and his mouth was curled into a smirk.

"Are you both calling yourselves detectives?" he asked.

Jade spun on her heel. "What do you want, Walker?"

He smiled. Tony sensed he enjoyed winding people up.

"What progress have you made on my case?" he asked, managing to put a sneer into the question.

"There is no case," Tony said.

"There better be. I told you I want my body moving. You've got no shame, you people."

Tony glared at Walker. "You died in the 1980s. They had gay Pride even then. The clue's in the name."

"And nothing's changed, except for the better," Jade added. "We've got rights in law, and homophobia's a hate crime."

"Decent people don't like having lesbians next door. Won't tolerate it." The nasty smile was back on Walker's face. "Ask them about the fire."

"What fire?" Tony asked.

"Ask that sly cow, Chris, or the bulldagger, Red."

Jade didn't respond, and neither did Tony. After a minute, Walker changed tack.

"Found that daughter of mine, yet?" he asked. "I want a word with her when you do."

"That's not going to happen. I won't be taking messages from the bastard that beat her," Jade said quickly.

Walker's eyes flashed. "Some kids need a slap to keep them on the *straight* and narrow. I don't care if you've got laws against it now—"

"We have," Tony said.

Walker carried on as if she hadn't spoken. "Lisa was off the rails. Hiding disgusting magazines under her bed. Some shit called *Shocking Pink*. It was a bloody shock. Didn't know my daughter was queer till I read it. Everything I did was for her own good. My only regret is not hitting her harder. Or sooner."

Jade took a breath. "The only thing to come from violence is hate. Children are full of love, but don't kid yourself. Deep down, they know what you're doing is wrong, and a part of them never forgives you. Never."

Walker made a sour face and vanished.

Jade sank onto the weathered stool.

The afternoon was turning to evening. The sun had streaked the sky yellow and gold. They stared at it without speaking. Tony would have given anything to go back and rescue the child Jade had once been. She'd had to learn skills no one should have to learn.

Tony reached across and took Jade's hand. Jade threaded her fingers through Tony's as the sun sank below the horizon, igniting a flame that consumed the clouds until there was nothing but fire.

❖

Chris's face hardened when Jade asked her about the fire. "Who told you about that?" She dropped her napkin on the table and pushed her plate aside.

Tony glanced at Jade, knowing they couldn't say it was Walker's ghost.

Chris stared at her untouched portion of cheese and potato pie in disgust. "Nick, I suppose." Her eyes came back up, furious and hiding something else, something that looked like fear. "He's got no business raking all that up."

She stood abruptly and left the room, letting the door slam shut behind her.

After they'd cleared the plates and Red had returned to the table with a pot of tea, Jade cleared her throat.

"I'm sorry," she began, but Red waved a hand at her.

"It's okay. The fire came during a horrible time, and someone got hurt. It was hard on all of us. But Bryony took it the worst."

"Bryony?" Tony sat up.

Red nodded. "Bryony thought it was her fault."

❖

2 November, 1985, Oak Springs

It was the sound that woke them. Cattle lowing and someone yelling. Red always slept lightly, and that night it was a good thing.

When Red got to the kitchen, they smelled the smoke. Outside, black clouds of it shot to heaven, swallowing the moonlight.

The barn was on fire. Red rammed on their boots and ran to it.

Disorientated calves staggered in the yard. The barn doors were open. Inside, Red saw gray smoke, a yellow, dancing mass, and glowing orange edges where the wooden stalls had gone up.

Cows cried out urgently. Oh God, there were animals still in there.

Chris appeared at Red's side, Bryony running after her.

"Get water. Call the fire brigade," Red said. "Get the hose, get all the women up. We need to douse it ourselves."

Not stopping to think about the sense of it, Red ran into the barn. A calf was heading for the doors, and a second one following. And something flopped to the ground behind the two cows.

A woman.

Red's breath was ragged, and the smoke was sandpaper in their chest. They pressed on, reaching for the body on the ground. The short distance was a world away.

They grabbed hold of her legs and pulled. Red's lungs screamed for oxygen, but they ignored them, focusing only on dragging the woman along the barn floor.

As Red stumbled into the yard, Chris took over. The women had formed a line passing buckets from one to the next. Bryony sprayed a hose into the barn. A thin, sad stream of water hissed at the edges of the flames.

Red looked at the woman on the ground and wished they hadn't. Leslie's arm was red raw. Half of her face and neck were still smoldering. One of the women threw a bucket of water over her. She didn't flinch.

Didn't move.

Red joined the line as sirens sounded in the distance.

❖

Red was looking down at their palms. There were pale lines and puckering that Tony hadn't noticed before. Red picked up their mug of tea and drank.

"Was she okay?" Jade asked.

"Leslie was in the hospital for weeks. We all went to visit. The hospital didn't like it, but we were stroppy dykes. They couldn't do much about it. Then Leslie said not to come. She'd only allow her lover to see her. One day she discharged herself and disappeared. She turned up in Todmorden a few years later. She'd had skin grafts, but you could still see the scars. It was bad luck both her and the cows were in the barn that night. It was only that day that Leslie brought the cattle in for winter. She was exhausted and had had a couple of ciders. She lay down to rest her eyes for a minute and fell asleep. But if she hadn't been in there, more cows would have died. Two did."

Jade poured more tea. "How did the fire start?"

"Well, that's the thing. We don't know, but we think it was Arnie Rawlings. I went poking around the next day. Found a lemonade bottle, and it smelled like petrol to me."

"Was there an investigation?" Tony asked.

"Chris and Bryony were against it. Bryony thought Arnie did it because she got together with Chris. Bryony worked in the Flying Horse with Arnie. They went on one date. Nothing came of it, but everyone could see Arnie was in love with her. Then Bryony came out as a lesbian, and Arnie took it badly. He was only nineteen at the time. A copper came up to the farm several times, keen to talk to Chris and me, but Chris said there was nothing to talk about. She told the detective it was an accident. She said she didn't want anti-lesbian policemen stomping all over women's land." Red smiled. "That's the kind of thing we said back then. Anyway, it was hard on all of us. None of the Oak Springs women thought it was an accident. We thought someone from the village had tried to burn us off the land, and that's a horrible thing to come to terms with. Took a long time before we felt safe. Chris isn't going to want to talk about it now. Not with Bryony gone and Arnie Rawlings back."

"And still homophobic," Tony said.

Red nodded. "That's right. It was a long time ago, but there are some feelings you never shake off. Being hated that much, it's hard to forget."

❖

Vera stood in front of the range smiling. Her eyes wandered over the cupboards and surfaces, resting at last on her son. "This kitchen feels a part of me," she said softly. "Hours and hours of my life cooking, washing up, chatting with Jed and Nick over a brew. I've sat in this room more than any other. All those years. Can you feel them?"

Tony nodded. The room hummed with Vera's presence. It was a warm welcome laced with sadness.

Nick was riveted to a website offering spiritual guidance. He had dark circles under his eyes. "Miranda won't take my calls," he mumbled. "She might get out of the business altogether, she said." He tapped the pristine countertop. "I don't know whether to sell up. It did me good coming over for dinner at Oak Springs. I wondered, maybe a change of scene…" He tailed off, sounding exhausted.

"Your mum's here now, Nick," Tony told him.

He shut the laptop. "Where?"

"By the range."

Nick jumped to his feet. "Mum…Mum?" He stopped a foot from the cooker, reaching his hands out.

"Vera's right here." Tony showed Nick the exact spot where his mum stood and then translated for the ghost.

"I don't want you to be so sad, Nick. I'm okay, and you will be, too."

Nick shook his head. "You don't understand."

"Maybe not," Vera said. "Nothing troubles me now except your pain. It's holding me here."

Nick bit his lip. "I'm sorry, Mum. I don't want you to go. I miss you so much." The years dropped away and Nick was a child, lost and confused.

Tony felt for him. She knew grief. How it can seep into the heart and take root, stripping hope away.

"I don't want to leave you, Nick, but that's how it is." Vera held her hand out to him. "I can see how much you're hurting. But, son, there is no love without loss. Some people protect themselves, putting a barrier around their hearts. But it's worth it. It's got to be. The alternative is all those days without love. A life without it."

"My past has gone with you, Mum. There's no one left to ask, and I can't remember all the stories."

"You'll remember what's important," Vera said.

"You were a good friend. The best." Nick's voice was choked with tears.

"I have to go." Vera's form flickered.

"Is this it, forever?"

"I don't know. I don't feel like it's the end." Vera put her arm around Nick's shoulders and began to fade. "When you think of me, that's where I'll be."

CHAPTER EIGHT

It had been a long afternoon pulling potatoes, carrots, and turnips in an intermittent drizzle. Tony's work clothes were in a soggy heap on the bedroom floor. She was standing in her boxers and a T-shirt deliberating what to wear when she glanced out of the window and got the shock of her life.

There was a group of people marching up the track with actual flaming torches. My God, Rawlings had stirred up the villagers. Tony stifled a scream. She scrambled into a pair of Red's pajama bottoms and ran barefoot down the stairs.

"Help! Help! A mob is coming," she shouted.

In the living room, Chris woke with a start. Tony ran past her to the kitchen and gawped at the sight of Red tenderly wiping tomato sauce from Jade's cheek.

She rushed past them too. Whatever was going on was none of her business, and she had more important things to worry about.

She shoved her feet into Wellington boots. And regretted it the second her bare, dry toes met cold, wet rubber. Ignoring it, she threw open the kitchen door, determined to meet the mob with a brave face.

"What's happening?" Jade had detached herself and was a step behind her.

Tony stopped dead. The mob was almost at the yard. It was a smaller group than Tony had thought, but the flickering torchlight threw eerie shadows on the advancing figures, distorting their features as they marched closer. There was a strange regularity to the line: one holding a smoking, flaming torch, the person behind carrying a huge, orange, supersized pumpkin.

What the hell did it mean? Were pumpkins the new pitchforks?

She searched the yard for a defensive weapon, found a trowel in a flowerpot, and grabbed it.

Jade was next to her now, with Red a step away. Chris pushed bravely past them into the yard.

Good. A united front. With all four of them, maybe they stood a chance.

They would need to dowse those torches. The whole house could go up. Tony ran to the coiled hose as the strangely silent group left the track heading for the farmhouse. Didn't mobs usually chant and shout? The strangers filed into the yard staring intently at Chris as she closed the gap between them.

"How do, Fiona," she said. "To what do we owe the honor?"

A tall, strikingly good-looking woman stepped forward. Torchlight played off her blond hair, and Tony caught a glimpse of intensely blue eyes. "We heard you had some trouble, and maybe you've not got the time or the inclination for it, but if you're willing, we'd like to bring the Harvest Fete committee meeting to you."

"The committee meeting," Chris said. "Of course. And the torchlight procession idea—we agreed to trial it tonight, didn't we? With all that's been going on, I'd forgotten. Forgive me. Come in, everybody. Come in."

Red took the hose out of Tony's hand, filled a bucket of water, and smoothly doused the four flaming torches.

Tony moved aside to let the women file past. One of them looked Tony up and down.

"Unconventional. I like it. You do you, girlfriend," she said with a wink.

As the committee followed Red into the living room, Tony tried to sneak upstairs, but Chris pulled her into the room.

"Tony, Jade," she said loudly, "can I introduce you to the Wooly Well Dressers."

"The who-is-it-now?" Tony spluttered, goggling at ten women of different ages, trying to squeeze onto the sofa or into chairs. No one was wearing wool, but maybe they were something to do with sheep. Fiona *was* well-dressed, as were many of the others. But one or two looked like they'd come straight from milking. Tony didn't want to be an urban snob, but were khaki dungarees high fashion in the Derbyshire farming community? Mind you, receiving company in a T-shirt, old pajama bottoms, and Wellington boots, as she was, Tony was hardly one to judge.

Fiona cleared her throat. "I speak for all of us when I say we want nothing to do with Arnie Rawlings. We're here in solidarity, and we want to hold our meetings at Oak Springs if you'll have us, as none of us want to meet in the room above the shop like we usually do."

"Oh, Fiona." Chris patted the woman on the arm. She slipped a tissue out of her pocket and wiped her eye. The business with Rawlings was getting to her. Several of the village women went to Chris, engaging her in conversation.

Tony tried to back out of the room, but the woman who had looked her up and down outside stepped in her way.

"Tsk-tsk. Don't go," she said. "I'm Penelope. You can call me Penny." She shook Tony's hand warmly.

"I was just going to get changed."

"No need," Penny said.

"But you're the well-dressed wooly women."

Tony was startled by a general outbreak of laughter.

"Oh, but you're charming," Penny said.

Tony hadn't meant to be. She shifted awkwardly.

Fiona smiled. "We assist another event, the well dressing or blessing of the well on the green. It's a tradition that goes back centuries."

"It's pagan in origin, and you always come, don't you, Red?" Penny said, rubbing her hand along Red's arm.

Red smiled. "We do. Chris and me, we both help out."

"You just missed it." Penny turned back to Tony. "You'll have to come back next August to see it."

"If this is the state of lesbian bars these days, we really are going to hell in a handcart," a familiar voice rang out. "Where are the mournful female ballads? The cheap lager? The unspeakably-stained barstools?"

Tony turned her head slowly. Sure enough, her spirit guide, Deirdre, was hovering in the kitchen doorway. She was distractingly dressed in a long red wig, a purple corset over a bright pink taffeta skirt, fishnet tights, and neon pink stilettos. Deirdre was from New York and had ruled the drag scene until she passed away in the 1980s at the height of questionable fashion choices. After being absent for weeks, it was typical she would turn up in the middle of a crowded room when Tony couldn't speak to her.

Jade twitched her head in the same direction.

The drag queen strutted literally through the crowd to float in front of Penny. "Why does this bar look like a run-down farmhouse? It's not a theme I approve of. If they tried to recruit me as a lesbian, I'd refuse. I couldn't be expected to rub shoulders with that furniture on a regular basis. And why are you wearing...I can't even think of a name for what you're wearing. Is this a cult? Have they forced you to pair tatty red flannel with green rubber? Don't they know that red and green should never be seen?"

Tony wanted to scream, "Tell it to Father Christmas," but that would have complicated everything. Instead, she muttered "Excuse me" to Penny and slipped away.

❖

In Tony's bedroom, Deirdre was still muttering about Tony's outfit, making Tony sigh. She needed help, and she needed a spirit guide whose main raison d'être wasn't to insult her. "We're on a farm. Get over it."

Deirdre took in the room for the first time and screamed.

Jade rushed through the door. "There are people downstairs, hush yourselves."

"I wouldn't worry. Who's going to hear Deirdre apart from you and me?" Tony said. "And Miranda, if she happens to be passing."

"Any of those women could be psychic."

"Fair point," Tony said.

"You said farm," Deirdre said in a shocked whisper. "You didn't say dusty chamber of horrors stuck in the…" Deirdre's eyes brightened. "Oh my, a nest of tables. Haven't seen one of those for the longest time. Oooh, a Terence Conran lamp. And that chest of drawers." Her voice took on a tone somewhere between nostalgia and awe. "Flat-pack furniture. Takes me back to the happy hours spent watching handsome men sweat over impossible-to-understand instructions. The fun we had finding the pieces at the end and throwing them away. This room is a tribute to the 1980s. I'd feel at home if it wasn't for the…" She squinted hard at the quilt. "Well, that certainly puts the L in labia."

"Deirdre." Tony clawed the ghost quickly back from memory lane. "Where have you been?"

"Trying to contact you. Didn't you get my message?"

Tony shook her head.

"The reception here is terrible," Deirdre said. "Ever since you ran off with no regard for your Guide."

"Or your best friend," Jade butted in.

"Or for Dr. Whatsit," Deirdre said.

Jade rounded on the ghost. "I've told you before if you're going to use that ridiculous analogy, I'm Sherlock Holmes, not Watson."

"Sherlock Groan it is. Tony's more of a Whatsit anyway," Deirdre agreed.

Tony sighed. "What do you mean, message?"

"The text I sent you."

"Text?" Tony picked up her phone, scrolling for messages.

Deirdre put her hands on her hips and huffed. "You were with the handsomely rugged, deliciously butch man."

Tony smiled. "That reminds me. I've decided to explore my butch identity. What do you think?"

"You might want to arm yourself with a magnifying glass. Or perhaps a microscope?"

"Tony is undeniably butch, and I'm proud she's embracing her identity," Jade chipped in.

Deirdre didn't look impressed. "Anyhoo, Tony, you were with the farmer with the tight butt cheeks messing about with a spirit board. I literally spelled out a message telling you I was trying to get through."

"That was you," Tony said, remembering furiously how scared of the Ouija board she'd been. "'Bad' and 'Tony Knows Who.' What kind of message is that?"

"Bad line, I was trying to say. And you do know who. How many spirit guides do you have?"

"I wish I had more. Just one more would do," Tony said through gritted teeth.

"Why I was saddled with a medium with the brain power of an amoeba, I don't know," Deirdre complained.

Tony glared at her. "The saddled feeling is mutual. I get more guidance from the chickens in the yard than you."

Deirdre huffed. "So, now that I've forced my way through, what's going on? Why are you here?"

"A ghost called Bryony asked me to come here and retrieve some jewelry. Only it turned out not to be jewelry, but a person buried out there." Tony pointed a finger in the direction of the copse.

Deirdre glanced out of the window. "She didn't come through me, and I don't like that."

"So what should we do?" Tony asked.

"Want some free advice? One, throw away those pajama bottoms, and two, don't try to understand the spiritual world. It's very different from the land of the living. Or, if your social life's anything to go by, the land of the half-living. Time passes differently. I can't help you with earthly matters, and the events here are distinctly earthly. You like to call yourself a detective, go detect."

"I've never called myself a detective." Tony picked her jeans up from the chair. Deirdre had a point about the pajamas. She should get changed, especially as Deirdre looked to be no more help than anyone else associated with this case.

"I've called you a super dick," Jade chipped in.

Deirdre put her hands over her ears. "Too much information, and not to mention completely implausible. Even with the help of silicone."

"As in detective. Get your mind out of the gutter, Deirdre." Jade laughed.

"As Oscar says, 'we are all in the gutter, but some of us are looking at the stars,'" Deirdre retorted.

Tony smiled. "I love that quote. Wait a minute, you said Oscar *says*, not *said*. Do you know him? Is he there, with you, in the ether?"

Deirdre pursed her lips together. "I couldn't possibly say. Now, I'm off to do some investigating myself. I want to look into this Bryony woman."

Tony zipped up her jeans. The T-shirt was relatively clean. She sniffed under the armpits ignoring Deirdre's shudder.

"I hear that soap and deodorant have been invented in your time zone, Neanderthal Nora. You might want to use them," Deirdre said before disappearing with a faint pop.

Jade was staring at the clothes Tony had left in a heap on the floor. "Those PJ bottoms look good on Red. Must be how you wear them," she said. "Though it could be your legs."

Just how familiar with Red's pajamas was Jade? "Hang on a minute," Tony cried. "What do you mean about my legs? I'll have you know, I've had compliments on my footballers' knees."

"Um-hmm," Jade said, heading through the bedroom door. "The footballers called. You're not using them. They want their knees back."

❖

Penny intercepted them at the bottom of the stairs. "Ooh, nice jeans, Tony," she said, "but you shouldn't have got changed on my account."

"Oh, I…" Tony went to say she hadn't, then worried that would sound rude, so she just followed into the living room.

One of the WWD women held a plate heaped with baked goods. Tony was suddenly ravenously hungry.

"Sausage rolls, yum," she said, making a beeline for the puffy, flakey, plump with sausage meat, delicious looking canapé. It tasted as good as it looked.

"Fiona's sausage rolls are the best. The meat is from her pigs." The expression on Penny's face suggested that was a good thing, so Tony swallowed, reasoning it was better for a meat eater to know the meat they ate. It was honest, at least. No anonymously butchered, plastic packets of flesh for these farming women.

"You should try my peach brown Betty," Penny murmured.

Tony hoped they were still talking about food. She nodded and chewed, avoiding Penny's eye just in case.

"I don't know if I'll be around long enough," Tony said, "I have to go back to London and look for a new job."

"Oh?" Penny said, "What do you do?"

"I'm a lighting technician for theater."

Penny clapped her hands. "I thought there was something theatrical about you. I used to be a dresser. Now I'm just a well dresser." She laughed at her joke. "But seriously, I worked at the Exchange in Manchester, the Theatre Royal, and several London theaters. I'm not in the business anymore, but you need to meet Mei. Come on."

Penny grabbed Tony's hand and pulled her through the crowd to a small, slim East Asian woman in an impeccably tailored suit.

"Mei, meet Tony. Tony's a lighting technician, and Mei's a producer for theater."

Mei smiled. "I'm looking for a lighting technician," she said. "Well, a lighting consultant, someone to advise me and work with the production manager. We should talk."

"That would be great. I don't know if you have anything to do with casting, but my friend Jade is a musical theater actor."

"Is she now?" Penny looked at Jade with interest and waved her over.

Mei shook Jade's hand. "Tony says you're a performer. I'm producing a panto in London. *Cinderella* on ice or roller skates, we haven't quite decided. Do you skate?"

"Oh yes," Jade said in the same crisp way she'd once told the director of *Black Beauty* she could ride a horse. That lie had come back to throw her in a pile of manure.

Fiona tapped her teacup with a spoon. "I want to say before we wind up this meeting of the Harvest Fete Committee that we have agreed not to involve the shop or the garage in our proceedings this year. We'll hold the celebration on the green as usual, and we'll do it without Arnie Rawlings's help or sponsorship. There's no place for homophobia in Wooly Mill. The Wooly Well Dressers are totally behind Oak Springs. I heard about the incident outside the pub, and you can call on me any time of the day or night. Chris and Red, please make sure your friends have my number."

"You can call any of us," another woman said. "Though Fiona's the one with the black belt in Tae Kwon Do."

Red and Chris looked moved. Tony smiled. This women's group was just what the Oak Springs lesbians needed.

❖

"I heard you coming back last night. And it's embarrassing. Grab that tool kit and follow me."

Tony blinked up at Red. She had been enjoying the smoothest, creamiest, most delicious cornmeal porridge. It melted on her tongue. It sang to her heart. It made her stomach sit up and beg. It was so different from Chris's and Red's porridge that the dishes shouldn't be in the same category. Theirs should be filed very carefully under Building Materials.

"Did you hear me, Tony? Ed's waiting in the yard. We're going to teach you simple bike maintenance. A butch of your age should be able to maintain your vehicles."

Jade breezed in from the kitchen, humming a salsa tune, and whisked the cereal bowl out of Tony's hands before she could refill it. Tony looked longingly at the pot of porridge but tripped obediently after Red. Jade smiled. Very broadly. So broadly, Tony stopped and looked her up and down to see if she had *that* glow.

Red tugged her sleeve sharply. Tony followed Red out into a sunny, autumnal morning, wondering if cycles *were* vehicles. She thought there had to be an engine for something to be a vehicle.

Ed had the bike leaning against the barn wall and was looking at it dubiously. "Nowt much been done to this for a long while," he said by way of greeting.

Tony thought about quoting Red's statement about butches and vehicles back to them, but one look at Red's face and she chickened out. Which got her thinking that whoever had invented that expression hadn't met Harvey, the chicken.

"It's no use being all muscles. You need to use your brain cells too," Red said to Tony, passing her a cloth.

Tony took it and grinned. Red had said she was all muscles.

"It's not as bad as it looks," Ed said. "We'll tighten the brakes and lubricate the gears and that chain. But first, you need to wash it down. There you go, Tony." He nodded toward a bucket of water.

Tony settled down in front of the bike that had faithfully squeaked her from A to B. She wiped off the dust, scrubbed at the dirt, and felt sad imagining the bike all neglected in a corner of the barn. She knew what it was like to feel abandoned. *Oh God, I'm Maya's rusty old bike.*

She scrubbed extra hard at the impacted mud on the frame, lavishing attention on the bicycle to make up for its tragic past.

"Any luck with the job hunt?" Red asked Ed, passing him a mug of tea.

"Bits and pieces, but nothing full-time and not local," Ed said, taking a drink. "Makes a good brew your new…" He raised his eyebrows at Red.

"House guest," Red filled in. "Jade makes everything taste better. About A1 Autos, though, what's Arnie Rawlings doing? He won't be able to cope alone, will he?"

"Arnie's Autos, you mean. He can, at the moment, anyway. No one's going to him."

"Are they not?"

Ed shook his head, examining the bike that Tony had made short work of cleaning. He showed Tony how to take off the chain, clean and degrease it, and how to check over the gears.

"Folks are riled up in the village about Arnie," Ed said casually. "People aren't happy he sacked me, and they don't think the trouble up here is right either."

Red frowned. The steam from their mug rose like a veil in front of their face making them look like someone in a misty, old-time photograph. "It's not pleasant it starting up again."

"But it's not like before, Red," Ed said quickly. "People know you now."

Red just nodded.

Ed turned his attention to whipping off the front wheel and releasing the stubborn brake pad. Tony grabbed her mug of rapidly cooling tea.

"Hey, Red, did you ever know a woman called Lisa? She was the girlfriend of someone who lived here, a Wiccan woman called Star."

Red looked curiously at Tony. "Didn't realize you knew any of the women from back in the day?"

"I don't. At least, I don't think I do. Except for Aunty Lena, of course. She wants to get in touch with the Lisa person."

"I see. Did you speak to Lena? What's her number? I'd love to catch up with her," Red said.

Tony quickly looked down at the bike, thinking.

"I say, *her*," Red was saying. "That's an assumption. What are Lena's pronouns?"

"Um, she/her, as far as I know," Tony said. It most certainly was as far as Tony knew on account of the fact she had never met the person. "The thing is, Aunty Lena happened to mention how she missed this Lisa woman when we were talking about me coming here to Oak Springs, but Lena's away at the moment."

In the silence that followed, Tony realized there needed to be a reason why being away meant a person couldn't be contacted. "Aunty Lena's on retreat. No phones or messages allowed." Tony invented wildly. "She's fasting. Loves it. She has very clear eyes."

Red stared at Tony. Even Ed looked up, and he'd been solidly engaged in trying to wrench off the rear brake pad.

"She's away for weeks at a time," Tony said, compelled to fill the awkward silence. "It's very remote. You have to get a ferry." She managed to stop herself from saying, "And a donkey" but couldn't help adding. "They have to leave their phones in a box by the door." *Shut up and stop talking now.*

"Is she Buddhist?" Red asked.

"That would make sense," Tony said.

Ed beckoned her over. "Here, you can fit this rear pad. I suppose if this place is remote, it's okay for them to leave all those phones by the door. You couldn't do that in London, could you?"

"No." Tony knelt by the bike, relieved to have a reason to stop talking. The new pad was clean and firm and looked like it would clamp down tightly onto the tire. Just what a person needed coming down one of the steep hills around Wooly Mill.

"I do vaguely remember Star's partner." Red drained the last of their tea. "I haven't seen Star for more than ten years. Bryony had a friend called Lisa, though. Pretty sure it's the same person. They used to meet up in the tea shop in Hatherwell now and then. Right up to when Bryony got ill. Didn't see her at the funeral or the wake. Well, look at that. It's a different bike."

Tony dropped the cloth, filing away the snippets of information. She stood back. The bicycle shone in the weak sunlight. The scratches and bumps were still there, but it was serviceable now.

"Good job, Tony," Ed said.

Red ran a finger along the crossbar. "We need a name for her."

"Like, Emily P, you mean?" Tony asked. "Do you think we could name her after a butch hero?"

Red thought. "There is Stormé DeLarverie. She was a Black butch who used to hang out at the Stonewall Inn. Stormé fought in the Stonewall uprising."

"Like Marsha P. Johnson and Sylvia Rivera?" Tony asked.

Red nodded. "Stormé was an entertainer, a drag king in the days when they were called male impersonators, and a bouncer. She patrolled Greenwich Village into her eighties to keep people safe."

"Stormé," Tony said, patting the bike. "An honorable name."

Tony took Stormé on a road trip to the tea shop in Hatherwell, musing on the amount of legwork involved. It was all very well for ghosts. They could float about, appearing and disappearing at will. But what about a supernatural detective's shoe leather? Or a vegan supernatural detective's synthetic shoe leather? Who paid for that?

It wasn't a lucrative profession. Money was going to be an issue, and soon. Word of mouth was everything in Tony's real job, the theater. Being let go may well have seriously damaged Tony's reputation. It wasn't fair. Twenty years as a lighting technician, and she was only as good as her last reference. Maybe her contacts would see her through. That would mean going back to London and facing the questions, the gossip, and the pitying looks.

Tony let out a sigh. And then she breathed in a lungful of country air. She didn't have to worry about that right now. The road stretched before her, bordered on each side by hedgerows bursting with juicy, ripe blackberries and scarlet hawthorn berries. The day was warm, the sky had a thin blanket of clouds, and Stormé was a different bike. The gears had actual power, the chain drove the wheels smoothly, and there was no squeak to ruin the peaceful symphony of insect and bird song. Tony felt the stretch on her calves and thighs. She was packing on muscle, and that couldn't hurt.

She reached Hatherwell in no time, left Stormé to her own devices, and pushed open the tea shop door.

The café was decorated in a traditional style with pretty, red-checked tablecloths on small round tables. There was a vase of fresh flowers, linen napkins, and a rose patterned sugar bowl on each table. Tony chose one near the counter with its array of cakes. She was aware that she was consuming far more fat and sugar than usual, thanks to the Wooley Well Dressers, but none of them had baked a big, gooey chocolate cake like the one nestling under a glass display stand. And she hadn't been able to taste proper Bakewell tart even though she was irresistibly close to Bakewell. The source of the original product must surely produce jammier jam, crisper pastry, and meltier in-the-mouth almond paste.

"Can I help you, duck?"

A generously proportioned, middle-aged white woman with short auburn hair appeared at the table. She wore a skirt and blouse with a white apron tied around her waist. She looked like she wasn't afraid to taste her wares—exactly the person you'd want creating the bounty of cakes and pastries.

"I'd like a cup of tea and a slice of cake, please. What would you recommend?" Tony asked.

"The coffee and the chocolate cake were both made this morning. Scones, too, of course. Carrot cake and lemon drizzle are both popular. I'm not blowing my own trumpet, but it is all good here and homemade."

"I'll try the chocolate cake, please."

"Coming right up."

While she waited for her order to arrive, Tony studied the room and wondered how to phrase her questions about Bryony's meetings.

"Is this your tea shop?" Tony asked when the woman returned.

"It is, love. My mother started it. I worked here with her and took it over when she passed away."

"I'm sorry," Tony said automatically.

"Thank you, but it's okay. Mum had a great life, and she's been gone for over ten years now. This place was her pride and joy, and I've kept it pretty much the way it was. Are you staying in the area?"

"I'm visiting at Oak Springs Farm in Wooley Mill."

"Oh yes. Chris and Bryony's place. Well, Bryony's gone, of course. How is Chris?"

Tony put her cup back down on the saucer. "Coping. I don't know, really. She doesn't give much away, to be honest."

"Well, it's nice you came up to see her. I heard she'd taken it hard."

Tony nodded. She wasn't about to go into the intimacy or lack of it of her relationship with Chris. "I wonder if you can help me, actually. I'm trying to find a friend of Bryony's, called Lisa. They met here from time to time, I believe."

The café owner looked thoughtful. "Bryony did meet a woman here sometimes. The name Lisa rings a bell. A blond woman? About my age?"

"Could be." Tony hadn't seen a picture of Lisa, and Bryony had been no help.

"They looked like old friends, except sometimes it seemed a bit heavy between them."

"What do you mean?" Tony asked.

"About a year ago, before Bryony got ill, they seemed tense. They spoke very quietly, almost under their breaths. Not that I was listening to their conversation," she said quickly. "When they'd met before, they'd been lighter, more jokey. Oh, and they came in another time. It was hectic that day, and I hardly noticed them except that Bryony was ill by then, and I wanted to get her seated at a table as quickly as possible. Poor lamb. The chemo had worn her out. The same woman was with her, and she didn't look happy. I put that down to Bryony being ill. We were all worried about her." The café owner nodded toward the teapot on the table. "Do you need some hot water in that, duck?"

"Oh, yes, please."

The café owner disappeared into the kitchen, leaving Tony to mull over the new information. Ghosts often didn't give out all the information a person might want. Things that mattered on the material plane didn't seem important, she'd been told. All the same, Bryony wanted Tony to act quickly, so why hadn't she mentioned these cozy café rendezvous?

The bell above the tearoom door tinkled, revealing Arnie Rawlings in the doorway. He was the last person she wanted to see. She hadn't forgotten his previous threats. Hopefully, he was sober.

"We don't want your kind in here," he said abruptly.

Tony thought he had a damn cheek, but she wasn't surprised. He was the sort of person to throw his weight about even if he didn't own the place. A brisk wind blew in, and she fought the urge to shiver, not wanting Arnie Rawlings to read it as a sign of fear.

The café owner returned. She put the teapot on the table with a glance at Rawlings.

"What are you serving her for, Mary?" Rawlings said. "She's one of *those* women, one of the Oak Springs lot. I told you they'd started up again, didn't I?"

"Arnie," Mary said, brushing past Rawlings to shut the door behind him. "I don't interfere in your businesses, and I'll thank you not to interfere in mine."

"Now, Mary—" Rawlings began, but Mary cut him short.

"I've never had a problem with Oak Springs or anyone who lives there. I was very fond of Bryony, as you know."

"Bryony was never the problem," Rawlings muttered.

"I support you in many things, Arnie. But not in this. This was my mother's tearoom, and now it's mine. We may be married, but you don't get a say in how I do things here."

Tony covered her surprise. If anyone had asked her, she would have presumed Mrs. Rawlings would be as homophobic as her mate. She was happy to be proved wrong. Rawlings, on the other hand, was not happy at all. He glared at his wife. Then he glowered at Tony before turning and marching back out of the door.

He didn't bother to shut it behind him.

❖

Tony wheeled the bike along the street to the house where she had last seen Madeline. She'd talked it over with Jade, and they'd agreed that Tony should try to speak to the care home nurse. They'd also decided that only Tony should go. It was better if Madeline didn't meet Jade, at least until Tony had some idea of what was going on with Sandra, the friend of Lisa Walker.

Tony found the house easily. She propped the bike against a wall, walked up to the front door, and rang the bell. There was a dull ding-dong inside.

No one came to the door.

Madeline could be at work. Tony remembered someone else had been there last time. She deliberated about what to say if a housemate answered the bell. There was something strange about Madeline. She had seemed to be the receptionist but wasn't. And the real receptionist had said she didn't know a patient called Sandra. On the other hand, Madeline had never actually claimed to be a receptionist. Tony couldn't think of a reason to explain the disappearing patient. Tony decided if a housemate answered, she wouldn't leave a message. She was wondering what she would say when she realized it had been ages.

Maybe the bell didn't work. Tony lifted the knocker and struck it against the door.

The sharp rap reverberated around the porch as the front door swung immediately and noiselessly ajar.

Tony waited a moment, but no one appeared on the other side. She tentatively pushed the door fully open.

A dark and silent hall stood empty before her.

Tony wavered. It was generally not prudent to walk uninvited into somebody else's house. It could be thought of as breaking and entering. Well, not so much breaking, but definitely entering.

Her instincts said to go in.

A second later, Tony was over the threshold closing the front door behind her. Memories layered the air. She felt footsteps and sensed a man walking through the hallway hundreds, maybe thousands of times. She saw him as a young man putting on a raincoat and picking up a hat from the coat rack by the door. She saw him older, putting it back, closing the front door, and walking to the kitchen.

There was a narrow console table next to the coat rack with mail stacked on it. She leafed quickly through it. The letters were all addressed to Mr. Thomas Fuller.

Tony walked along the hallway. The kitchen was straight ahead beyond another small passage, but something called her through a door to the left into a study.

There was sadness in the room. Snapshots of the man's life hung in plain wooden frames on the walls. There was a black-and-white photograph of a young white man in a suit with a young white woman in a wedding dress. The man and woman a little older with two children. The man older still at a party with a mixed group that didn't include his wife. The man, middle-aged, at an official function shaking hands with another white man with a mayoral chain around his neck. The man, now old with snowy white hair standing next to a slim, impeccably dressed old man. The other man in the photograph looked vaguely familiar.

There was a computer on an office desk next to the window. Tony didn't want to go anywhere near it. The energy around it was so unpleasant Tony felt queasy.

A scuffling sound came from the other side of the wall. It sounded like someone banging into a piece of furniture.

She crept to the doorway and saw a man holding onto the kitchen table. He was bent over, taking great, labored breaths.

She could run out. All she had to do was turn right, and she'd be through the front door in seconds. The man was in no shape to pursue her.

Except she couldn't ignore the horrible rasping sound he made as he struggled to breathe.

She approached cautiously. He was another older white man, although he wasn't the man in the photographs. He was younger, in his late fifties. She guessed he was medium height, although it was hard to tell as he was bending forward with one hand on his chest. He was balding with gray hair, and his complexion was pale, with beads of sweat on his forehead.

His watery blue eyes fixed on her. "Who…you?" he struggled to say between breaths.

Tony debated what to tell him.

"What…are you…doing here?"

Tony recognized the voice as the heavy breather from the creepy phone call.

"You called me, didn't you?" she said.

He fumbled around in his jacket pocket, fished out an inhaler, and took a puff. Then he gasped for several long seconds. "I'm Detective…Adam…Hutchins," he got out eventually.

Shit. The man was a policeman.

His breath eased a fraction. He took another puff. "Why are you looking for Lisa Walker?"

He remembered who she was. Tony itched to leave, but two things kept her standing in the room that smelled as if it hadn't been lived in for months. Detective Hutchins might know something, and he looked extremely ill.

"I can't tell you that," she said.

He coughed, spitting something into a handkerchief that he stuffed into his trousers pocket. "You working for someone?"

She nodded. "What about the man who owns this house? Is he all right?" The house was empty; she felt it. Sorrow seeped through the walls like damp.

But when Detective Hutchins went to answer her, he started coughing and couldn't stop. His skin was gray. His lungs rattled, and his lips were turning blue. He struggled to lift the inhaler. Tony helped him get it to his lips, and he managed to press it but didn't have the breath to inhale.

Tony took out her phone and dialed 999.

The paramedics came quickly. They hooked Detective Hutchins up to an oxygen tank and bundled him onto a little chair with wheels on the back. They trundled him through the narrow hallway and out the front door.

The old lady Tony had met previously came over as the ambulance pulled away. "So where are they taking him? Hospital?" she asked.

Tony nodded.

"Taken bad, has he?"

Tony nodded again. The old lady looked Tony up and down and then back at Mr. Fuller's front door.

"You house clearance, then?" She waved a hand to where the ambulance had been a moment before. "He's your boss, is he?"

Both seemed plausible explanations, so Tony nodded once more. "Has Mr. Fuller gone away?"

The old lady gave her a sharp look. "That's one way of putting it. He's dead, duck."

Tony thought the old lady must be calling Tony *duck*, as in term of endearment like *love*. Rather than calling Mr. Fuller a dead duck.

"The home rang and told me. It's a shame. Fifty years he lived in that house. I've been next door for thirty. He was a good neighbor. Quiet. He had friends call around sometimes. He had a wife once and kids. I never met them. She left him, I think. Never came to see him, any of them."

"Have you seen any health professionals go into the house?" Tony asked.

"Just those paramedics," Fuller's neighbor said. "Well, happen you'll have things to do. Itemizing or whatever. And I can't stand here talking all day." She walked away, tipping her head at the house.

The house seemed to acknowledge the payment of her respects.

Tony went inside to the kitchen. She shut and locked the back door, and then took a quick look upstairs. There was a bedroom that hadn't been used for some time. And a very cobwebby guest-cum-box room. The taps on the bathroom sink squealed when she tried to turn them. No one had lived in the house for months and months.

Tony let herself out of the front door and closed it firmly behind her.

❖

Nick was topping up the water and feed bowls for his chickens when Tony dropped in on him later that day. He had a similar informal setup to Oak Springs, and no one could deny these birds were free-range. His hens looked a happy bunch pecking contentedly in a short-cut, grassy paddock containing a wooden, wire-fenced coop. A squark alerted Tony that Nick had a rooster, too, but this one eyed Tony briefly before ignoring her. The sawdusty-warm-straw smell from the coop mixed with the scent of grass and the occasional whiff of manure.

Nick looked less tired. Tony hoped he was sleeping better.

"I've brought you some baked goods," Tony said. "The Wooly Well Dressers have taken it upon themselves to ensure we don't run out of food. We have more scones than we can shake a tassel at."

Nick raised an eyebrow. "Is that a southern expression?"

"A queer one, I think."

"We would say we've got scones to cobble dogs with."

"I think we're even in the nonsensical phrase department."

Nick smiled. "Got time for a cuppa?"

Tony nodded happily. She had an ulterior motive for the visit. "I bring gifts of sausage rolls also."

"Not Fiona's?" Nick said as they walked to the farmhouse.

"The very same."

"She's a busy woman. What have you done to deserve such lavish attention?"

"Not me. Chris and Red. The WWD are looking after them to compensate for Rawlings's behavior." Tony pushed off her Wellington boots, leaving them outside the back door.

"Ah, Arnie, right." Nick filled the kettle and set it on the range to boil. Tony passed him the bag of pastries. He put a couple of sausage rolls in the oven to warm and perched on a high stool at the breakfast bar. "I don't condone his behavior now, but something happened years ago that helped make him the way he is. Arnie started all the trouble back in the day. Him and his mates messed with stuff on the farm, tried to ruin their crops, let their livestock loose, that kind of thing. He tried to get me involved, but I didn't want anything to do with it. One night, Chris and a woman called Jay caught Arnie pouring sand into their tractor's fuel tank. Chris had her shotgun. They made Arnie strip down to his boxer shorts and drove him off their land. He came over here in a state. He was crying, Tony. I lent him some clothes. I don't approve of what they did, but it got him off their backs at the time. He left the area the next morning."

The kettle whistled. Nick lifted it and filled the teapot. "How's the spooky sleuthing going? Jade mentioned your Paranormal Investigation Agency."

Tony groaned. Jade had a thing about creating acronyms. The more ridiculous sounding, the better. PIA was a case in point. She slipped the name to clients now and then despite Tony's best attempts to preserve the true title of the Supernatural Detective Agency. Tony didn't and never would work for an organization called Pee-er.

"I want to pay you. I don't believe I would have got to speak to Mum if it hadn't been for you. I've been sleeping better. Even if I never connect with her again. Spirits need to pass over, don't they?"

Tony shrugged. "Ghosts are cagey about what happens next. I don't think we're supposed to know."

Nick nodded. He pulled the sausage rolls out of the oven and left them on top to cool. "Well, I feel lighter. You have a real gift. So, please tell me, what's your fee?"

Tony thought of Mystic Miranda. Nick had paid out plenty already. As broke as she was, charging Nick didn't feel right. "I don't want to charge you. But you might be able to help me with information."

"Okay. Fire away."

"Do you have an address or contact details for Star?"

"I thought you were looking for her partner, Lisa?"

"We are. Maybe Star knows where she is."

"I see. Well, Star did send me a condolence card when Mum died. Let me get it." Nick put the sausage rolls on a plate, passed the plate to Tony, and began riffling through a pile of cards and letters next to a shelf of cookery books. "I put them away when they started collecting dust. Mum would have hated it. Ah, here it is." Nick opened a card with a picture of a white lily against a purple background on the front. He turned it over. "No address, I'm afraid. There was nothing on the envelope, or I would have kept it. I've got a number for her in my phone, though." Nick passed the card to Tony.

Inside, Star had written that she was sorry for Nick's loss and hoped to visit him at the farm sometime. That was it. Vague and unhelpful for Tony's purposes.

"Would you text her, perhaps ask her if she *can* come and visit? If you don't mind, I mean," Tony asked.

"Sure. This is an old number, mind." Nick composed a text and pressed send.

There was a ping almost immediately. Nick pulled a wry face. "The text is undeliverable. Sorry."

Tony sighed. This case had more dead ends than a maze.

❖

After an uneventful morning, Helen called.

"Hi, I remembered something," she said.

"About Lisa?" Tony asked hopefully. Time was passing, and Walker was a loose cannon.

"No. It's about Star. I wasn't sure if you knew Star's second name?"

"Actually, I don't."

"It's Young. Star Young. Will that help you find her?"

"Possibly." Tony didn't want to break it to Helen that she'd already explored the only avenue she had to find Star. And improving Helen's love life by putting her back in touch with an old flame wasn't top of her list of priorities. Star might have an address for Lisa Walker, but how were they supposed to find her with only a last name to go on?

"I also remembered Star's dead name. That's what they call it, isn't it, when people change their name?"

That was interesting. "I think so."

"Lisa would forget sometimes and call her Maddy."

Tony sat up. "Maddy," she repeated. As in short for Madeline. "Do you know what Star's job was, by any chance?"

"Sure. She was a nurse. Still is, probably. If you find her, you will pass on my details, won't you?" Helen said.

"Yes," Tony replied, already picking up her coat.

❖

The same smartly turned-out and impeccably manicured receptionist was on duty at Forest View Care Home. She was still called Aisha, according to her name tag. Tony wondered if name-tag wearers ever swapped tags if only to see if anybody noticed. Tony would be tempted to do that if she had to pin her name to her shoulder.

"Hello, Aisha," she said brightly.

Aisha pushed the microphone headset away from her mouth, smiled, and chirped, "Hello."

"I've come to see Madeline," Tony said confidently.

"Oh, dear. That's a shame. Did you find the other one? Susan? Sarah? Simone?"

"Sandra. I haven't, actually, but I've come to talk to Madeline today." Tony thought keeping Aisha on point was her best chance of achieving something this side of the next millennium.

"I thought after you left, but there was no way to contact you. Hillside Care Home has a very similar layout and the same color walls. Did you try there?"

Tony took a breath. What kind of person opened a care home on a hillside? Hopefully, Hillside was as much on a hill as Forest View was by a forest. "Yes," she lied. "It would be really good if I could talk to Madeline."

"She left for the day. Not long before you got here." She dropped her voice. "In a bit of a hurry. Maybe you can get her at home."

And how would she get Madeline's number? Tony took a breath. "I'm a private investigator. It's essential that I speak to her. Can you give me her number?"

Aisha's eyes widened. She leaned forward. "Are you working for Mr. Fuller's family?"

Tony blinked back at Aisha. Madeline had been at Fuller's house, and she remembered Fuller's neighbor saying the home had rung her when Mr. Fuller died.

"How long was Thomas Fuller here?" she asked, ignoring Aisha's question.

"Nearly a year. But you'll know that. I mean, the family knows that already."

Tony was aware that Aisha was frowning, but she'd suddenly remembered something else, and she looked up to the room on the first floor, where she'd seen Madeline with a resident on that first visit.

"Was that Mr. Fuller's room?" Tony asked.

Aisha followed Tony's gaze, only now she shifted uncomfortably in her chair. "You *are* working for the family, aren't you?"

Tony shook her head. "There's an investigation, though, right? Is Madeline being questioned?"

Aisha sat up straight. "I can't discuss it, I'm afraid. If you're not the actual police and you're not representing the family." She glanced over her shoulder toward a closed office door. "My manager won't want me talking to you."

Tony racked her brain for a second, trying to think of a way to get more information. But the look on the friendly receptionist's face told Tony that ship had sailed.

"Sorry." Aisha turned her face firmly to her computer screen. Tony took the hint and left.

❖

Tony cycled through Hatherwell without incident and stopped at the sheltered accommodation block to chain the bike to some railings. No doubt the human Stormé would have appreciated the significance.

On the way to the main gate, Tony was drawn to an elderly white man sitting on a bench. He looked familiar. And then she remembered he had been sitting on another bench by the school on Mr. Simmonds's road. As if he felt her gaze, he turned and waved a hand in greeting.

She realized then that she had also seen him in a photo at Tom Fuller's house. She walked over. He might know Simmonds, and if not, he obviously knew Fuller. So, he might know where Lisa was.

"Hi," she said. "Do you live in this block, by any chance?"

"I do." He had a polished accent with barely a trace of Derbyshire in it. He was smartly dressed, wearing a jacket, trousers, shirt, and tie. All of which were clean and pressed. In contrast to the confidence of his clothes, he had an apologetic look. Her *something's not right here* bell tinkled in her ear.

She ignored it. "Perhaps you can help me. I've come to speak to someone who lives here, and you might know him, Mr. Donald Simmonds?"

The man smiled. "I am Mr. Donald Simmonds."

Tony eagerly sat next to him. "I'm so pleased I came over. I'm looking for someone who worked for you, a home help called Lisa Walker. Do you remember her? Maybe you have an address for her?"

Don Simmonds had been nodding away happily a moment ago. Now he looked sad. "Nopa Ata," he said.

Tony stared at him. "I beg your pardon. I don't understand."

"Nopa Ata," he repeated.

Tony wondered if he was confused or perhaps had a form of dementia. "I don't want to trouble you. Please don't worry if you don't have an address for her. Do you remember when you saw her last?" she asked gently.

"Nopa Ata," he said again.

"Are you feeling okay?" Tony looked for signs of heart attack or stroke. He looked remarkably well, although he was trembling and pale, and there was an urgency in his eyes that scared her.

He stood up. "Nopa Ata." He spoke slowly and carefully this time, and then he walked quickly away.

"Mr. Simmonds, I don't understand," Tony called after him.

But he didn't turn around. He walked elegantly at a good pace. He didn't seem ill at all except maybe for the confusion. Tony wondered about following him until she noticed a woman with a baby in a buggy staring at her. Tony didn't want people to think she was harassing the old man.

How strange. She'd found Simmonds, and maybe he did know Lisa Walker. It was hard to tell. Her warning bell had been correct, but what exactly was wrong, she had no idea.

CHAPTER NINE

Tony traveled up to the third floor of the Peak Royal Hospital in the lift. Jade had phoned, posing as Hutchins's niece, and discovered that he was in Bluebell Ward and visiting times were between two p.m. and eight p.m.

The lift opened out into an anonymous corridor. Everything was very gray, and it all looked the same. If it wasn't for the signs, how would anyone find their way around hospitals? Could there not be some relief from the institutional feel of it all? Perhaps different themes for the wards. If Tony were a designer, she'd decorate one ward like a fifties diner. Another could be regency-style with four posters around the bed. Or they could have themes from nature, like under the sea. Though that might be alarming for patients coming around after surgery. Anyway, the details would need working out, but there was nothing wrong with the general idea of getting rid of the frightening starkness. And they could do something about that peculiar stomach-clenching smell of disinfectant combined with mushy food.

Not that Tony was criticizing the wonderful folk of the NHS. They worked their butts off for little pay and scant thanks. They, too, should be allowed a themed environment if they wanted one. It was the least designers could do.

Tony reached Bluebell Ward. There was a list of patient names with bed numbers scrawled beside them on a dry wipe board. Adam Hutchins was in bed five.

Tony nodded at a woman sitting up in bed three, reading a book. The woman frowned, and Tony didn't blame her. If a total stranger walked past Tony's bedroom, she'd frown too. Bed four had the curtain pulled entirely around it, and bed five was obscured by bed four's curtain. Tony took another couple of steps forward and froze. A visitor was sitting in a big blue armchair beside the bed. Tony recognized Detective Hutchins's receding gray hair and side profile, but it wasn't him that stopped the breath in her throat. The face of the woman talking to him was burned into Tony's memory from Maya's Facebook page. Tony stepped back quickly, her mind racing.

Her name was Eve, something. My God, even from a glance, the woman was sickeningly fit. More importantly, what was she doing here? And how did she know Detective Hutchins?

Tony couldn't visit him now. She stepped backward, not quite sure what to do, but instinctively moving out of sight of bed five.

Tony's neck prickled, telling her she was being watched. She turned to bed three, and sure enough, the female patient was looking over her book at her.

She had to get out of the ward. The walls were closing in. Her breath was coming hard and fast, and Tony was terrified she'd burst into tears. Damn, Maya. Damn her. Tony could try to shut down her feelings all she liked, but Eve's face had smashed that box right open.

She walked quickly along the corridor to the lift. She pressed the button taking big, slow gulps of air. Her brain was struggling to make sense of what she'd just seen.

What the hell was Maya's new London girlfriend doing at the bedside of a Derbyshire detective?

Tony woke with the sense that icy fingers were gripping her shoulders and shaking her.

"Wake up," Bryony yelled.

"What's wrong?" Tony murmured. She was tired and had no desire to get up. Whatever Bryony wanted could wait.

"Someone's outside." The urgency in Bryony's voice made Tony open her eyes again.

This time she sat up and swung her legs over the side of the bed. It was dark outside, and Bryony had vanished. Tony was confused. Had Bryony been there or not?

She went to the window and opened it. Tony couldn't see the yard or barn properly from this side of the farmhouse. Her bedroom had a view of one of the fallow fields, the track, and beyond that, the copse. A fact that Tony did not find comforting.

There were the usual sounds: the rustling of leaves and grasses in the wind, a lonely bird warbling—wait a minute, what time did birds get up around here? She grabbed her watch from the bedside table.

It was three a.m. The middle of the night, even by Red's and Chris's standards. Harvey was quiet, so it must still be nighttime.

Except he wasn't. He gave a loud, urgent cry. And the chickens were clucking in alarm.

Tony threw on her jeans and a T-shirt, shoved her bare feet into her trainers, and ran down the stairs.

The chickens were still squawking when Tony flew out of the kitchen into the yard. But an odd noise gave her pause. It sounded like something rattling or clanking. When a sharp hiss followed it, Tony recognized the sound of a spray paint can. And now she made out the scuffle of footsteps.

The barn loomed ahead dark and squat. Someone else moved inside, throwing things around. A chicken flapped out through the open door, agitated and distressed.

The spray-painting sound came from around the corner. Tony hesitated, deciding which of the invaders to tackle first. Maybe she should go back and wake the others. She padded back into the kitchen to the toolbox she'd meant to put away. As she riffled through it quietly for a weapon, Jade appeared confused and half asleep.

"Bryony woke me," she said.

Tony put a finger to her lips. "There are people outside," she whispered. "Go get Red and Chris."

Jade disappeared as Tony found the hammer. She gripped it for dear life and crept back outside, keeping to the shadows.

Tony followed the serpentine sound of spray paint. The sky was heavy with cloud making it difficult to see beyond a few feet ahead. Tony could only make out the outline of the side of the barn and broad shapes: a tree, a bush, and a human moving in front of the barn wall. She smelled the fruity acetone scent of the paint.

"What the hell are you doing?" The words came out in a rush and sounded strangled even to Tony.

The person turned with a muffled yell. Tony walked toward them, puzzled by a strange, rounded shape where their head should be.

The vandal ran at her. Tony swung the hammer, and it smashed into a bike helmet. The person reeled. Tony reached to pull the helmet off, but they straightened up and kicked out. Tony fell back, and the vandal took off.

On the track, the vandal was already swinging one leg over a motorbike. Tony broke into a run, vaguely aware of Red shouting and the sounds of a scuffle.

Footsteps thudded behind, getting louder. Before she could turn, she was shoved so hard she went down, her face hitting the dirt. As she tried to roll over, a boot smashed into her back. She yelled, her kidney on fire. She pulled her knees up, writhing in pain.

Bikes roared to life as more footsteps ran past her. Tires scrabbled away on the dirt track with Red and Chris shouting after them.

And then Jade was kneeling next to her. "Tony, what's wrong? Talk to me, are you hurt?"

But Tony just gripped her knees while Jade murmured beside her in worried tones. All Tony could do was breathe through the pain, furious at herself for letting the bastards escape.

❖

Tony woke surprisingly late. She stretched, winced, gingerly rolled her legs over the bed, and straightened up with a groan. Her back complained at the movement, but it permitted her to get washed and dressed, albeit carefully. The kick had been well placed. It had put her out of action for a good ten minutes. Jade had wanted Tony to go to hospital, but it had been obvious to Tony that all she needed was a good night's sleep.

Before she put on a T-shirt, she went to the antique mirror above the chest of drawers. The mirror would have been charming in the 1930s with its Art Deco fan shape, but enthusiastic cleaning, or perhaps preening over the years, had distressed the mirror work. Twisting her body around and trying to make out her image through the mottled surface, Tony was also distressed. A vivid purple bruise covered the middle of her back.

Red and Jade were at the breakfast table, talking in subdued voices. Red jumped up when Tony appeared.

"Here she is, the hero," they said.

Jade kissed her teeth. "Some might say, damn fool."

"Jade, that's not nice. Tony was brave last night."

Jade cut her eye at Red. "Tony has a habit of running into burning buildings, jumping into freezing canals."

"Going after a friend that's disappeared and needs help," Tony said pointedly.

Red looked from Jade to Tony and back again but said nothing.

Jade dipped her eyelids. But then she patted the chair beside her. "Come, sit and have breakfast. How are you feeling?"

Tony had made it down the stairs, but she needed to keep moving. "Stiff. I need to walk. Stretch a little. Are the chickens all right?" She wasn't sure she was up to dealing with slaughtered poultry.

Red nodded. "I don't think going after the chickens was part of their plan."

Tony stepped out into brilliant sunshine. From the back of the farmhouse, the barn looked normal. Both doors were open. The hens in the yard looked up and drifted quickly away like children in the playground melting away from the school bully. Harvey flew out of the barn and flapped halfway across the yard before stopping abruptly. He glared at Tony but then gave a curious head dip. If Tony didn't know Harvey better, she would have thought Harvey was acknowledging her part in the night's proceedings.

Tony walked past the rooster and peered in. Boxes were scattered across the dusty concrete floor with rusting nuts and bolts lying alongside half-empty lubricant bottles and paint-splattered screwdrivers. She bent over to right a paint can that had started to leak out and winced at the stab of pain. She threw a bit of old cloth over the congealing red pool. It would protect the chickens until someone could deal with it.

Tony went outside, around the corner of the barn, and stopped in horror. Jagged white letters had been sprayed onto the flaking gray surface of the barn wall. *Gay = Sick* was written above *Homos go home*. To the right of that, the word *Dyke* had been scrawled. Some of the paint had dripped. Tony supposed it wasn't easy spray-painting in the dark. Yet the words were unpleasantly clear. All in a night's work for a homophobe-vandal-cum-graffiti artist.

From the way the paint sprayer had moved the night before, Tony guessed they were young. They'd had a head's height on her, even allowing for the helmet, so an older teenager, perhaps? She hadn't seen the second person. If the police were interested, they might be able to get a boot print from the bruise on her back.

She studied the graffiti for a moment and took a photo with her phone. *Homos go home*, indeed. Chris and Red were home, so where did the painter want them to go to? Lesbos?

Tony decided the painter was ignorant, probably young, and a motorbike rider. She'd got pretty close when she'd chased them. The vandal's build didn't match Arnie Rawlings, and it was unlikely Rawlings would move that fast. He might have been the person inside the barn, but they'd legged it pretty sharpish as well.

The air next to her wavered, and Bryony appeared frowning at the barn wall.

"This is the last thing Chris needs," she said. "There's damage at the front gate, too. Let me show you."

Tony snuck a look at the ghost as they started along the track. Bryony looked well, much like the photo of her propped on the mantlepiece above the fire. Maybe ghosts got younger the further away from death they got. On the other hand, Tony was getting decidedly older and nowhere fast with finding Lisa Walker.

"We're running out of time," Tony said. "Every lead goes to a dead end. All I can tell you is where Lisa isn't."

Bryony sighed. "I know. But I'm sure Lisa's still in the area."

"I need more than that to go on, Bryony. Maybe it's time to tell Red and Chris."

"You can't do that." Bryony looked horrified. "Red will move the body, and if they get caught, or if the body gets found with Red's DNA on it, the courts will have a field day, and so will the media. An old, Black, butch lesbian. And they'll come down heavily on Chris as well."

Tony grunted in frustration. "Maybe we go to the police. Volunteer the information."

"Are you stupid?" Bryony didn't bother to mince her words. "Have you forgotten he was one of their own?"

Tony had been about to mention Detective Hutchins, but Bryony's reaction made her hesitate. Tony wasn't even sure if *she* trusted Hutch, not after seeing Maya's girlfriend at his bedside.

They had reached the part of the track that meandered through the copse. Bryony steered away from the area where Walker was buried, walking quickly to the entrance gate. "By the way, a drag artist tried to talk to me on the other side," she said. "Mentioned you. She was dressed very strangely."

"Sounds like my spirit guide. Was her name Deirdre?"

Bryony nodded. "Which I also didn't understand. She had a New York accent. Not an accent I associate with the name Deirdre."

"She called herself after Deirdre Barlow."

"The character from the soap opera *Coronation Street*?"

"The same."

"I'm not sure I want to know why. She was wearing a tweed cape and deerstalker hat over a long, blond wig. Did she die a very long time ago?"

"In a way. She died in the eighties."

Bryony tutted. "That's not a long time ago. I meant Victorian times. She asked me what my intentions toward you were."

Tony was about to reply when she saw vivid, red spray-painted letters on the *Danger Keep Out* sign ahead. *Keep Out* had been over-painted so that the message read *Danger Dykes Here*.

Faggots had been sprayed with white paint onto the tree trunk where the *No Hawkers. No Cold Callers* sign was nailed. That had been resprayed to read *No Queers. No ugly dykes*.

The gate was stuck in a furrow of mud in a mostly-open position. It had been daubed with paint. The *Oak Springs Farm* sign was still swinging from one nail. Someone had carefully altered it to read *Yak pis Farm*. Not far away, the *No Trespassers* notice predictably now said *No queers*.

Two paint colors had been used, and Tony had seen two figures the previous night. The red painter was cleverer. They'd made new words and put some thought into their messages. The white painter was more ignorant and vicious. Words had been sprayed on another tree saying *Go Home*.

Tony wondered at the mentality of spraying those words at someone's house. Why not *Go Away*? Either way, the painter was making it clear they didn't want lesbians living in their area. She worried it was a racist message meant for Red and maybe Jade. Anger bubbled inside her, and she wished more than ever she'd got her hands on the spray painter last night.

Bryony had vanished, and Tony felt suddenly lonely, surrounded by the messages of hate. The trees and vegetation at the entrance to the farm made it cool and shady, and they also screened the entrance from the road. The vandals would have been able to take their time. Tony felt their energy lingering: fear, anger, and excitement.

She shivered and turned back to the farm. The whole business was distasteful. Tony needed a cup of tea and something to settle her stomach.

❖

The wind blew gently as if to soothe Tony's nerves and blow the images of the graffiti from her mind. If she was feeling crap, how much worse must it be for Red and Chris? It was good Tony and Jade were there for solidarity. Although Tony had to admit she wasn't feeling safe at the moment. Which was precisely what the homophobes wanted, of course. Well, bugger them.

There was an animal up ahead walking oddly toward her. As it got closer, she saw it was a black and white dog about the size of a Labrador, and it was walking strangely because a sign was tied around its neck.

Tony stopped mid-step. Her instincts told her to be cautious with a stray dog, even one that looked perfectly friendly. It had seen her now and ran awkwardly to her, its tail wagging behind it.

When the dog got closer still, Tony tensed. The sign read *I hate homos*.

What a horrible thing to do to a dog. This one couldn't have been more friendly. Tony itched to remove the offensive sign. She reached her hand out only to freeze again, seeing blood on the dog's fur.

She shrank instinctively away when the dog tried to lick her. She couldn't tear her eyes from the congealing blood stains around its mouth. There was a smaller amount of blood on its chest and legs.

Tony bent down cautiously. She wanted to get the sign from around the dog's neck and use the string to tie its collar to a post. She gingerly reached out, expecting the dog to sink its teeth into her at any moment. It continued to look adoringly up at her. Its sweet expression was a macabre contrast to the blood on its fur, lips, and mouth.

The dog didn't flinch as she removed the sign. She moved her fingers slowly through the fur around the dog's neck, feeling for a wound.

She didn't find one.

The dog shook, splattering Tony with droplets of blood. She shuddered. Whatever had happened, whatever the dog had bitten, it had been recently. She loosened the knots in the string, peeled it away from the cardboard, and carefully tied the string around the dog's collar, ensuring the collar wouldn't tighten if the dog pulled against it.

"Come on, pooch," Tony said gently. Holding the end of the string like a lead, she walked to the small gate of a fallow field next to the track.

The dog looked up at her, sitting down on its back legs in a gesture of patience.

Tony pulled her phone from her pocket and called Jade's number.

"Is everyone all right?" she said the second Jade answered.

"Yes." Jade's answer was short and confused.

"No one's bleeding?"

There was a slight pause before Jade replied. "No. Should they be?"

"This isn't funny, Jade. There's a stray dog outside the fallow field, the one nearest the entrance to the farm. It's covered in blood, and it's not the dog's blood, I've checked."

There were footstep noises and the sound of a door opening followed by more hasty footsteps, this time outside on rough ground.

"Oh, thank goodness, they're all right." Jade panted for breath. "Here, Harvey, Harvey. Are you okay, my darling?"

The dog hadn't been at the chickens. Tony thought about the other farm animals. The dog wouldn't go after pigs, surely. They were huge. But it might go after, oh shit, the sheep.

"I've tied the dog up. I'm going to the sheep field. Get Red and meet me there." Tony didn't wait for a reply. She was already running.

The dog howled after her.

❖

Tony knew something was wrong before she had the gate fully open.

The sheep were huddled in the far left corner. That wasn't unusual. But their shivering, protective, bunched-together appearance was.

And then she saw the cotton wool pillow lying in the middle of the field. A lone sheep lay on her back. Her four black-socked legs stiffly flexed as if she was stretching vigorously from sleep. There was red on the fluffy white body. Tony broke into a run.

The sheep was still breathing, but the wound on her neck was deep, and blood had spread, soaking into the wool on her chest and back. Tony wanted to cry. The sheep's eyes were closed, and she was very still. Tony knelt beside her and, not knowing what else to do, just stroked her leg and shoulder gently, murmuring, "Help's coming. You'll be all right." Although she didn't believe the sheep would be okay. Not with those wounds.

Red ran into the field, then stopped dead, looking at the fallen sheep with anger and horror. Jade came behind slowly and hesitantly.

"Tony, I need to get the vet out. Can you go to the Plough and fetch Chris. You'll have to ride there on the bike. Chris has taken Emily P." Red sounded matter-of-fact, not a tremor in their voice.

Tony looked at Red and wondered how they could be so calm? And then she realized that that was all they could do. It was the best thing for the little sheep taking shallow breaths on the ground.

Tony nodded and set off for the barn to pick up Stormé.

❖

The car park at the Plough was almost empty, and the roomy, comfortable, and highly polished saloon bar was deserted, so Tony was surprised to find a sizable group of men in the tap room. The tap was the smaller and plainer of the two rooms, with no cushions on the chairs, no curtains, just half-frosted windows, and old, rough furniture. It was, what Tony's dad would call, a spit and sawdust bar. There was no sawdust on the wooden floor and, thankfully, no spit.

Chris was speaking loudly and angrily. Tony hovered in the doorway between the two rooms, not wanting to interrupt her. Chris had planted herself in a prime position halfway between the door from the car park and the long, wooden bar. Arnie Rawlings was perched on a worn barstool, but she wasn't addressing him. All her attention was on the landlord, a burly, balding man with a sour expression.

"I shouldn't have to put up with it. People coming onto my property, causing damage, scaring my chickens." Chris looked at the end of her tether.

The landlord smirked at a beer mat on the bar, not bothering to meet Chris in the eye. He rubbed at a spot so ancient it was never coming out while Chris exhaled loudly, her anger growing.

Bryony appeared at Tony's shoulder. "Is it starting again?" she asked.

Tony shrugged.

"They're all Arnie's pals or his dad's," Bryony said, tossing her head at the men in the tap room. They were a motley crew. Tony guessed the old men were friends of Rawlings senior while the middle-aged ones were likely Arnie's. All of them were riveted on the action unfolding in front of them.

After thirty seconds of pointless polishing, the landlord flicked his eyes to Chris and away again. "No one's saying it's right," he said to the beer mat. "But we've all had problems at some time or another with kids making a nuisance of themselves."

There were noises of agreement from the assembled old and middle-aged cronies. "Maybe you should suck it up and quit whining, Chris. You can't accuse people just because you don't like them. Arnie's a grown man. Do you really think it was him painting stuff on your barn wall in the middle of the night?"

Two men sitting near the window laughed.

"They'll be from Sheffield, one of those estates, lots of kids knocking around with nowt better to do," one of them said.

"Exactly," the other old man chipped in. "Some of them are a bad lot. You read about it. This business won't have anything to do with Wooly Mill. I'm surprised at you, Chris Webster, for even thinking it. My grandchildren would never behave like that. They've been brought up to know right from wrong."

Chris grunted. Tony took a step into the room, but no one noticed, including Chris, despite Tony trying to subtly get her attention.

Chris glared at Arnie. The grin disappeared from his face.

"Maybe it was kids, just like you said. But if so, he's behind it. Why would they pick on my farm all of a sudden? What they wrote was nasty and homophobic, and how would some kids from Sheffield even know lesbians live at Oak Springs?"

One of the younger men sniggered at the word lesbian. Some of the others shifted uncomfortably, stealing glances at Arnie. The idea of him being behind the vandalism had sunk home, then.

Arnie squared up to Chris. "How do you know it's homo-whatsit?"

"Because of what they sprayed on the barn wall."

"That's just words, Chris," the landlord said. "What did they write? Lesbian? You are one, aren't you? I don't come crying to you when some bored youth sprays 'dickhead' on my pub wall."

"He's got a point," the old fella on the window table said.

"I've not come *crying to you*." Chris's face was flushed. "I'm saying that someone's stirred these kids up. Or paid them, maybe. And that person is Arnie Rawlings."

"Now then," the landlord threw his polishing rag onto the bar and faced Chris properly for the first time. "You can't say things like that in my pub. I won't have it. Arnie's a friend of mine and a good bloke."

The atmosphere in the tap room changed, moving from quiet stonewall to simmering hostility. Tony sensed the men in the bar all supported Rawlings. They might not be openly homophobic, at least not in front of Chris and Red, and they most likely wouldn't paint words on walls themselves, but they were rallying around Arnie to a man. Homophobia comes in many forms. Their complicity was the fuel for Rawlings's actions.

Tony walked through the bar. Chris noticed her then and frowned, but she turned back to the landlord.

"If he's such a good bloke, why did he sack Ed?" Chris said.

There were mutterings then amongst the cronies.

Rawlings plonked his pint down on the table. "You accuse me of stirring things up when you've been turning people against me in the village. Some of them won't come in my shop because of you."

"Chris," Tony said, trying to get her attention, but Chris flapped a hand at Tony, batting her away.

"Because of me? They're boycotting your shop and garage because you sacked Ed."

"And I wouldn't have done that if he hadn't stolen that part for you." Rawlings was half on his feet now.

"Chris," Tony said more insistently.

"Stolen? A part that's been sitting on a shelf for more than thirty years. I'll pay for it. How much was it?"

"Now you're just being ridiculous," Rawlings said.

"Happen you shouldn't have sacked Ed," one of the middle-aged men spoke for the first time.

The others threw him disapproving looks.

"Ed made his choice," Arnie said.

"And so have you, Chris," the old man sitting by the window said. "You chose your lifestyle. We've come to accept it in the village, but you must know others won't. Word's got out again, maybe to folks in Hatherwell or even to Sheffield. Perhaps you should think twice about starting that women's land up again."

Chris straightened up, fixing the old man in the eye. "Are you saying this is what I deserve?"

There was total silence in the bar. Arnie and the landlord smiled. The blood rushed to Tony's head along with images of the hate-filled words and the devastation in the field.

"They killed a sheep," she blurted out. "You think it's okay for people to be terrified in the night? When are you going to think it's not all right? When they kill one of us?" The acceptance of the homophobic actions sickened her. And it wasn't even just acceptance. She felt it. She knew in that weird extra-sensory way that people who experience prejudice know, that some of the men were happy about the damage and fear provoked at Oak Springs. And that incensed her.

Arnie Rawlings stared at her, narrowing his eyes. "What are you talking about 'killed a sheep'?"

"A dog got into the field," Tony told him.

He grunted in an exasperated way. "Another one throwing accusations. You can't blame the kids for that, girl. A coincidence, I'll bet."

"People are always letting their dogs off the lead. Day-trippers usually," the old fella by the window chipped in quickly. "I'm sorry about your sheep, Chris, but for goodness' sake, have a word with your woman there."

Chris walked over to Tony, shaken and concerned. "What makes you think it was the two lads from last night?"

"Because there was a sign tied around its neck, and someone had written on it, I hate homos," Tony said.

No one sniggered, no one spoke, and all eyes turned to Rawlings. He shifted uncomfortably, fronting up to them with blazing eyes even as the color drained from his face.

❖

Back from the pub and having cleaned out the chickens, Tony kicked off her trainers, poured herself a steaming mug of tea, and turned her attention to the slab of cake cooling on a wire rack. It was Jade's handiwork. Tony took in a lungful of the sweet, spicy scent. Jade was liberal with the powdered ginger and cinnamon in her ginger cake.

Was there a way to slice a piece from the cake without Jade noticing? Perhaps if Tony pulled off a chunk or bit it, she could persuade Jade that an animal was responsible. Unfortunately, Chris and Red didn't have a cat. Didn't all farmers have several cats, chickens, ducks, and a squirrel or two? But maybe that wasn't farms. Maybe that was arks?

The loaf cake was sizable. Could she even fit it in her mouth? Tony was standing over the cake, seeing how wide her mouth could get, when the kitchen door swung open.

"Get your damn mout' away from my ginger cake," Jade snapped, flapping at Tony with a tea towel.

Tony jumped out of the way of the towel at the same time that a Range Rover pulled into the yard. The producer, Mei, got out with two children.

"Make yourself useful." Jade shoved the kettle into Tony's hand.

Chris and Red appeared at the kitchen door with Mei and the children in tow. Jade slid the ginger cake onto a plate and led them into the dining room.

Mei and her younger child sat down, but a young teenager stood awkwardly looking anywhere but at the Oak Springs lesbians.

"No, thank you, Jade." Mei waved away a slice of cake but nodded at Chris, who was pouring tea into fine china teacups. Tony suspected Jade had been finding things in cupboards again. "Lee has something to say."

The teenager, Lee, was staring at the floor. He looked about thirteen. His hands were shoved into his pockets, and his body was rigid. Tony assumed he was angry until he lifted his head, and she saw shame in his eyes. He glanced at Chris and then at Red and cleared his throat.

"I'm sorry," he said, a flush creeping up his neck.

Tony was confused. She guessed this was something to do with the vandals, but she was as sure as she could be that Lee wasn't one of them. He wasn't tall enough. Had it been him that had trashed the vegetables?

"What are you sorry for, Lee?" Chris asked.

He swallowed. "He won't like me telling you this, but someone's paying a lad called Martin and his mates to come up here and mess things up, you know, smash things up, write nasty stuff, try and frighten you, that kind of thing."

"Who's paying them?" Red asked.

"It's okay, Lee. Don't be frightened," Mei said.

"I'm not frightened," Lee said quickly, even though he clearly was.

"It's that man that's just moved back here," Mei's younger child said.

Lee shot his sister an angry look.

"Arnie Rawlings?" Chris asked.

Lee nodded slowly.

"But why didn't you tell us, Lee?" Red said.

Tony heard the hurt in Red's voice. Lee hung his head.

"I didn't want them to do it, Red. I don't agree with it," he said in a rush. "They asked me to help them because I know my way around here at Oak Springs. From when I worked up here in the spring, and you showed me how to drive the tractor." He looked pleadingly at Red. "That's how I know. I would have told you all. It's just…it's just you don't want to get on the wrong side of Martin."

"How do you know what he said?" Chris asked.

"Because I was on the green a few weeks ago. Martin and his friends were hanging out near me and my mates. Arnie Rawlings came over from the shop with some cans for Martin's lot."

"Cans of alcohol?" Mei asked sharply.

Lee nodded.

"What did Rawlings say then?" Chris said.

"Stupid stuff. You don't want to hear it." Lee looked embarrassed.

"I think we've seen it painted on our barn. Spit it out, Lee. We'll have heard worse, I'm sure," Red said.

Lee looked at his mum.

"It's all right, Lee, tell them," Mei said, her voice a great deal softer than when they'd first arrived.

"Well, it was old-fashioned ideas like it's not natural what you do, and it's against God. I could tell they were humoring him at first. Drinking their beer and nodding but looking at each other like Arnie was off his head."

Tony flinched at the casual prejudice toward people with mental health issues but decided this wasn't the moment to discuss it.

"It was only when he said the lesbians at Oak Springs would take all their girlfriends that they started to listen."

"You didn't believe that, did you?" Red asked.

Lee frowned. "Well, maybe. I mean, I know you two are old." He tipped his head at Chris and Red. "But those two are middle-aged. They could be after…" He quickly looked at his mum, "Well, people's mothers or something."

Mei glanced at Tony and Jade, looking embarrassed.

"And if more women come here, some of them might be our age, and, you know, that might affect us," Lee said earnestly.

Red struggled to hold back a smile. "It doesn't work like that, Lee. As devastatingly attractive as lesbians are, in general, the only women interested in us are lesbians and bisexual women."

"Oh." Lee looked down at the ground.

"You haven't even got a girlfriend," Lee's sister said.

Lee glared at her. "Martin believed him, and also, he wanted the money. But none of his mates were interested. He came to me because I know my way around here, but I turned him down." He looked at Red again. "No way would I do anything like that."

"So Martin Dewsbury is responsible for killing my sheep," Chris said coldly.

Lee's eyes widened. "It, it wasn't him, Chris. He couldn't get anyone from the village to go, so he asked his cousin from Sheffield. He doesn't know anything about farming. His cousin brought a stray dog with him and let it loose on the farm."

"So Martin and his cousin are responsible for two animals' deaths. That dog had to be put down," Chris said.

"Put it down. You mean kill it?" Mei's daughter asked, full of alarm. "Who did that?"

"The vet, love," Chris said gently. "They have to when a dog attacks sheep."

"But why? It's not the dog's fault."

Mei hugged her daughter. "I know. Unfortunately, that's how it is, darling."

"I'm sorry I didn't tell you sooner." Lee looked ashamed, and Tony felt sorry for him. He was a good kid.

Mei smiled at her son. "You've done the right thing, love. What now? Do we go to the police?"

"Thank you, Mei," Chris said, getting up. "We'll handle it from here. Appreciate you coming over."

Mei gathered her bag and children. "Let me know what you decide, will you? And, Tony, Jade, the musical I mentioned is opening in London in six weeks. They go into rehearsal soon. Here's my email. Send your CVs, will you, and, Jade, your spotlight reference number."

Tony's spirits lifted at that, and Jade beamed. After a horrible day, maybe it was a sign their fortunes were changing at last.

❖

When Tony returned from waving Mei off, Chris was sitting in her favorite armchair, staring at the wall. She looked grim.

"Rawlings has gone too far this time." Red eased into their armchair on the other side of the fireplace.

"Happen." Chris sounded tired.

"The police can deal with him." Red sat forward. "Criminal damage, two animals dead, and harassment or whatever. There are laws against it now, and the evidence is right there on our barn."

Jade and Tony looked to Chris for her response. She sighed. Her eyes drifted to the photo of Bryony on the mantelpiece. "I don't trust them. The law may have changed, but I don't know if law enforcement has. They can drag their feet, not find enough evidence, decide not to prosecute. And meantime, we've invited them onto our land. I don't want them here, Red. I've seen what they do to butches, to Black lesbians."

Red and Jade exchanged a look.

"I've known women sanctioned for speaking out, just for trying to defend themselves," Chris went on.

Tony wanted to scream, "This is bigger than us." There was only so much they could do, and there were good people in the police force, like Sergeant Lewis. Officers who joined the force to help and protect. Even so, Chris was right. They didn't want to draw police attention to Oak Springs.

"There is someone I trust," Jade said into the silence.

Chris pressed her lips together, then she looked around at Jade and Tony. "Many years ago, we helped women here, women who had no one to turn to. It wasn't exactly illegal, but people could have made it hard for us. I don't want any of that coming back to haunt us."

Tony avoided looking at Jade. Chris had no idea how haunted she already was.

Chris sat back in her chair and nodded across at Red. "We'll deal with this ourselves."

Tony frowned. Red stared back at her, looking as concerned as Tony felt.

But Chris was more than grown. It was her land and her decision. Tony only hoped "dealing with it ourselves" wasn't about to bring a world of pain crashing down on their heads.

❖

Tony was getting ready for bed when her phone rang.

"Hello, is that Tony Carson?" a deep, moderately breathless voice said.

Tony tensed, recognizing the voice. "Yes, this is Tony. Are you feeling better, Detective Hutchins?"

He took a couple of shaky breaths. "Better than I was. I'm out of hospital anyway. I'm sorry if I gave you a scare. The paramedics said I was lucky you called them when you did."

"You weren't looking too clever."

"Well, thank you. The thing is, I think we should meet." He took a labored breath. "It's easier for me to talk in person. I'm recuperating at home. Can you come to me?"

"Perhaps." Tony didn't want to commit. "Where are you?"

"Hatherwell. Five, Lawrence Drive. Can you come tomorrow?"

"I don't think so," Tony said. "I'm helping with the Harvest Fete. Maybe we can meet the day after."

As if he felt her reluctance Hutchins's tone became more insistent. "We need to talk, Ms. Carson, pool our resources." Hutchins paused to take several short, sharp breaths.

"Sounds like maybe you should rest, Detective Hutchins. I'll phone you tomorrow and confirm," Tony said, ending the call.

Tony had done some digging around. Maya's new girlfriend was a police officer, so it was conceivable that she knew Hutchins, perhaps she was even working with him on a case. But the whole situation made Tony uneasy.

He was a good lead. Following it up made perfect sense. Why, then, was she so reluctant?

Was Tony being ridiculous? Letting personal feelings cloud her judgment? She didn't trust Eve Phee, though when she broke that line of reasoning down, that wasn't fair either. This Eve person might never have known Maya was involved with Tony. And, even if she did, Tony wasn't her responsibility. It was Maya that Tony couldn't trust, not the woman she'd betrayed Tony with.

And none of that had anything to do with finding Lisa Walker.

So why did Tony want to go anywhere else, follow up any other lead, see anyone else rather than go to five Lawrence Drive?

❖

The following day dawned sunny and bright. By early afternoon Chris had rushed them through the farm's daily chores, which included loading hay bales onto the back of Emily P. With Red at the wheel, they cruised through Wooly Mill. There had been an overwhelming response to the Harvest Fete, so much so that the WWD had moved it to the larger recreation ground.

Red slowed down as they neared the village shop. The shop and Arnie's Autos both had banner signs advertising *The Original and Only Harvest Fete, on the Village Green where it always has been and always will be.*

"Surprised he managed to find such long signs," Chris said wryly.

In the small triangle of grass nestled in the middle of the three buildings opposite, Arnie set up a gazebo by himself. It had seen better days, and even though Arnie was tacking a sign to it, it was already sagging on two of its four sides. The sign read, *Beer Tent, proper cheap prices, nowt fancy.*

"Well, you've got to give it to him, he doesn't give up easy." Red pressed down on the accelerator, pulling away.

Traffic had built up on the road outside the village. And as they got nearer, they saw why. Everyone and her dog were on their way to the rec.

The large open field was by a pretty bridge where a brook splashed over cobbles. The playground was screaming with excited children allowed to play while their parents were occupied.

Fiona, the chair of the WWD, directed arrivals. She wore a quilted jerkin and jeans she made look catwalk fresh. She saw them and waved them forward onto the grass. "We need the bales outside the real ale and cider tent," she said, pointing to a chichi striped canvas affair draped with festoons. There was a proper wooden bar inside the tent complete with draught pumps.

A large white marquee had been installed in the center of the field for the judging of the best of the harvest. Competition was fierce amongst the Well Dressers, many of whom were dropping off jars of pickles, enormous vegetables, and Tupperware bursting with baked goods. There was a hubbub of activity around the smaller stalls that flanked the marquee with lights, bunting, elaborately carved pumpkins, and signs going up. A pop-up pizza truck edged carefully past Emily P. The Wooly Well Dressers didn't do autumn fetes by halves.

Penny came by just as they'd moved the second bale into place. She pulled a strand of hay from Tony's hair and pushed a bite-sized square of tray bake into Tony's mouth. "Try this," she said. "It's my entry for the Autumnal Cake Creation category. Tell me what aspects of autumn it captures?"

Tony chewed. Or tried to. A generous caramel layer had glued her jaws together. *Mud* was the word that came to mind. She didn't express it. "Sticky leaves," she managed after a couple of minutes.

Penny frowned. She looked away and was distracted by a white minibus cruising slowly over the bridge. The legend on the side of the vehicle read *Sappho Rentals, Todmorden*. The firm could have been Greek-owned. But given that Todmorden was packed with more lesbians than the lager tent at Pride, it was more likely to be a woman-owned company.

The bus pulled into the car park. Before it had drawn to a halt, the side door slid open, and a long, cool drink of water peeled out. She was tall, tough, and taut, with a physique to rival Red's. The white woman had dark hair peppered with gray, adding to her charm. She slapped a rounders bat in her hand, assessing her surroundings with narrowed eyes.

Six more lesbians of varying ages piled out of the minibus behind her.

"Now that's what I call a magnificent seven," Jade drawled. She headed for the car park, attracted to the new arrivals like filings to a magnet.

But Tony held back, reading the tension in their bodies and the hostility on their faces.

When Chris and Red began to move toward the Todmorden lesbians, Tony went with them.

Chris walked straight to the tall woman. "How do, Joan? Good to see you. Why are you here?"

Joan gazed cooly down at her. "We heard about the homophobia in Wooly Mill, and we've come to sort it. Where is the garage the fucker owns?"

"And how is that going to help exactly, J?" Red looked pointedly at the bats dangling from each lesbian's hand.

"Too many people about you think?" Joan replied. "That's okay. We can stay till it gets dark. We're here to support you."

Penny skipped up at that point, pushing Tony aside in her haste to get to Joan. "Did I hear that you've come to volunteer? Oh, that's wonderful," she gushed. "And you're a rounders team. Sporty *and* fun." She rested her hand on Joan's arm. "Come help me, will you? I need someone tall to strap up my bunting."

❖

The WWD Harvest Fete was a success. The weather held with the afternoon turning into a mild, dry evening, and Chris managed to persuade the Tod women not to confront Arnie Rawlings. They walked together in the torchlight procession through the village.

"This weather is lovely," Jade said. "Just goes to show that God loves gays and also heterosexual people who fight homophobia."

"Like to see you get that onto a badge," Tony muttered at her side.

"You could use the same printing firm as Arnie. They're bound to have enormous badges to go with their huge banners." Red smiled wryly as they passed Arnie's fete on the green.

Two men were queuing at a BBQ manned by the landlord of the Plough. The only stall was the beer tent which looked to be populated by the tap room regulars.

The smell of sizzling patties and onions made Tony hungry. As soon as the procession reached the rec ground, she peeled off, heading for the Feted Burger Van, where she bought a vegan mushroom burger.

She met up with Jade at the competition judging tent. Jade was focused on trying to hear the results. It was too packed to fit inside. The whole village seemed to be there, and half of Hatherwell too.

Tony chewed on her burger, savoring the umami goodness with only half an ear on the announcements coming through a speaker perched above one of the tent poles. She couldn't remember the last time she'd gone to a village fete. Wooly Mill had gotten under her skin. She'd been there far longer than she'd meant to, and they were no nearer to finding the elusive Lisa Walker. She resigned herself to having another conversation with Detective Hutchins.

Loud voices to her left grabbed her attention.

"I won't leave you to sort this out alone."

It was Joan's voice. She was standing by the guess the weight of the pumpkin stall, yelling at Chris. The discussion looked heated, and Tony moved closer.

"It's better we sort this out ourselves," Chris said.

"That isn't how we do things, and you know it. We never leave a woman in a vulnerable situation."

Tony had to admire Joan's sentiment. The rest of the Todmorden dykes were standing by the pizza van, also keeping a close eye on the conversation.

Fiona walked over at the same moment that Red and Jade emerged from the competition tent.

"Well done for bringing home the rosette for your Autumn Cake Category win, Fiona. Again," Red called. "I tried to get a slice, but everyone knows your reputation with Victoria sponge cake."

"What made your cake autumnal?" Jade asked.

"Home-made blackberry jam instead of strawberry, a hint of nutmeg in the sponge, and a dusting of cinnamon in the buttercream," Fiona said.

"What, no pumpkin?" Tony teased her.

Fiona expressed mock outrage. "In a Victoria sponge cake? That breaks seventeen Women's Institute bylaws." She turned serious as Chris approached, lowering her voice. "I took a stroll to the green a while ago, and there's no one there but Arnie and his friends getting tanked up on cans from his shop. Hopefully, he'll go home soon and sleep it off."

Joan had rejoined the Todmorden group. Chris and Joan had history. She wondered how far back it went and a thought occurred. "Is Joan's second name De Silver?" she asked Red.

Red shook their head. "Jones."

"Her name is Joan Jones?" No wonder the woman was impossibly cool.

"Yes. That's why people call her Jay or JJ."

"Did she ever live at Oak Springs?"

Chris nodded. "In the early days. She was close with Bryony. Joan was around for the first dose of homophobia. She went through it at Oak Springs before and feels obliged to get involved now."

Arnie's wife, the woman who ran the tea shop in Hatherwell, strolled by sporting a second-place rosette on her coat. She waved. Arnie's son was with her eating a hot dog. Fiona shouted hello, and Mrs. Rawlings stopped to talk, pulling Red and Chris into the conversation.

Jade held a slice of pizza out to Tony. Steam rose from it in the cold air. "So that's Bryony's Long Joan? There was a nugget of truth in the tale, then. They were non-monogamous, weren't they? You think Chris resents her?"

"Why would she? Chris stayed at Oak Springs with Bryony. Joan went to live in Todmorden. There is an undercurrent of something, though." Tony's mind ticked over. Somebody else had mentioned the name Jay.

The crowd separated then, and a second later, Tony saw why. A group of men marched toward them with Arnie in the lead. The atmosphere changed, becoming menacing. Arnie noticed his wife, and his face turned crimson, but he stopped in front of Chris.

"Let's have it out then. You think you're a man. Let's see how you do in a proper fight."

Arnie's friends waited silently behind him. The Tod women materialized in a second, and the tension grew.

Until Arnie threw the first punch.

The blow caught Chris on the chin. She staggered back, but before she could react, Joan slipped between them.

Arnie looked at her with hate in his eyes. "I'll never forgive what you did to me." He came in swinging with both fists, aiming for her face.

Joan kicked out, sweeping Arnie's legs from under him. She followed with a martial arts punch, and the next second he was sprawled on the ground, eyes wide with shock.

The pub landlord pushed forward. The other men hesitated, but the Tod women and Oak Springs lesbians moved in around Chris and Joan.

"Stop this, Arnie," Ed called from the edge of the crowd.

Arnie spat on the ground. He looked up at Chris. "You think he's such a good friend. It wasn't me that started the fire in your barn."

Chris's forehead wrinkled in confusion. She turned to Ed.

His eyes dropped to the ground. "It was after what you did to him, you and Joan. I was a kid. I was angry. I never meant for anyone to get hurt."

The silence stretched until Fiona walked calmly to Arnie extending a hand.

"Get up," she said. "The village has changed, and it's time you did." She faced the rest of the men. "Go back to your homes and know this. Hate has no place in Wooly Mill."

The men and the Tod women began to leave. Arnie allowed Fiona to help him up. After a last, confused look, he, too, walked away.

CHAPTER TEN

Adam Hutchins's house was a cottage on a small road not far from the high street. The slope to Hutch's house was steep enough to set Tony's heart racing. How did the detective manage the incline with his breathing issues, and why on earth hadn't he moved? The cottage was built from slabs of sandstone. There was a tiny window just below head height to the right of the equally small front door. The cream wooden door was glass-paneled with a slate-tiled porch above it. The cottage could have appeared exactly as it was in a seventeenth century painting if it wasn't for the video doorbell and the small but incongruous camera perched on the slate porch.

Tony pressed the bell and waited, musing about the reach of Big Brother even to historic villages. Ironically, the State didn't even need to provide surveillance equipment when so many citizens were installing it for them. She was surprised that Adam Hutchins wanted to spoil the look of his picturesque property until she reasoned that the detective was probably more interested in recording criminal activity than conserving heritage.

Hutch's voice came out of the doorbell.

"Come in, door's open."

Tony pushed the door, and it swung inward. So much for high-tech security. Tony stepped straight into a small kitchen with the range that appeared mandatory in these parts, a porcelain apron sink, and a stone-flagged floor. The makings of tea were set out on a tray next to the fridge.

"I'm up here," Hutch's voice came faintly through the ceiling.

Tony went through a second door into a tiny hallway just wide enough to access a set of narrow stairs.

"Up here," Hutch called again a little hoarsely.

Tony climbed a flight of stairs and crossed a landing containing three doors. Two were open, revealing a bathroom and a single bedroom with no one in it. She knocked on the paneled door directly ahead of her.

"What kept you?"

Tony found the detective propped up in a double bed with a brass frame, smiling at her. The bedroom was furnished with a chest of drawers and a wardrobe from the last century. It was charming, with exposed beams and a sloping ceiling.

"You find me somewhat inconvenienced," Hutchins said. "Hope you don't mind conducting our meeting in unusual surroundings."

Tony would never have agreed to meet a man she'd barely met in the bedroom of his house, but looking at Hutchins, she felt no threat. A clear plastic tube in his nostrils was being fed by an oxygen tank propped next to the bed. "I shut the front door properly," she said.

"Perhaps you can put it back on the latch when you leave," Hutch said mildly. There was a breathy quality to his voice, but it lacked the disturbing frothy sounds Tony had heard in the hospital ward.

"Really? I saw you've got security equipment out front, and I don't mean to be rude, but if someone walks in, someone unsavory, you don't look in a position to defend yourself."

Hutchins chucked. "Kind of you to worry, but there's nowt to fear on this street. And that's not my equipment either. The care people put that doorbell in so I can talk to visitors when the home help isn't here. I get muddled up working it, to tell you the truth, so I'd be grateful if you leave the door on the latch."

"As you wish, Detective Hutchins."

"Call me Hutch, and take a seat. You're making the place look untidy."

Tony sat in a small armchair by the window. "This is a very nice house. It seems very old."

Hutchins smiled. "Eighteenth century. My parents bought this house more than seventy years ago. I was born here, in this very bed." He patted the duvet cover affectionately.

Tony glanced at the bed, hoping it had had several changes of mattresses since that happy occasion.

"They wanted to put me in a nursing home till I was better, but I wasn't having any of it," Hutch said, his eyes as sharp as a bird's. "Checked myself out of hospital as soon as I could walk, well, stand. Told them I had people here, but even so, they imposed a home help woman on me and a nurse. At least the nurse only comes every other day. I don't know how they've got the staff to spare, but I don't care as long as I'm not paying for it."

"*Have* you got people here?"

Hutchins frowned. "Don't need anyone. The neighbors drop in, and I've been looking after myself for a long time. I don't like strangers in the house. Present company excepted."

Tony nodded. She'd yet to meet anyone who welcomed carers into their own home, at least until they discovered how truly helpful they could be. "So that's how you're out of hospital so quickly."

"Hmmm." Hutchins pursed his lips. "They can't do owt. I've got emphysema. It will see me out. But not today, mate" He shook his head quickly. "Luv, sorry."

"I'm butch. I don't mind what you call me." The words were out of Tony's mouth before she thought about them.

Hutchins blinked at her and then nodded. Tony doubted he understood, but it didn't matter. She was trying on the new identity for size.

"Lisa Walker," Tony said.

"Lisa Walker," Hutch repeated, studying her carefully. "Why are you looking for her, and why were you at Thomas Fuller's house?"

Tony sensed they were playing investigators' poker. She wanted to direct the same questions back but had a hunch she needed to reveal her hand. "I was following a lead that took me to Thomas Fuller's house. How about you?"

Hutch pulled himself up against the pillows. "A report fell onto my desk four years ago. Fuller was named in it along with a friend of mine."

"Donald Simmonds?" Tony guessed. It wasn't a great leap of deduction. Hutch had called her after she'd left her number at Simmonds's accommodation.

Hutch nodded. "Have you come across a group called the Avengers?"

Tony shook her head.

"It was a vigilante group active at that time. We don't know much about them or who was involved apart from our mutual person of interest, Lisa Walker."

"Vigilante group?"

Hutch nodded. "They claimed to use acts of entrapment to target pedophiles online by posing as children in chat rooms."

"Lisa Walker did this?"

"They were very clever. The accusations were mailed anonymously. The first ones we received were just transcripts of web chats. We couldn't do anything with those. But we did start a file and logged the names of anyone they accused. After a few months, the group began luring people to meet them offline. They sent film of these encounters. We followed up on the men. Someone had gone to great lengths to identify them, and I'm not sure how they did it. We prosecuted three of them after finding indecent material on their computers, but for most of them, the evidence against them remained circumstantial."

Tony thought back to Fuller's house. "Did you look at Thomas Fuller's home computer?"

"I was going to. Didn't get the chance."

Tony thought. "And Fuller was a friend of your friend, Donald Simmonds?"

Hutch looked uncomfortable. "Yes. From the photos in Fuller's house, I deduced as much. Don is missing. I was supposed to meet him over a week ago."

"I saw him."

"You did? Where?"

"On a bench outside his sheltered accommodation block. Has he got dementia?"

"No. His mind is as sharp as a razor."

"Something's happened then because the man I spoke to seemed confused. He was saying words I didn't understand. Is he Italian? Or Eastern European?"

Hutch shook his head impatiently. "He's British. I think he speaks a smattering of French."

Tony was puzzled. "I recognized him from the photo in Fuller's house. And he knew his name. He said he was Donald Simmonds."

Hutch sighed. "I don't understand. Maybe he was concussed. Did he look like he'd been hit? Or fallen?"

"No obvious bruising or wounds." Thinking back, Simmonds had seemed well enough. He just didn't make a lot of sense.

"But you've seen him. That's a relief."

"Yes. Hang on a minute. How did you know Lisa Walker was involved with the Avengers group?"

"Ah, yes. The team assigned to the case traced the web activity to a computer registered to her. She was interviewed, and she said she was only involved for a short while and had since left the group. When an officer tried to contact her again, she'd moved, leaving the computer behind."

Strange behavior. Very organized. Tony wondered about mentioning the nurse, Madeline, and the survivors' group, but she didn't want Hutch digging around and linking Lisa Walker with Oak Springs. At least not until they'd resolved the Raymond Walker problem.

"Now then, Tony, I've given you a lot of info. What can you tell me?" Hutch stared at Tony shrewdly from the bed, managing to look intimidating despite the oxygen tube in his nose and the sweet pink roses on the pillowcase at his back.

"Nothing helpful, I think. I'm looking for Lisa Walker for a client. It's a personal matter and has nothing to do with vigilante groups or child abusers." That wasn't strictly true. Ray Walker was a child physical abuser, but Tony couldn't see a link with Hutch's case.

"If you find her, will you tell me?"

Tony shifted on her chair. "Why are you looking for her?"

"I want to talk to her."

"You know that she worked for your friend Don Simmonds?"

"I do."

"Do you know there's an investigation into Thomas Fuller's death at the care home?"

Hutch nodded. "You have been doing your homework. What took you to Forest View? And while we're at it, why were you at Fuller's house?"

"Leads that didn't pan out."

Hutch looked as if he didn't believe her.

"I promise you, all I'm doing is looking for Lisa Walker," Tony said. "Have you any idea where she might be?"

Hutch sighed. "My hunch is she's left the area again."

That wasn't what Tony wanted to hear. "Will you tell *me* if *you* find her?"

Hutch smiled. "I'll consider it."

Tony got up. "I'll be off then. Do you need anything before I go? Want me to make you a cup of tea?"

"That's kind, but no. I'll sleep now for a bit." Hutch looked and sounded worn out.

His eyes were already fluttering closed when Tony left the room, quietly shutting the bedroom door behind her.

Tony processed the new information as she walked down the stairs into Hutch's kitchen. None of it was relevant to her case, but it was interesting. She was thinking so hard she barely registered Bryony standing in front of the fridge.

"Did you find out where Lisa is?" Bryony looked worried, and the ghost's face fell further when Tony shook her head. "What about him up there? Do you think he's lying?"

Tony was taken aback. She hadn't considered that possibility. "I don't think so," she said hesitantly.

"Well, I do. I think he's hiding something."

"Do you know that in some ghostly way, or is it just a guess?" Tony asked.

"I've got news for you. Being dead doesn't give you the answers to everything."

Tony was highly disappointed to hear that.

"If anything, it makes it harder because so many things don't matter anymore. But this does, and I think he's lying."

"Why do you think that?"

"He's a policeman," Bryony said.

Well, that was helpful. Tony stared back at Bryony, feeling annoyed. *She* didn't entirely trust Hutch, but some of that was because Maya's girlfriend had been talking to him in the hospital ward. And some of it was instinct based on what he was and wasn't telling her. None of it was blanket prejudice.

"And there's an address scribbled right there." Bryony drifted over to a pad next to an old-fashioned landline phone.

Tony went to the phone. Fifty-three Beech Lane was written on the top sheet of the pad.

"Maybe that's Lisa's address," Bryony said.

Tony shook her head. "That's a leap. It could be anywhere and could mean anything."

"Some supernatural detective you are. You're not making much headway, are you? And we're running out of time, in case you've forgotten." The pleasantness had disappeared from Bryony's voice, and her eyes drilled into Tony's.

Tony stared coldly back. Bryony was right, Tony hadn't discovered much at all, but that was hardly her fault. And, quite frankly, she was doing the ghost a big favor. If it weren't for the fact that she'd grown to like Chris and Red, she would be walking out of the house and straight to the train station. Well, maybe back to Oak Springs to pick up her stuff and tell Jade, but then she'd be going straight to the train station.

Bryony dropped her head, her anger deflating. When she looked up, her eyes were full of tears. "I'm sorry, Tony. I'm worried and don't trust the police to be fair with Chris. She was living at the farm when it happened."

Tony couldn't help sympathizing. She was worried for Red and Chris, too. "Well, I suppose I could go to the address. It's probably nothing to do with Lisa, though. I wouldn't get your hopes up."

"I won't," Bryony promised, smiling far too broadly for someone measuring their reaction.

Fifty-three Beech Lane was at the end of a quiet street away from the rest of the houses. If Lisa Walker lived there, it was behind a heavy, two-door gate. A notice painted in big letters across the doors told anybody who might consider leaving a vehicle in front of them that there should be *NO PARKING AT ANY TIME*.

There was no padlock or other sign of security. After a glance around, Tony pressed her eye to a crack between the doors.

Beyond the gate was a small forecourt in front of a row of garages.

Tony pushed down the catch holding the two doors of the gate together and swung the right hand one open.

She peeked in, ready to back off if challenged, but there was nobody in sight. She was one step inside the forecourt when the letters on the left-hand door grabbed her attention like a flashing neon sign.

The message had been painted across both doors. *NO PARKING* was the top line with *AT ANY TIME* underneath. With the gate split, the left-hand door read *NO PA AT A*.

Donald Simmonds's nonsensical phrase.

Tony went cold. Simmonds had been here. And something felt very, very wrong.

Cautiously, she walked onto the forecourt, leaving the right-hand gate open. She was drawn to the garage at the end of the row and walked toward it, her pulse quickening.

She put her hand on the garage door's T-shaped handle.

And twisted it.

But she couldn't lift the door, not with the voice in her head screaming, *Run.*

She registered a light footstep and then a sharp pain at the top of her arm. She turned, but she was already falling.

❖

There were low sounds, both muffled and resonant as if she was inside a thick metal box. Tony lay in the dark, listening.

Something pattered faintly across the ceiling. Somewhere in the distance came the faint rumble of a vehicle.

She shivered. There was a musty smell. The surface she was lying on was hard and cold, and her shoulders ached. Her arms were behind her back. She tried to stretch, but they wouldn't move. She flexed her fingers experimentally, and rope cut into her wrists.

She tried rolling and ended up face down in dust and concrete. She turned again, attempting to get onto her back, and bumped into something hard but not dense. It gave a little. She got her back to it and felt along with her fingertips. It was some kind of textile. Wool maybe. A rolled-up rug? With great effort, pulling herself up by awkwardly gripping the thing, Tony wrenched herself into a sitting position.

Bile rose into her throat, and she thought she was going to be sick. The room spun. Even though she couldn't see anything. It was like being horribly drunk. She leaned back against the carpet roll and breathed slowly in and out.

After a few minutes of blinking and breathing and staring in front of her, she realized something or someone else was in the room with her. A human-sized shape slightly raised from the ground.

Her eyes adjusted agonizingly slowly as she stared in front of her, gripped with terror, not daring to move. The person was sitting on a chair, but she couldn't determine who it was.

"I told you. Nopa Ata," they said.

Tony recognized Donald Simmonds's voice immediately.

She replayed the moments before she'd collapsed. There had been a light footstep just before the sharp, stabbing pain at the top of her arm. She'd turned, but a hand had pressed down over her eyes, preventing her from seeing her attacker's face.

Had it been this old man?

Her throat was bone dry. "What are you doing here, Mr. Simmonds?" she croaked out tentatively.

"I don't know," he replied, sounding as vague as the last time they'd spoken. "I've been here a while. It's so cold. Do you feel it?"

"Yes," she said.

"I came to meet someone. Was it you?" Don Simmonds sounded anxious as well as confused.

"No. I saw you near your home, and we talked for a while. Do you remember?"

"Oh, yes. So, who did I meet here?"

"I don't know, Mr. Simmonds. Did somebody hurt you? Did they inject you with something?"

"I can't remember."

Tony's eyes had adjusted well enough for her to see that Simmonds's feet weren't tied, and his arms were flat at his sides. "Can you move your hands?" she asked urgently. Maybe there was a way out of this. Before, whoever had lured them here reappeared.

He shook his head sadly. "I'm too stiff. I think it's the cold. I'm so cold."

"You said that." Tony bit back disappointment. She forced herself to be patient. He was old and confused, and he'd probably been injected with God-knows-what, the same as she had. Tony scanned the room, searching for something she could use to cut through the rope binding her wrists. Simmonds could have been here for a couple of days, and he would be dehydrated. He could even be hypothermic.

The shapes of old furniture loomed out of the dark: a wardrobe, a bookcase, a chest freezer. That was the last thing they needed. Simmonds was right. It was freezing in the room. Maybe the ancient freezer was leaking cold air.

Though, maybe it had a sharp corner.

She pushed herself away from the roll at her back onto her knees. She felt immediately sick but made herself press on. Someone wanted them both in this out-of-the-way place. Whatever their plans were for them, they wouldn't be pleasant, and they could be back at any moment.

She struggled to her feet. The room transformed into a merry-go-round that wasn't merry at all. Tony swayed on her feet, trying to keep down the contents of her stomach.

It's not just me. There's a confused, ill old man who needs my help. She held onto that fact until the room slowed, and her breakfast retreated.

But with each step toward the freezer, she was filled with a terrible dread. She turned her head to the old man sitting patiently on the chair, looking at her now with big, round eyes. Eyes so sad, so concerned for her.

She forced her feet forward until she brushed up against the freezer. Gulping down her fear, she turned her back, got her fingers under the lip of the lid, and pulled. It was stiff, and her fingers were awkward and numb, but she pushed against the vacuum until it started to lift.

It was a strange recognition the feeling that built within her. A premonition. A sixth sense. A putting together of puzzle pieces.

She knew she was right. But she hoped against hope she was wrong. Tony turned around and looked down.

To stare into the eyes of Donald Simmonds stretched out in the freezer gazing up at her, blue, stiff, and very, very dead.

❖

The concrete floor was cold and hard. Her head lolled against something metallic.

The freezer.

She bit back a scream, remembering what was in it. She rolled away as far as she could along the dusty ground and lay catching her breath.

Why was she on the floor again? She'd turned her back and slammed the lid down. She'd tried rubbing her wrists against a corner of the freezer, and it had hurt, and then there'd been a rushing in her ears, and her legs went out from under her.

She'd collapsed then.

She was back where she'd started when she'd woken the first time, and a quick pull revealed her wrists were still bound. They hurt, and there was something wet on her fingertips. Blood.

A scuffling noise on the other side of the garage door got her sudden, sharp attention.

She froze. Maybe it was a cat or a fox.

Footsteps came closer. Someone whispered. Someone else mumbled a reply.

Two of them. Not good.

The door clunked. The handle started to turn.

Her heart pounded clear through her chest. The garage door started to lift.

Daylight rushed into the room, and she screwed her eyes up against the glare of it, staring at two figures silhouetted in the space where the door had been.

Tony breathed fast and shallow, pulling at the ropes around her wrists, not caring what damage she was doing to herself. Had she managed to fray the rope at all? Dear God, she hoped so. She stood no chance against two assailants, bound and groggy with drugs.

There was a click, and torch light assaulted her eyes. Pinpricks of light hurt like real pins, hurt so bad she had to shut them.

Choking back a whimper, she vowed she wouldn't passively meet her fate. She struggled against the ropes again, opening her eyes, forcing her lead-heavy legs into action. She needed to be on her feet. She needed to be able to kick and head butt and bite. She wasn't going to make it easy for them. She was not going to be their next victim.

"Tony!"

The torch clicked off. On her knees, Tony looked up at Jade and started to sob. All she felt was relief as two sets of arms lifted her.

They walked her onto the forecourt where Emily P was waiting. Red got her inside, and Tony sank back against the soft, padded headrest. She needed to tell them something important, but the seat was so comfortable, and the rushing sound in her ears pulled her into a dreamless sleep.

❖

Tony didn't wake until the truck stopped. A pounding headache drummed in her temples, and her brain wasn't working properly. Everything was jumbled, and she couldn't hold onto her thoughts.

Tony fluttered open her eyes. Red was standing outside the passenger door, waiting to help her out of the vehicle.

"Are you okay, Tony?" Jade squeezed her arm gently.

Tony shook her head. Regretted it. Winced. "I just need to lie down," she managed. "My throat is so dry. Need water." She managed to stand, but the yard span, and she gripped Red's arm.

"Let's get you inside," Red said, their strength shoring Tony up. And then Jade was on the other side holding her too. A stiff breeze whipped through the yard. She gulped down lungfuls of the cold air concentrating on making her shaky legs move across the packed dirt. It darkened overhead.

"Storm's blowing in," Red muttered.

"I don't like it. We should get Tony to hospital." Jade sounded anxious.

"No," Tony spat out. There was something urgent she had to do just as soon as she'd rested a little. "Want to sleep, just for a moment. Someone injected me. Need to tell the police." Donald Simmonds's face flashed under her closed eyelids. "Body. Freezer," she muttered.

"She's cold. I think you're right, Jade. We're two steps from the back door. Let's sit Tony inside for a moment and grab Chris. I want to tell her about Raymond Walker. We can go to the hospital and then the police, tell them all of it together."

A splattering of rain helped push back the fog in Tony's head. She managed to stand practically straight as they neared the farmhouse. What had Red just said?

They knew about Ray Walker and were going to go to the police. It was the right thing to do. It had got too serious for two amateur detectives to handle. Tony breathed a sigh of relief.

❖

But when they walked into the kitchen, Chris was sitting at the table with a strange look on her face.

When Jade shut the back door, a woman stepped out of the pantry behind Chris holding a handgun.

"Lock it behind you and give me the key," she said.

"Sandra?" Tony said. It was the woman Tony had spoken to at Forest View nearly a week ago. But her hair was a different color.

"Hello, Tony," she said pleasantly. Her accent had changed too from London to Yorkshire. "Why don't we all go through to the sitting room," she said. It didn't sound like a request.

"What's going on, Chris?" Red asked.

"Best do as she says." Chris pulled herself up and led the way. Tony moved the slowest, and Sandra followed behind, her gun at Tony's back.

In the sitting room, Red helped Tony sit on the sofa, their gaze on Sandra. "I know you, don't I?"

"Yes, Red. Our paths crossed briefly. I've aged since then, gracefully, I hope." Sandra smiled.

Red frowned. "You weren't called Sandra then."

Sandra's smile deepened. "You're right." She turned to Jade. "We haven't met. Allow me to introduce myself. My name is Lisa Walker."

❖

Tony was astonished. "Have you changed your name?"

Lisa Walker shook her head. "Forgive my intrusion, but I couldn't let the situation go on any longer. I've been looking for you, Tony."

Tony blinked. "I've been looking for you." Her head was pounding.

"As soon as I found out Tony was here at Oak Springs, I had to come."

"With a gun?" Red said coldly.

"Don't be concerned, Red. The gun is for your protection."

"Give it to me then," Red said wryly.

"It will all make sense when the police come. I'll explain then."

"Explain now." Red didn't seem worried about the firearm pointing at them or about goading the person holding it.

"Tony's dangerous," Lisa said tersely.

Jade, squeezed in next to Tony on the sofa, gave a tense, annoyed snort.

But Chris's eyes darted to Tony strangely. "Lisa showed me a film of you at Forest View Care Home saying you were in a survivors' group in Hackney. She said you killed a man at Forest View that day."

What? Tony thought back to that day. "Wait a minute. I was talking to Lisa. She was pretending to be a woman called Sandra. Couldn't you see that in the film?"

Chris shook her head. "There's just you and the back of a blond woman's head. Your face is very clear. And she also has film from a video doorbell of you going to visit Adam Hutchins."

Why did that matter, and why did Chris sound so annoyed? And how had Lisa gotten footage from Hutchins's doorbell? She replayed the conversation with Hutch. He'd said the care agency installed the doorbell.

"Why are you working with that man?" Chris asked sharply.

"I'm not working with him. He contacted me. He's looking for Lisa Walker too. He's got a file on her."

"On us, Tony, on the Avengers, as you know," Lisa said.

Tony ignored the bizarre comment. "Why shouldn't I trust Hutch?" she asked Chris.

"Because he worked with Raymond Walker, the man Lisa says is buried on our land." Chris sounded like she had the day they'd met: hurt, angry, and suspicious.

Hutch worked with Walker?

"Detective Hutchins is dead," Lisa said quietly. "And Hutchins's friend, Donald Simmonds, is dead too. Thomas Fuller and Don Simmonds were pedophiles. I understand why you did it, Tony," she said softly. "They were bad men. But your name's recorded in the logbook at Forest View on the day that Fuller died, and your DNA is on Simmonds. I could have helped you if you'd come to me sooner, but not now that you've left a trail of evidence. What were you thinking, love, talking to people who will remember you, even leaving your contact details? I'm sorry. I wish it could have been different." Lisa spoke to Tony like they were friends.

Pieces of a puzzle were sliding together, but Tony couldn't make sense of the picture. She thought back to the man in the photographs in the creepy house where she'd first met Hutch. He was the old man the nurse had been injecting the first time she'd gone to Forest View. "Madeline," Tony said. "She killed him with an injection." She looked at Lisa. "Your ex-girlfriend."

Lisa started. "What?"

"The nurse, Madeline. She's your old girlfriend, Star."

"You're confused." Lisa pulled out a phone and tapped it several times, frowning. "Why isn't there any signal?"

Red smiled. "You won't get one in this room. You'll have to go upstairs to the back bedroom."

Lisa waved the gun at Chris. "Go call them."

But Chris shook her head. "No, Lisa. I don't think I will."

Lisa flushed. "For God's sake, Chris, you've always been stubborn. I've told you, Tony's dangerous. She's killed three men already. And she's clever. Look how she fooled you."

"You said. All the same, I'm staying right here." Chris sat back in the armchair. "So what are you going to do, Lisa? Shoot us all?"

The sky outside thickened, and rain began to beat against the window. Lisa glared at Chris. The clock on the mantle ticked loudly as Lisa looked at them, one by one.

"You," she said.

Jade stiffened beside Tony.

"Bring me that bag."

Unusually, Jade did as she was told, though not with good grace. She picked up a sports bag in the corner of the room with two fingers and dropped it unceremoniously at Lisa's feet.

"Open it."

Cutting her eye at Lisa, Jade knelt and unzipped the bag. Metal glinted inside.

And then Red stood and strode quickly toward Lisa. "I've had enough of this. Give me that bloody gun."

Red was two steps away, one hand reaching for the weapon, when Lisa fired.

❖

The gunshot rang in the small room.

Red crumbled, clasping their leg. Blood soaked through the blue denim of their jeans.

"Get Red over to the water pipe," Lisa barked.

"What?" Jade stared at the deepening pool of blood in shock.

"Get Red over to the pipe on the floor over there, above the skirting," Lisa repeated, her eyes cold. "Help her, Chris."

Chris jumped from the armchair and edged past Lisa, her eyes on the gun.

No one spoke. Tony hardly dared breathe. They weren't in any doubt now whether Lisa was prepared to shoot.

"Cuff them both to the pipe," Lisa told Jade.

Jade backed away, shaking, dragging the sports bag with her. She fastened Chris's hands to the pipe, then hesitated. Red gripped their leg with both hands.

"Red needs a tourniquet," Jade said.

Lisa narrowed her eyes. A second later, she nodded toward a work shirt draped over the sofa. Jade wrapped it tightly around Red's thigh, making Red groan. Jade gently cuffed Red to the water pipe, and Red closed their eyes, taking long, slow breaths.

"You two, come with me," Lisa said to Tony and Jade. "Upstairs to wherever the phone signal is. Keep in front of me."

Tony stood. The room spun, and she stumbled. Jade looked worried. Behind her, Red rested their head against the wall, the color draining from their face.

"Move," Lisa said.

Tony started for the door, desperately trying to find a way out of this situation.

Because she had a bad, bad feeling about it.

❖

The stairs had never felt narrower or steeper. Jade went first, with Tony following and the barrel of Lisa's gun uncomfortably in the middle of Tony's back.

Tony dug her fingernails into her palms, trying to wake up her sluggish brain. Lisa was setting her up, that much was clear. But how?

Someone. Madeline? Had killed Thomas Fuller while Tony had been at Forest View, and she'd been lured to Beech Lane. But Lisa hadn't told her to pretend she'd been in the Avengers. That had been Bryony. The address for Fuller's lock-up had been at Detective Hutchins's house.

A step ahead, Jade stumbled. She tipped backward.

Tony caught her.

"Keep her talking," Jade muttered quietly.

"You filmed me at Forest View. Why?' Tony stopped in the middle of the next step, her eyes on Jade mounting the stairs quickly now.

The tip of the barrel pressed against Tony's spine. Seconds passed, punctuated by the sound of Lisa's breath. And then that breath was at Tony's ear.

"I needed to have you say you were in the Avengers," Lisa whispered.

Jade had reached the landing. Tony turned so they were face to face. "Why are you setting me up for those murders?"

"It's nothing personal, Tony." Lisa looked deep into Tony's eyes. "The work needs to continue. Fuller and Simmonds were pedophiles. We sent evidence to the police, and they did nothing. Do you know how I got Simmonds to meet me? By pretending to be a twelve-year-old girl." There was weariness and pain, and regret on Lisa's face. "I've tried other ways, Tony."

"When you were a social worker," Tony said.

Lisa gave a quick humorless laugh. "You're a better detective than I was led to believe. It's a shame."

"The police won't believe I had anything to do with those murders."

"Are you sure about that? Hutchins's file has your name all over it now in an excellent approximation of his handwriting. And everyone *will* believe you murdered him."

The video doorbell the agency fitted. Hutch was discharged with a home help. Lisa.

But even so, how did she get Tony to Beech Lane? The address had been left in the kitchen. Lisa probably wrote it, but Bryony pointed it out. Just like Bryony told her to go to Forest View. And Bryony gave her Simmonds's address.

Lisa's expression changed. She pressed the gun against Tony's chest, and her voice took on a dangerous tone. "Upstairs. Now."

Jade had disappeared. Tony started up the stairs, holding tightly onto the banister, her mind working furiously. The adrenaline pumping hard in her body was dispersing the drugs at least.

The temperature dropped as both Bryony and Raymond Walker materialized simultaneously.

Walker glowed. His attention was all on Lisa. "There you are, you treacherous bitch. You'll not get away with it this time. There's another psychic. I'll go to her."

You won't get away with it this time. A succession of images flashed through Tony's mind.

The matted mess on the back of Walker's head.

Bryony's story. How she'd faced Walker as she hit him.

On the landing, Tony turned to Lisa again. "You killed him," she said. "You killed your father, not Bryony."

Walker gave a wicked, nasty laugh. It echoed in the cold, draughty corridor.

Lisa cocked the gun, but Bryony was between them in Lisa's face. "This isn't the way. This isn't what we agreed. I won't let you do it."

The ghosts knew something. And Tony's brain caught up at last.

Lisa meant to kill them all.

Walker sneered. "Stupid girl. Useless, ugly freak of a girl. Never could get anything right."

Lisa went rigid. "Shut up, shut up, shut up," she shouted. Which was very odd because no one but Lisa had spoken.

No one living that is.

Lisa shoved her hard.

And she shoved Tony again, hurtling her toward the bedroom door.

❖

Tony barreled through the doorway into an empty, freezing room.

The window was wide open. Gusts of wind and rain poured through it.

"Police," Lisa said into her phone. She went to the window.

It was dark outside, but Jade was lit by the light spilling from the window. She dangled on the edge of the roof, scrambling onto the drainpipe.

"Oak Springs Farm, Wooly Mill," Lisa said, then she raised the gun and fired.

Tony couldn't breathe. Couldn't think. The shot reverberated, ringing in Tony's ears. Lisa blocked her view of the window. Tony tried to push her out of her way, but Lisa shoved back.

"She's got a gun. Oh God, she's shot someone." Lisa dropped the phone. Tony pushed past her.

Jade clung to the drainpipe. A bracket moaned, inching away from the wall.

Lisa raised the gun again, and Tony launched herself at her.

They grappled for the handgun. Tony tried to force it up, away from the window, away from Jade, away from herself. Lisa snarled, forcing it back, and Tony couldn't stop it as the barrel slipped, inching toward her.

There was a dull thud behind, but Tony was completely focused on the barrel aimed at her face. She pushed back. She wasn't going out like this. Set up by this bitch.

There was a crack, and Lisa's eyes widened. She staggered. She put a hand to the side of her head. Blood tricked through her fingers.

Jade was standing at Tony's side, soaking wet, magnificent, a Lesbos paperweight in her hand. She took the gun from Lisa.

Lisa shook her head. She took a breath, but Tony didn't wait. She jumped between Lisa and Jade, and she punched and punched until Lisa dropped to the floor.

Jade snatched the cord from a dressing gown. She bound Lisa's hands together as sirens screamed outside.

"They're here, thank God. That's why I ran ahead," Jade said.

Tony ran to the window. Police cars and an ambulance screeched into the yard, and Tony yelled, "The shooter's disarmed. She's up here. Someone's been shot below."

Beneath them came the sound of the back door splintering and heavy boots on the stairs.

Tony turned to Jade. "Why did you come back?"

Jade wiped the rain from her face. "For you. I thought she needed you alive. But she was going to shoot you."

A voice yelled outside the bedroom door: "Armed police! Armed police!"

Jade was already on the floor. "Get down, Tony," she cried, reaching up.

Tony threw herself over Jade, her hands in the air as the door burst open, and the room filled with black flak jackets and carbine rifles.

CHAPTER ELEVEN

With the following morning came a gentle breeze that chased the rain clouds from the sky. Mild autumn sunshine fell across the veg field. Reeling from the night, Tony leaned against a raised bed with her back to the activity in the copse.

She should have been feeling relieved. Lisa had been arrested, and Tony hadn't. At least not yet. But Tony didn't feel relieved. She felt stupid. Gullible. Angry.

It had never been convenient and hardly ever pleasant being able to see ghosts, but Tony had helped them all the same. She'd endured some hard knocks in the last few months, and this felt like rock bottom.

It wasn't the worst thing, she reminded herself. That would have been losing Jade.

After the police had arrived, Tony and Red were taken to the hospital. Red was admitted, but after blood tests and an assessment, Tony had been released. She'd given a preliminary interview to the police and returned to the farmhouse in the early hours of the morning.

The area around Walker's grave had been sealed off. A seasoned, patient officer had said digging would start soon, and they were to keep away. Tony was more than happy with that.

She nursed a mug of tea and focused on the solid and ancient hills in front of her. The sky, and grass, and earth had seen countless humans come and go, and they were still standing. Or hanging, or whatever it was that sky did. The point was everything changed even as it stayed the same.

A lone figure walked lightly across the wilted potato stalks toward her. Bryony.

Tony did not want to talk to the ghost.

Bryony stopped a few feet away. Tony coldly met her eyes.

"I was trying to protect Chris and Red," Bryony said.

Tony sipped her tea. It was cooling quickly in the chill air.

"Lisa lied to me." Bryony bit her lip.

Tony had believed Bryony without question before. More fool her. There was no reason to believe her now. "Lied to you, did she? There's a lot of it around."

"I was going to give you the name of a lawyer we know in Hebden Bridge. She specializes in abuse cases. Especially survivors who fight back. She would have got you off. That was the plan."

Tony was unmoved. More than that, she was angry, and she didn't care to hear Bryony's excuses.

There were questions she wanted answers to, though. Lisa had to have had something on Bryony apart from Walker's grave. Why were they meeting right up to Bryony getting ill otherwise? "Were you in the Avengers?" she asked.

Bryony nodded.

"Did you help kill those men?"

Bryony sighed. "I knew about the plan, but I passed away before their deaths. Tony, do you have any experience of abuse?"

"No."

"I don't know if you'll understand. Maybe survivors wouldn't even understand. The thing that drew Lisa and me to each other was our need to stop it. When I hear about a case, it's like I'm in the room, and I have to do something. We concentrated on young women, but I care about the boys too. I'd get them all away if I could. The abuse that the authorities know about is a tiny percentage of what's happening in this country. All those kids with no one to help them."

Tony let the words settle. "Even if I agreed with what you did, it wasn't just abusers you hurt, was it? You were prepared to wreck my life. And I was trying to help you."

Bryony stared at her feet. "Lisa was going to tip off the police about her father's remains. She would have set Chris up if I hadn't..."

"If you hadn't what? Lured me here, sent me to all those places to incriminate myself?"

A tear rolled down Bryony's cheek, but Tony was unmoved. "Why me?"

"After I died, I knew Walker's remains were a ticking time bomb. I went to Lisa and, to my surprise, she could communicate with me. But she refused to move her father's body. I needed someone else, and suddenly there you were. My mistake was telling Lisa. I didn't want to go along with her plan, but she made it clear it was either you or Chris." Bryony's voice trembled. "I couldn't let that happen to Chris."

A twig snapped behind Tony. She turned to find Chris behind the planter, looking strained. "Who are you talking to?" she asked.

"Bryony."

Chris shivered. "I don't understand what's gone on, and I need you to tell me honestly. Did you truly never know Bryony when she was alive?"

"I never knew her." Tony stood and drained the last of her tea.

Chris looked out over the field. "They want you down at the police station in Hatherwell."

"Okay," Tony said and started back toward the house.

But Chris grabbed Tony's arm. "Where is she?"

Before Tony could speak, Bryony floated between them, putting her arms around her partner. Chris closed her eyes. Then she dropped her head and began to cry.

❖

Tony was ushered into a small room at Hatherwell Police Station by a constable who opened the door and told her to wait.

Hutch was inside, leaning against the pale gray wall. His skin was practically the same color. Ghosts' complexions usually reverted to a similar shade to when they'd been alive. It was early days for Hutch. Maybe he was still transforming.

"So," he said by way of greeting, "Lisa Walker, eh?" He gestured toward a monitor on a table in the center of the room.

Tony pulled up a chair looking at the screen. Lisa was sitting in a similar, slightly bigger room, staring straight out front with a resolute expression. Her face was bruised, her lip was cut, and the skin under one eye was puffy and discolored. Tony guessed she'd done that with all the punching. She knew she'd had to but felt sick anyway.

"I didn't recognize her," Hutch said. "So many years had passed, and she was still a kid when I last saw her. Not that I saw her much. I worked with Ray, but we weren't good friends. Happen, that's how I missed…" his voice trailed off. "Completely accepted she was the home help." He shook his head, looking embarrassed.

Tony grunted. "Don't feel bad. She's good at taking people in. Good at setting them up too."

"She's been spinning quite the tale," Hutch said. "Given us a heap of evidence implicating you. Luckily, it doesn't hold up to proper investigation. You were at the care home the day Thomas Fuller was killed?"

Tony nodded. "I saw the nurse inject a patient that day. Later, after I'd been to Fuller's house, I realized the man was Mr. Fuller. Have they caught up with Madeline? She was part of the Avengers and also known by the name Star."

Hutch smiled wryly. "The Madeline Young with the social security number your nurse friend was using died in 1984. All activity on her phone and credit cards has stopped. Her bank account's been cleaned out, and she's disappeared."

"Have they found Donald Simmonds?"

Hutch looked down at the floor. He nodded almost imperceptibly. "Oh, Don," he said under his breath, and then he met Tony's eye. "I'm not feeling too proud of myself. I missed Ray Walker's violence all those years ago, failing that girl in there. And I never knew my friend was doing despicable things. Not much of a detective, am I?" He bit his lip and turned away, but not before Tony saw the tears in his eyes.

Hutch cleared his throat. "One thing that's puzzling me. You said you'd seen him when you couldn't have. The pathologist thinks Don was killed over a week ago."

Tony looked at Hutch, wondering why he hadn't put it together for himself. But then ghosts sometimes took a while to adjust to their new circumstances. "As you are now aware, I can talk to ghosts. I just didn't realize he was one at the time. People don't look all that different in the afterlife, you know."

Hutch's brows knotted together in a question mark.

The door opened, and the constable that had shown Tony in entered with a mug of tea.

"Here you go," he said, handing the mug to Tony.

Tony reached for it as the constable turned to Hutch. "If you're finished here, we're ready for you now, Detective."

Tony nearly dropped her tea. She stared at Hutch.

"We'll talk more about that last statement, anon," he said. "Meantime, watch the interview. One of my colleagues will be watching with you. If anything occurs to you, let them know."

❖

Hutch was still alive. Thank heavens. Had Lisa been lying? Tony took a deep breath focusing on the monitor screen in front of her. A young woman came in and sat next to Tony. She turned the volume up on a speaker.

Tony heard the interview room door open. Lisa Walker sat up, squaring back her shoulders, and then her eyes widened.

"What's the matter, Lisa?" Hutch's voice said. "You don't look pleased to see me."

Lisa opened her mouth and shut it again. She shifted in her seat. Hutch announced himself and a colleague. They both sat in the two chairs opposite Lisa Walker, and Hutch announced the day and time for the recording.

"Do you remember me, Lisa? I don't mean from working as my home help. I mean from years ago when I worked with your father."

Lisa's face hardened. "I've told you everything I know, and I think I've been forthcoming. I wish I'd come to you earlier, but I didn't believe Tony Carson would go through with her plan to kill those men." Lisa leaned forward, her eyes on Hutch. "She wanted to kill you. The same way she killed Tom Fuller." She sat back again.

Tony wished she could see Hutch's reaction. The back of his head didn't move. Lisa's face was in full shot, though, and the look in her eye sent a shiver down Tony's spine. Mrs. Mackey had described her as a kind, caring child. She'd been a brave teenager who'd asked for help to escape a horrible situation. Helen knew her as a campaigning woman working to protect others. When had she turned into this ruthless killer?

"We found a syringe in your bag," Hutch said.

Lisa's expression didn't change. "What bag?"

"The one you brought to the farmhouse, the one with handcuffs and rope in it."

"I didn't have any bag."

"Four witnesses say different. Four witnesses say a lot of things that contradict your story. We've tested the contents of the syringe and found ketamine, midazolam, and thiopental. The hospital took blood and urine samples from Tony Carson last night. We should get the results soon, and I'm betting we will find those drugs in the samples."

Lisa said nothing.

Hutch's shoulders shifted upward as he took a breath. "I don't think Tony Carson had anything to do with this. I think it was you that committed those murders. You and Madeline Young."

Lisa stared impassively forward. The seconds ticked by.

Until Lisa leaned against her chair's hard, plastic back and folded her arms. "I want a lawyer," she said.

❖

Tony let the entrance doors of Hatherwell Police Station close behind her and stood on the top step drawing cold, fresh air into her lungs.

She felt sullied. It had been a nasty case. *Case*. Was that what she did now, detect?

Hutch had officially informed her they would be taking no action against her.

She was free to return to London. To no job. To no access to her child.

She let out a sigh. There was nothing to be gained by feeling sorry for herself. Action was needed.

Tony took a bold step forward and froze a second before she walked slam into Eve Phee.

Maya's new girlfriend stared at Tony and paled. She opened her mouth. Shut it again. Blinked and sidestepped around Tony, then walked quickly into the police station without a backward glance.

Tony swallowed, breathing hard. What the hell was *she* doing here?

Eve Phee knew Hutchins. She had been at the hospital visiting him.

Did it matter who she was? Tony wasn't a suspect. Eve Phee was the last person Tony wanted to see. Well, actually, it was Bryony, followed by Lisa Walker, followed by Eve Phee.

Tony had been humiliated in every area of her life. She didn't know what she felt for Maya anymore or whether she even cared that Maya had moved on.

But the connection was strange. Tony deliberated, still standing on the second-to-top step. She looked across the high street at people shopping and going about their business, one or two eyeing her curiously. And Tony began to simmer with rage.

She was done with being hapless and hopeless and taken for a ride.

Tony swung around back through the entrance doors.

Eve Phee was at the desk talking with Detective Hutchins. They looked up as her trainers squeaked on the polished floor.

"Who is this woman? How do you know her?" Tony said crisply when she was a few steps from the pair.

Hutch frowned. "This is DS Yvette McPherson. I work with her."

The desk sergeant stared at Tony. DS McPherson drew herself up, her spine rod-straight, her gaze ice cool. Tony would have doubted her instincts if it weren't for the flicker of fear in her eye.

But her gut was singing loud and clear. Something wasn't right, and she was going to find out what it was.

"Why?" Hutch asked.

Tony's gaze remained on DS McPherson. She held it long enough for McPherson's eyes to widen. And then, without a word, Tony turned and walked away.

She was done for now, but this wasn't over.

Chapter Twelve

Tony couldn't stop thinking about Yvette McPherson. She knew she would have to call Maya. But there was someone she wanted to call first. She took a walk to the chicken barn for privacy, perched herself on a hay bale, and called Helen, the woman from the Hackney Survivors Group.

"Did you find Star?" Helen asked as soon as she picked up.

A hello would have been nice. "No. But I found Lisa Walker."

"Oh, that's great. How is she?"

Disturbed? Murderous? Tony thought about how much to tell Helen and decided to say nothing. "She's okay. No one knows where Star is."

"Oh." Helen's disappointment reached through the phone. "Well, thanks for letting me know."

"Hang on. Was there anyone in your Hackney Group called Eve or Yvette?"

There was a pause. And then Helen said, "Fee."

"Fee?" Tony sat up straight. Harvey cast her a suspicious look. Tony ignored him.

Fee, as in Eve Phee, the name on Yvette's Facebook page.

"Yes. She introduced herself as Fee, but Lisa called her Eve. Lisa and Star made a fuss of her. She only came to a couple of sessions, but Lisa met her at the pub sometimes. They'd huddle into a corner, and once or twice I saw them talking outside. Someone else might have thought they were together, but I didn't get that vibe. And then, well, it was sad actually because Fee disappeared a couple of months later. It turned out she wasn't eighteen like she'd said. Star told me she'd run away from a children's home. The police were looking for her because she was fifteen and underage."

Tony turned the words over. Was the young woman Helen remembered Yvette McPherson?

Maybe there was a way to check it out. "I'm going to send you a link to a Facebook page," Tony said. "Will you take a look and tell me what you think?"

"Of course. Hey, Tony, is there something I don't know about? I used to feel like that back then. I was always on the outside with Lisa and Star."

"I don't know anything for sure right now, Helen. But I can tell you this, your information has already prevented a major crime. A horrible thing was being done to me, and you've helped stop that. Maybe I can tell you one day. Right now, things are still unfolding."

There was silence on the other end of the phone.

Tony let it play out.

It stretched so long that she was about to end the call when Helen said, "They were important, you know, those groups."

"Yes?"

"Yes. I wasn't alone. I wasn't just damaged goods. What happened to me was wrong. What happened to all of us."

Tony swallowed. Her head span with all the pain. How could anyone think abuse didn't leave its mark? How could anyone survive it? Not just survive but thrive. Go on to live, succeed, and love?

"I don't know what you've been through, Helen," Tony said. "But I'm starting to understand why people will go to such lengths to stop it."

Helen's voice caught. Tony didn't say any more. She did the phone equivalent of holding Helen. She didn't turn away from the horribleness of it all.

"Thank you," Helen said softly.

❖

The text from Helen confirmed Yvette McPherson was the young woman from the Hackney Group.

Her stomach in knots, Tony called Maya.

She answered on the third ring.

"Tony! I'm really glad you called—"

Hearing her voice hurt like hell. Damn it. Damn her. Tony swept pleasantries aside. "I need to talk to you about Yvette McPherson," she said.

Maya didn't answer. There was a shuffling noise as if Maya was shifting from one foot to another. "Well, I'm not sure there's a point to—"

"This isn't about us," Tony interrupted her. "Something serious has happened. I'm not going to tell you about it. You can call Jade. Has DS McPherson mentioned anyone called Lisa Walker or Madeline Young?"

Maya exhaled the way she did when she was thinking. "Yvette has never talked about anyone called Lisa," she said after a moment. "Young, you say? Yvette has a friend called Star Young. Please tell me what this is about, Tony? Are you in trouble? How do you know Eve's a detective, by the way?"

Tony clenched her jaw. This was typical Maya. She was freaking out, thinking that Tony was obsessing about Maya's girlfriend. She knew why Maya compulsively searched her lovers and ex-lovers for signs of mental illness, but Tony couldn't find it in her heart to make allowances anymore.

"I have to go, Maya. Thanks for the information," she said, ending the call.

❖

Emily P hooted coming along the track.

Jade jumped up mid-sentence, practically knocking her mug of coffee over. She brushed away a crumb that had avoided the previous vigorous scrubbing of the table and ran to the dining room to check her appearance in the mirror. Jade had been cleaning and baking since Harvey had shattered the calm of dawn with his terrible squark four hours previously.

"Is the kettle on, Tony?" she yelled.

Tony stopped, one hand on the back door. "I was going to help. I thought they might be on crutches."

Jade sprinted into the kitchen so fast Tony jumped out of the way to avoid being mowed down.

"I'm on it." Jade wrenched the door open.

"Do you think maybe you fancy Red a little?" Tony asked.

Jade swung around, her face serious as hell. "How can you say that?" She looked at her clothes, pulled at her top to straighten it, and looked Tony in the eye. "As a fellow butch, I would have thought you would want to make Red comfortable in their own home, a fellow butch, I might add, who was shot by a highly disturbed individual." Jade planted both hands on her hips and squared her shoulders into an affronted position.

Tony nodded at the cake on the table. Jade's trademark Trinidadian concoction of sugar, alcohol, spice, and everything very, very nice. "I've been attacked by several highly disturbed individuals over the years, and you've never made me black cake."

Jade kissed her teeth, flapped a hand at Tony, and stepped out into the yard.

Red was struggling with two crutches trying to get down from Emily P while waving Chris away. They hobbled toward the house awkwardly until Jade slipped her head under Red's arm.

"Welcome home," Jade said after Red was safely ensconced in a chair at the kitchen table.

Red smiled. "It's good to be back." Their glance fell on the back door patched up but still bearing the damage from the police battering ram.

"Carpenter coming from Tod on Tuesday," Chris said.

Red nodded.

Tony made coffee and tea while Jade laid a spread on the kitchen table to rival anything served to the Famous Five. Cheese and plain scones, sweet bread, and in pride of place on a lesbian symbol china cake plate, was the Trini black cake.

Red whistled. "Did you make all this?"

"The Wooly Well Dressers baked the scones. The rest is all me." Jade beamed at Red over the coffee pot.

Chris sat in the chair next to Red. "Tony, Jade, I want to say something." She placed a white envelope on the table. "I can't pretend this has been easy." She swallowed. "I've found out things Bryony kept from me, and that hurt. I don't condone what she did, working with the Avengers. But I understand why she was doing it." Chris looked from Tony to Jade. "We were all trying to help in the old days, and I was part of the original rescue network along with Bryony."

"The ReSisters group?" Tony asked.

"Yes. Now then, the WWD women have been doing more than baking lately. Unbeknownst to me, they started some fundraising thing online to cover the damage done here at Oak Springs. The shocking thing is they've raised over twenty thousand pounds. The first thing I want to do is to pay you two for your services. Not sure what your normal fee is, so if this doesn't cover it, let me know." Chris pushed the envelope toward Tony, who immediately gave it to Jade.

Jade handled the agency's finances. She opened it and did a quick mental calculation. "There's a thousand pounds here."

"Is that enough?" Chris asked.

"Of course," Tony said. "But, really, we don't need—"

"Yes, you do," Red chipped in. "Chris is absolutely right. Now, let's honor this good woman by eating her delicious food." Red beamed at Jade and lifted a slice of cake.

❖

Tony was mucking out dirty straw in the barn when her phone rang.

She tensed seeing Maya's name on the screen, and her finger wavered between Decline and Accept.

Finally, she accepted the call but couldn't bring herself to say hello.

"Tony, is that you?"

"Yes."

"Thank goodness. Tony, I'm so sorry about what's happened. I had no idea, and I'm horrified. Are you all right?"

"Yes," Tony mumbled. Phones were weird things. Hard bits of glass and plastic. Very cold.

"I hate to think of you being in so much danger."

When Tony didn't reply, Maya lapsed into silence. For a moment, there was just the sound of Maya inhaling and exhaling while Tony felt weird. Numb. Confused.

"Anyway,' Maya dropped into the silence. "I thought you should know that after we got together, Eve asked a lot of questions about you. She was particularly interested in Louise and your childcare arrangements, how you were managing, that sort of thing."

"Did she?" The anonymous letter claiming that Tony was neglecting Louise jumped to the forefront of Tony's mind and did a Highland jig to get her attention.

"You know what Lisa Walker tried to do to me, right?"

"Yes," Maya sounded upset and anxious.

"I think your girlfriend knows her. You said she knows Star Young. And I've met Star. She's a friend of Lisa Walker, and she was well into this whole frame Tony Carson business."

Maya gulped so hard the sound could be heard through the phone. "Ex-girlfriend, Tony. As soon as Jade told me what's been going on, I realized I couldn't trust Eve. I finished with her."

Tony didn't know what to do with that piece of information. Interestingly, her heart didn't leap for joy.

"Thanks for letting me know." There really wasn't anything more to be said.

❖

Tony found Jade in the kitchen. The air was fragrant with sugar and spice.

"I think you are preparing baked goods in the requisite quantity to be accepted into the Wooly Well Dressers," Tony said. "In fact, the WWD should change their name to the Wooly Well Bakers. Or the Well Good Milly Bakers. Or the Wooly Baking Well Dressers. Or—"

"I get the idea," Jade interrupted her, pushing a wooden spoon around a pudding basin, stirring coconut into vividly red sugar.

"What are you making now?" Tony asked.

"Coconut roll." Jade infused the words with full Trinidadian flavor. "I'm wondering about getting a range or an Aga for myself. What do you think?"

"On your narrowboat?"

Jade sniffed. "Maybe they make real small ones. What about a wood stove with an oven in it, you think someone makes one of those?"

It was on the tip of Tony's tongue to say *Yes, and East London is known for the vast quantities of free wood lying around*, but who was she to stomp on Jade's flight of fancy?

"It would be a nice reminder of your time here," she said instead.

Jade stopped stirring and sighed. "I guess we have to go back."

"Well, I do. I need to find some work, and I need to move on from all this."

Jade brushed a sheet of pastry with butter and sprinkled it with the scarlet coconut mixture.

"Maya called," Tony said into the silence. "DS McPherson asked Maya about Louise and my childcare arrangements, apparently."

Jade's eyes widened. She rolled up the pastry and brushed it with more butter. "Put the kettle on. We need to sit down and talk."

By the time Jade had put the coconut roll into the oven and dusted herself down, Tony had made a pot of tea. She poured them both a cup.

Jade looked thoughtful. "DS McPherson knows Lisa Walker. Helen confirmed it?"

"Helen recognized her from her Facebook page, yes. Maya said Yvette had recently been in touch with Star Young."

Jade frowned. "You think she was sent to seduce Maya?"

Far-fetched, maybe, but it could fit. "Lisa Walker was fanatical about protecting the Avengers. DS McPherson worked with Adam Hutchins. What's the betting she told Lisa about the file he had on them? Lisa was looking for a fall guy. Breaking up with Maya isolated me. And so did losing Louise. Don't forget someone sent that anonymous letter to Amy."

"You think that was Yvette McPherson too?"

"Or Lisa. Or Star. It could have been any one of them. But it would have been easy for Yvette to get the information from Maya, and Maya sent Louise's birthday present last year, so she has Amy's parents' address."

Jade shook her head. "A real tangled web."

"Hmmm." Tony took a sip of tea. "I'm not sure what to do about it. Maybe I'll speak to Hutch."

"Or Sergeant Lewis? Hey, it was good that Detective Hutchins was okay. I talked to Bryony. She said Madeline was supposed to inject him after you left his house, but she balked at it and took off instead."

"That explains why Lisa was shocked to see him alive. How did you find me at the lock-up, by the way?"

Jade looked sheepish. "I sewed a tracker into your jacket. You were so late getting back, I was worried. I checked the location app, and there was no reason for you to be there."

Tony squeezed Jade's hand. "Thank God for your obsessive love of spy gadgets."

"Can you blame me? We've been getting into some real messy situations lately. You want a scone or some ginger cake?" Jade asked.

"No, thank you. I'm still full from the doubles at breakfast," Tony said, patting her stomach. "Jade, why are you cooking so much?"

Jade picked at a scratch on the table. "I think I'm a nervous eater."

"But you're not. You're not even eating what you bake. Are you a nervous flirter? Is it whatever's going on between you and Red?"

Jade nodded slowly. "I like Red. But I'm scared."

"I'm not surprised." Jade knew what it was like to be completely taken in and abused. How could she trust her feelings after the horrors Jade's last girlfriend put her through? Tony swallowed hard. "Does it get easier?" She needed to know if this sickening feeling would pass. Would there be a time when she didn't feel so gullible?

Jade must have read Tony's mind because she said, "It's not you. You mustn't feel it's you. I'm not glad you were tricked, but I'm glad you were able to be tricked."

Tony frowned in confusion.

"You're kind and sweet, and you trust people. You would help anybody. Tony, what hope do we have if we don't have people like you in the world?"

Tony's heart lifted. She took Jade's hand and squeezed it. "We've got each other anyway. We could change the name of our agency to the Stupidly Conned Two. What do you think?"

Jade smiled. "No way. Conned maybe. Stupid never."

Chris came through from the dining room looking serious. "Come talk with me, Tony," she said in a voice that defied opposition.

❖

Chris walked away from the house along the track to the sheep field. Tony followed her onto the thick grass, and she closed the gate behind her, remembering how she'd tied the dog to the post just a few days ago. Tony felt sad for the little dog despite the awful wounds it had caused.

Chris stared out at the sheep, the dry stone wall, and the magnificent view beyond. The sun broke through clouds the color of charcoal, throwing shafts of light onto the green hills below.

Chris turned. "I want you to stop investigating Yvette McPherson."

"You know her?"

Chris frowned. "You don't understand."

"Are you in the Avengers?"

"God, no. I didn't know they existed before the other night." Chris sounded affronted.

That was something, at least. "Why then?"

Chris swallowed. "There are things you don't know."

"Try me."

She stuck her hands in the pockets of her gilet. "The night Raymond Walker died, we were helping Lisa get away from him."

"You were in the ReSisters?"

Chris nodded. "Happen, Bryony told you."

"She did. So?"

"The group shut down a few years later."

"Bryony told me that too."

"Okay. Did she tell you that Star formed a new group shortly after the millennium?"

"No. Another rescue network?"

"That's right. Yvette was one of the first girls we helped."

Tony remembered that Yvette had run away from care. "This underground network, they helped Yvette get away from something?"

"Yes. Abuse. I've spoken to Eve. She had nothing to do with the vigilante murders, and she had no idea what Lisa and Star were doing to you."

"You believe her?"

Chris met Tony's eyes. "I do. She's a good copper. I know, I know, you don't expect to hear that from me. If they were all like her, I'd have no reservations. Lisa told Eve you were connected to an abuse ring, and that's why she agreed to help get your child taken away from you. She never would have…"

Tony sucked in a breath, hardly believing what she was hearing. But at the same time, unsurprised at the lengths Lisa Walker had gone to. "Well, the police can work out how involved DS McPherson was or wasn't," she said, not feeling sympathetic toward her.

Chris grunted. "It's not as simple as that. It would finish her career. We need people like her in the police force."

Tony was yet to be convinced. She looked away.

Chris sighed. "Oh, for God's sake, Tony, the group's still active. Lisa and Star won't be involved now. If Eve has to pull out too, it will fold."

Tony didn't reply. Chris's words rang in a silence broken only by the wind and the occasional bleat from the sheep. Tony didn't want to let the words affect her, but they weighed down on her anyway. Anonymous, invisible kids in horrible situations, pulled at her heart.

"I'll not ask again, Tony. Do what you need to do. If you go to the police, I'll deny everything I've just told you."

Tony nodded. She would have expected nothing less. She watched the sheep with their heads down chewing the grass and wondered what they would make of the lies and the sorrow and the treachery of it all. None of them looked up, and no answers drifted back on the wind.

❖

The Adams Family theme tune rang out on Tony's phone.

A lifetime ago, when she'd been playing Happy Families with Amy, Tony had set the tune as Amy's ringtone. After they broke up, she'd found it ironically fitting.

Amy was video calling.

Was that a good sign? Steeling herself in case it wasn't, Tony pressed accept.

"Mum persuaded me to call you," Amy said. "I watched the vids that Jade sent me. And I talked to Louise." That sounded promising, but Amy looked tense. Though she never did like talking things through.

"The letter was a malicious lie," Tony said.

"Jade said as much. So, who have you been pissing off?" Amy arched an eyebrow.

Tony was too raw to roll with Amy's flippancy.

Amy shrugged. "Anyway, I think it's time we made a formal arrangement. I've engaged a solicitor."

Tony saw her half of the £1000 fee disappearing fast. But it would be worth it. "Okay. How do we do this?"

"My solicitor will write to you or maybe email. I'll check. Where are you living now? You look like you've traveled back to the 1990s. Via the eighteenth century."

Tony smiled, turning the phone so that Amy could see her bedroom. "I'm on a farm in Derbyshire temporarily. They can write to my London address if they need to. Is, um…can I?"

Amy's face softened. "Yes, of course. I thought you might want to talk to her. Louise!" she called.

There was the sound of running footsteps, and then Louise rushed in front of Amy, grabbing the phone. "Tony! Are you okay? I miss you. When can I come to London? Where are you? What is that place?"

Tony laughed at the torrent of questions. "It's a farmhouse."

"Is it far? Can I come there?"

"We have to work some things out first, Louise," Amy broke into the conversation. "Until then, we'll stick to phone calls."

That hurt, but Tony was in no position to make demands. She made the most of the call, listening as Louise talked about school and swimming and martial arts and her friends and what she wanted to wear to a party next week.

After the call ended, Tony held the phone in her hand for a long time, knowing she was only thirty miles away from her child. It might as well have been thirty thousand.

❖

"Putting all the dead veg in the compost? Really? Let me see that list." Tony grabbed the scrappy back of an envelope that Jade was peering at. "This is a farm. Don't they just let it go back into the ground naturally?"

Jade zipped up the waterproof jacket borrowed from Chris, stamped her foot to get some feeling back into it, and pursed her lips. "You'd think. So, you want to pick up squashed tomatoes or sweep out the chicken barn?"

It was an overcast, drizzly day with a stiff breeze blowing in from the peaks.

"That barn hasn't been swept in a decade. And what does that say?" Tony stabbed a finger at Chris's spidery handwriting. "Checking the dry stone walls for loose stones?" Tony stared out at the craggy, gray borders curving away for miles. "It's like Chris doesn't want to spend time with us on our last day."

"Some people hate good-byes."

"Maybe she wants to make sure we don't come back. 'A few little jobs. Take no time at all,' she said," Tony complained.

Immediately after breakfast, Chris had presented them with "work clothing" and a list. Tony narrowed her eyes at the veg field as if it was the inventor of the last-day jobs.

"I'd rather be in the kitchen, but Red wants to cook for us today," Jade said. "And who am I to deny a butch's heartfelt desire?"

"You've often denied my heartfelt desires."

"But you don't have Red's broad shoulders and real long fingers," Jade said, smiling sweetly.

"Yes, well. Less said about that, the better. I like this shirt, though." Tony pulled at Red's old blue, checked flannel overshirt. It was baggy. She should do more push-ups. She'd start when she got back to London.

"What are you going to do about Detective McPherson?" Jade asked softly.

Tony burned with anger just thinking about what had been done to her. "Don't know. I want to tell Hutch, at least." She watched a cloud moving slowly across the sky. "Maybe I will." Was Yvette to blame for Maya's betrayal? And the detective had thought she was protecting Louise with her lies to Amy. "I'm still thinking about it."

The air wavered outside the barn, and Deirdre appeared in a high-necked, ankle-length floral print dress, matching bonnet, and improbably matched high-heeled boots.

"Dare I ask what you're wearing and why?" Tony muttered, glad of the distraction.

Deirdre frowned. "Far more worrying is your outfit. Is this the saddest costume party of all time? What did you come as, a filthy lumberjack? And as for you, Miss Thing." Deirdre turned to Jade. "That jacket's seen better, cleaner days. I, on the other hand, am blending in with the farmland."

"I think you've got the wrong farm," Tony said. "Oak Springs couldn't be further from the *Little House on the Prairie* if it tried."

"Quite. This is the Falling Down House on Animal Poo Hill." Deirdre's gaze drifted over Tony's shoulder. "It's beautiful, though." She stood for a moment drinking in the view. "But far too quiet. I think I can hear the air moving."

Jade listened. "That's someone using a power saw in the valley."

Deirdre arched her eyebrows. "Impressed. I'd be more impressed if the hems of your pant legs weren't stained slurry brown, and you'd thought to pull the straw from your hair."

Jade flapped at the bottom of her trousers and her head simultaneously. Tony laughed.

"I haven't finished with you yet." Deirdre turned to Tony, looking her up and down, her lips moving soundlessly. "There are no words for what you are wearing."

"My clothes are ready to go back to London tomorrow." Tony huffed.

Deirdre clapped her hands together. "Thank the angels and their delightfully tight butt cheeks. Flying's great for quads and glutes. You should try it. Oh, you can't. You don't have wings. Anyway, it's good news the big city awaits. As does a tailor and a hairdresser, hopefully."

"Why are you here?" Tony asked Deirdre.

"It's an intervention. You've become addicted to peace, quiet, and fresh air. You need noise and pollutants. The buzz of urban life will help you over this unfortunate series of incidents. Both of you."

"Well, you needn't have worried. We are coming back. Although I don't agree that I need a strictly urban life." Tony took a deep breath of clean air, trying to hold onto the peace and the space.

"I'd have visited sooner, but this place has terrible reception."

"Not for evil ghosts," Tony said. "Or lying, conniving ones, or lovely ones like Vera. Those spirits have been popping up like rabbits at twilight."

Deirdre snorted. "Even your references are rural. I blame it on the lack of preservatives in your food. I've met Vera, and she *is* lovely, full of quaint country advice, a bit overfond of haystacks but very good at poker."

"You couldn't make this stuff up," Jade muttered.

"Pretty sure Deirdre does," Tony replied.

Deirdre pouted. "Charming. Anyway, mazel tov, Tony, on claiming your butch identity at long last. It's been sitting in lost property with your name on it for so long they were about to throw it out. Anyway, I'll be in touch. Let's do drag brunch." Deirdre pouted but then turned back. "Oh, and I'm sorry about me not being there and the damned nastiness of it all." Her face softened for the mili-est of milliseconds.

And then she straightened, snapped her fingers together, and vanished.

❖

Jade slapped dust from the knees of her trousers as Tony petted the brown-speckled chicken called Lavender Menace. The bird couldn't have been sweeter. "You're not a menace at all, are you," Tony cooed to her. The chicken tipped her head to one side, clucking softly.

Heavy footsteps announced Chris's arrival. She squinted at them and the barn wearing her trademark dour expression. Tony's heart sank. She'd hoped their hard work would brighten Chris's mood.

"Looks tidy in here," she said roughly.

"We've stripped out all the old tomato plants and bean vines and what-not," Jade said brightly.

"I saw." Chris nodded without smiling, her eyes still on Tony. "What about the walls? How far did you get with inspecting them, up to the ridge, maybe?"

Tony raised herself from the barn floor to her full five foot seven inches. She matched Chris's truculent expression and raised it to recalcitrant. "There wasn't time."

"Humph. Well, you'd best come in and get cleaned up. Red's been cooking all day. Anyone would think they had a soft spot for you." Chris tossed a knowing look in Jade's direction, who suddenly found the broom handle fascinating.

Tony followed Chris out of the barn. She wanted a shower, her properly-fitting and clean clothes, and a hot meal. It hurt that Chris was so grumpy. Tony thought they'd moved past the "We're not partial to strangers in these parts" stage. It might only be days, but it felt like months since she'd trekked up the soggy track in the rain, hurting, lonely, and vulnerable. Tony hadn't known just how vulnerable she'd been. She let out a sigh. It would take some time to get over, but things were better now despite all that had happened.

She would have liked to leave on better terms with Chris, though.

Near the yard, Chris sped up without a word. She didn't seem to care if they were behind her or not. Tony plodded behind, supposing it wasn't like they were proper friends.

"SURPRISE!"

A chorus of voices stopped Tony in her tracks. She gasped.

The back of the farmhouse was crowded with people spilling into the yard. The Wooly Well Dressers were there, Nick and Ed, Red, of course, and some of the Todmorden lesbians. Festoons were strung from the gutter, and sparkling fairy lights twinkled over the porch. Tony smiled at the flaming torches stuck into planters. The work of the WWD, no doubt.

Penny pushed her way through the crowd. "We love you. Both of you, our honorary well-dressers. Though perhaps not in those outfits." Penny smiled, holding out a plate of little balls that smelled cheesy and delicious.

Tony popped one into her mouth as warmed by the appetizer as the sentiment. People here did care.

Chris pressed a foaming mug of home brew into her hand, beaming. "Did I fool you? Do I get the Academy Award?"

Tony nodded, spontaneously hugging her. Chris hugged her back.

Nick appeared with a plate of sausage rolls. "I'll be sorry to see you go," he said. "You've done me a good turn, and I won't forget it. You're welcome to stay with me any time. Keep in touch, won't you?"

Red clapped Tony on the back, sending her shooting forward. "When they visit, they'll be staying with us, of course. And you won't be leaving it too long, I hope," Red said.

Jade pulled Tony into the house then to talk to Mei Chen about *Alice's Adventures in Barking* (an urban tale for our times).

Much later, full of good food and bonhomie, Tony found Jade in the yard, standing alone, her back to the house.

"Everyone's been saying 'thank you' to me tonight, and I realize I haven't told you how grateful I am that you planted illegal trackers on me. Thank you for being paranoid and obsessive," Tony said.

Jade smiled. "It will be all right, won't it, going back to London?" She sounded nervous.

They would both have issues after the last couple of weeks. "You and me, we're a team, right? Whatever happens?" Tony murmured.

Jade put her arm around Tony's waist, snuggling in close. "Whatever happens," she repeated. She rested her head on Tony's shoulder, and they looked at the purple sky.

Stars shone over the ancient hills and the old, stone farmhouse, blown by wind, beaten by rain. Still standing.

THE END

About the Author

Crin Claxton is the author of the butch/femme vampire novel *Scarlet Thirst* and the Supernatural Detective ghost mystery series, all published by Bold Strokes Books. Short stories have been published by Diva Books, Bella Books, Bold Strokes Books, Diva magazine, and Carve webzine. S/he has recipes in *The Butch Cook Book*. Poems have been published in Onlywomen Press and La Pluma.

The Supernatural Detective won an honorable mention in the Foreword Indie Fab book of the year awards (2013, Gay & Lesbian section) and was nominated for the American Library Association Over the Rainbow booklist (2013). *Death's Doorway* was an Indie Fab Award Finalist (2015) and won an honorable mention in the 2015 Rainbow Awards.

Crin is a proud butch lesbian. S/he is a lighting designer and production manager for theater. Crin lives in London with hir partner and son.

Website: www.crinclaxton.com

Books Available from Bold Strokes Books

An Independent Woman by Kit Meredith. Alex and Rebecca's attraction won't stop smoldering, despite their reluctance to act on it and incompatible poly relationship styles. (978-1-63679-553-9)

Cherish by Kris Bryant. Josie and Olivia cherish the time spent together, but when the summer ends and their temporary romance melts into the real deal, reality gets complicated. (978-1-63679-567-6)

Cold Case Heat by Mary P. Burns. Sydney Hansen receives a threat in a very cold murder case that sends her to the police for help where she finds more than justice with Detective Gale Sterling. (978-1-63679-374-0)

Proximity by Jordan Meadows. Joan really likes Ellie, but being alone with her could turn deadly unless she can keep her dangerous powers under control. (978-1-63679-476-1)

Sweet Spot by Kimberly Cooper Griffin. Pro surfer Shia Turning will have to take a chance if she wants to find the sweet spot. (978-1-63679-418-1)

The Haunting of Oak Springs by Crin Claxton. Ghosts and the past haunt the supernatural detective in a race to save the lesbians of Oak Springs farm. (978-1-63679-432-7)

Transitory by J.M. Redmann. The cops blow it off as a customer surprised by what was under the dress, but PI Micky Knight knows they're wrong—she either makes it her case or lets a murderer go free to kill again. (978-1-63679-251-4)

Unexpectedly Yours by Toni Logan. A private resort on a tropical island, a feisty old chief, and a kleptomaniac pet pig bring Suzanne and Allie together for unexpected love. (978-1-63679-160-9)

Bones of Boothbay Harbor by Michelle Larkin. Small-town police chief Frankie Stone and FBI Special Agent Eve Huxley must set aside their differences and combine their skills to find a killer after a burial site is discovered in Boothbay Harbor, Maine. (978-1-63679-267-5)

Crush by Ana Hartnett Reichardt. Josie Sanchez worked for years for the opportunity to create her own wine label, and nothing will stand in her way. Not even Mac, the owner's annoyingly beautiful niece Josie's forced to hire as her harvest intern. (978-1-63679-330-6)

Decadence by Ronica Black, Renee Roman, and Piper Jordan. You are cordially invited to Decadence, Las Vegas's most talked about invitation-only Masquerade Ball. Come for the entertainment and stay for the erotic indulgence. We guarantee it'll be a party that lives up to its name. (978-1-63679-361-0)

Gimmicks and Glamour by Lauren Melissa Ellzey. Ashly has learned to hide her Sight, but as she speeds toward high school graduation she must protect the classmates she claims to hate from an evil that no one else sees. (978-1-63679-401-3)

Heart of Stone by Sam Ledel. Princess Keeva Glantor meets Maeve, a gorgon forced to live alone thanks to a decades-old lie, and together the two women battle forces they formerly thought to be good in the hopes of leading lives they can finally call their own. (978-1-63679-407-5)

Murder at the Oasis by David S. Pederson. Palm trees, sunshine, and murder await Mason Adler and his friend Walter as they travel from Phoenix to Palm Springs for what was supposed to be a relaxing vacation but ends up being a trip of mystery and intrigue. (978-1-63679-416-7)

Peaches and Cream by Georgia Beers. Adley Purcell is living her dreams owning Get the Scoop ice cream shop until national dessert chain Sweet Heaven opens less than two blocks away and Adley has to compete with the far too heavenly Sabrina James. (978-1-63679-412-9)

The Only Fish in the Sea by Angie Williams. Will love overcome years of bitter rivalry for the daughters of two crab fishing families in this queer modern-day spin on Romeo and Juliet? (978-1-63679-444-0)

Wildflower by Cathleen Collins. When a plane crash leaves eleven-year-old Lily Andrews stranded in the vast wilderness of Arkansas, will she be able to overcome the odds and make it back to civilization and the one person who holds the key to her future? (978-1-63679-621-5)

Witch Finder by Sheri Lewis Wohl. Tamsin, the Keeper of the Book of Darkness, is in terrible danger, and as a Witch Finder, Morrigan must protect her and the secrets she guards even if it costs Morrigan her life. (978-1-63679-335-1)

A Second Chance at Life by Genevieve McCluer. Vampires Dinah and Rachel reconnect, but a string of vampire killings begin and evidence seems to be pointing at Dinah. They must prove her innocence while finding out if the two of them are still compatible after all these years. (978-1-63679-459-4)

Digging for Heaven by Jenna Jarvis. Litz lives for dragons. Kella lives to kill them. The last thing they expect is to find each other attractive. (978-1-63679-453-2)

Forever's Promise by Missouri Vaun. Wesley Holden migrated west disguised as a man for the hope of a better life and with no designs to take a wife, but Charlotte Rose has other ideas. (978-1-63679-221-7)

Here For You by D. Jackson Leigh. A horse trainer must make a difficult business decision that could save her father's ranch from foreclosure but destroy her chance to win the heart of a feisty barrel racer vying for a spot in the National Rodeo Finals. (978-1-63679-299-6)

I Do, I Don't by Joy Argento. Creator of the romance algorithm, Nicole Hart doesn't expect to be starring in her own reality TV dating show, and falling for the show's executive producer Annie Jackson could ruin everything. (978-1-63679-420-4)

It's All in the Details by Dena Blake. Makeup artist Lane Donnelly and wedding planner Helen Trent can't stand each other, but they must set aside their differences to ensure Darcy gets the wedding of her dreams, and make a few of their own dreams come true. (978-1-63679-430-3)

Marigold by Melissa Brayden. Marigold Lavender vows to take down Alexis Wakefield, the harsh food critic who blasts her younger sister's restaurant. If only she wasn't as sexy as she is mean. (978-1-63679-436-5)

The Town that Built Us by Jesse J. Thoma. When her father dies, Grace Cook returns to her hometown and tries to avoid Bonnie Whitlock, the woman who pulverized her heart, only to discover her father's estate has been left to them jointly. (978-1-63679-439-6)

A Degree to Die For by Karis Walsh. A murder at the University of Washington's Classics Department brings Professor Antigone Weston and Sergeant Adriana Kent together—first as opposing forces, and then allies as they fight together to protect their campus from a killer. (978-1-63679-365-8)

A Talent Within by Suzanne Lenoir. Evelyne, born into nobility, and Annika, a peasant girl with a deadly secret, struggle to change their destinies in Valmora, a medieval world controlled by religion, magic, and men. (978-1-63679-423-5)

Finders Keepers by Radclyffe. Roman Ashcroft's past, it seems, is not so easily forgotten when fate brings her and Tally Dewilde together—along with an attraction neither welcomes. (978-1-63679-428-0)

Homeland by Kristin Keppler and Allisa Bahney. Dani and Kate have finally found themselves on the same side of the war, but a new threat from the inside jeopardizes the future of the wasteland. (978-1-63679-405-1)

Just One Dance by Jenny Frame. Will Taylor Spark and her new business to make dating special—the Regency Romance Club—bring sparkle back to Jaq Bailey's lonely world? (978-1-63679-457-0)

On My Way There by Jaycie Morrison. As Max traverses the open road, her journey of impossible love, loss, and courage mirrors her voyage of self-discovery leading to the ultimate question: If she can't have the woman of her dreams, will the woman of real life be enough? (978-1-63679-392-4)

Transitioning Home by Heather K O'Malley. An injured soldier realizes they need to transition to really heal. (978-1-63679-424-2)

Truly Enough by JJ Hale. Chasing the spark of creativity may ignite a burning romance or send a friendship up in flames. (978-1-63679-442-6)

Vintage and Vogue by Kelly and Tana Fireside. When tech whiz Sena Abrigo marches into small-town Owen Station, she turns librarian Hazel Butler's life upside down in the most wonderful of ways, setting off an explosive series of events, threatening their chance at love…and their very lives. (978-1-63679-448-8)